# CHROMIUM RISE

# CHROMIUM RISE

## THE INVASION OF THE CHROMIUM SERIES

## WILLIAM LJ GALAINI

### Anthology

*Last Night at the Jolly Chicken*


<u>Misplaced Mercenaries</u> by Kevin Pettway

*A Good Running Away*

*Blow Out the Candle When You Leave*

*Big Damn Magic*

*Illusions of Decency*

*Heroes Kill Everyone*


<u>Hettie Stormheart series</u> by Jen Bair

*One Good Eye*


<u>Huntress and Harvester series</u> by Jessica Raney

*A Seed Once Sown*


<u>Wrong Way series</u> by Kevin Pettway

*Wrong Way to Heaven*


<u>Invasion of the Chromium</u> by William LJ Galaini

*Chromium Rise*


<u>Pick's Pocket</u> by C.M. McGuire

*Beer For My Corpses*

Gullhome
Oldam's Temper
Norrik
Icebite
Raiders Sea
Spirit Oyster River
Vikkan
Summervatn
Krysuvik
Badron
Majton
The
Disn
Tyrran
Summer Trades
Knarrax
Gradron
Mirrik
Pippa
Green
Low
Wood
Bruinland River
Sheaf
Watchpost
Rousea
Rousland
Dalry
The Arlean
Arlea
Steed
Sejent
N
W
E
S
Sedrios
Whene
Southen
Bangui
The Paradisals
Runfish
Port Placid
Pelf

Full-color map at KevinPettway.com

*To all of us who don't have magical powers or special destinies. It's up to us to fix these messes.*

# CHAPTER
# ONE

Visteria

The alabaster chamber flickered with the uneven light of torches and braziers. During the day, the Skullhew clan hauled away crumbled stone and mounds of dust, so Visteria held her experiments at night to avoid coughing. She figured that prior to the expedition, no one had entered this chamber in centuries. Who knew what ugly illnesses could be kicked up from the floors, to say nothing of the contained reek of dozens of sweaty laborers.

In the relative quiet, she marveled at the alabaster floor. With ornate copper inlay, periodic blue slates mounted into the walls at regular intervals, and architecture so precise that a feather couldn't fit between any of the stones, the ancient technological mastery of the sprawling ruins still caught the breath of every tribesman that descended into them.

For tonight's experiment, she had decided to test her theory regarding the crystalline pods that populated the chamber she waited in. Only four out of the forty pods glowed with dormant power, and each had a rectangular stone of blue embedded on the end. They were vaguely translucent with the imperfections expected of crystalline growth, but within, Visteria could see intersections of copper wiring all throughout.

Around her waist, Visteria carried a leather-wrapped book of detailed notes and observations. It clung to her by a small chain along with a bag of charcoal for writing and copying the runework she found throughout the halls. Her laborers were taking longer than expected to deliver her test subjects, and she pondered what other work she could accomplish in the meantime.

Then she heard the echoing of approaching footsteps from the stairwell at the end of the chamber. "M'lady, we are bringing down the animals now," a man said as he raised a wriggling sack.

"What did you bring?" she asked, glad the wait was over.

The man hesitated awkwardly. "Well, rats. We caught a bunch in the upper levels of the ruins and around Tent City. So here's them." He shook the sack a little and it pulsed, filled nearly to the brim with squirming bodies.

She had made it clear that the four test subjects were all to be radically different. If the laborers had their way, they would have just delivered rats but Visteria wanted to capitalize on the four operational pods as much as possible. She didn't know how much magical power remained in each pod, and she also had no idea if one species had better odds of survival over another. Hence four different animals of radically different make and size.

"I assume you will pluck one out at random and eat the rest, yes?" she asked pointedly.

He smiled with joy at the thought of a hearty stew. "We can keep the rest?"

She rolled her eyes. "Yep, all yours. And the other three animals? Where are they?"

"Thems coming behind me in a bit. We bought a fancy bird from a traveling merchant topside. Perfectly white, from some fancy city somewheres."

"Excellent, and . . .?"

"A true treat, Lady Skullhew." He beamed with pride. "A bear!"

"A bear?" She hadn't seen a bear in Tent City above or anywhere in the ruins—or even in real life. No breed she had read of were indigenous to the *desert*.

"A bear from the woodland regions well to the north beyond the mountains."

Visteria turned her attention to the rows of silicate pods that populated the chamber. Each was large enough to fit two men at once, but a bear was a creature of varying size depending on both the season and the breed. She had read of them exhaustively in the Matron's archives when she was a little girl. The truth was, she was excited to see one, and while the size would provide a challenge, she was eager to experiment.

"What kind of bear?" she asked, trying to judge if a pod could hold such a thing.

"Gold-tip."

She sighed. "They are huge. Can it fit into the pod?" He nodded confidently without even looking. "Certainly!"

"And getting it down here won't be a problem? They are strong and can kill—"

"Oh no!" he interrupted. "This one is morose. Sad. Will barely eat and won't even put up a fight. It's less than six hundred pounds. It will fit."

Few things raised Visteria's blood faster than a man interrupting her, but she let it slide. "Fine. Just, nobody die from the bear."

"Can you imagine?" he bounced. "A bear! In Vastard!"

"Likely not for much longer. And last?"

"Last?"

"What is the last animal, so I can finish this conversation with you and never have another one."

"A spotted spunt."

Visteria paused. "A *spunt*? That's a fish..."

"Yes, m'lady. Big one too. Caught two days ago in the mountains upstream."

The people of Vastard, and the region of the Yellow Sea in general, weren't known for their academic insights and wise philosophy. But even *this* was a startling low for Visteria to observe.

"How is the"—she struggled to say the word—"*spunt* fairing? Currently?"

"Oh, it's dead." The obliviousness on his face melted away as he processed Visteria's flummoxed frown. "But it's an animal all the same. Should do nicely."

She did her best not to cup her face into her palms. She privately complained about the imbecility of some of the men under Evrick's banner, but this was too much.

"So, for the sake of the experiment, I'd like to only run it on *live* animals. And since I only have three, you'll just be the fourth." She pointed toward one of the four glowing silicate pods. "Climb on in. Go on."

He blanched. "M'lady! No! I . . . You didn't say anything about them being alive. I can find you something else. A bird? A spider? Oh! There's a fighting badger up in Tent City. Let me run to the surface and fetch it. He's perfect."

He turned on his heel and bolted off toward the stairs. He nearly plowed into four more laborers descending with a chained Gold-tip bear in tow. The beast lumbered, its golden fringed fur loose since most of its fat reserve was gone. With its nose to the ground, it didn't even look up at its rough handlers as they shoved it over to the nearest open, active pod.

"Yes," Visteria said. "That one. That one still has power. See if you can get it in without breaking anything."

The men shoved on the bear's rear, pushing her up over the silicate lip of the pod. She obeyed, climbing in slowly, and settled herself down inside as her excess mass filled it like a mold.

As the men recovered their breath, one said, "Would have thought the bear would give us the trouble, what with the teeth and claws and such. But the damned swan has been the issue. Phigar offered to carry it down, brave man that he is."

The others nodded in solemn agreement as a hissing echoed through the chamber. A man, presumably Phigar, ran down the steps with his arms outstretched. He tossed his head from side to side, the massive swan in his grip at arm's length, trying to keep it from pecking out his eyes.

"That pod! Here!" Visteria shouted, directing him.

The other men fell into a guiding formation for Phigar. "Follow my voice, lad!"

"Almost there!"

"Believe, boy! Believe!"

He threw the hissing, snapping swan into one of the open pods, and Visteria pushed the top shut. It pressed against a rubber seal and something clicked secure, but the shadow of the swan thrashed around inside and pecked about.

Phigar wiped the blood from his face. "Scratched me up good. All quiet until you got it in yer hands then *pow*, hissing and nipping and flapping!"

Visteria couldn't help but laugh at the jovial nature of the men. The excitement of the impending experiment was taking hold, and it appeared to be infectious. "You, close the bear in. Make sure not to pinch any of its skin. And where's the rat?" She spotted the roiling sack on the ground. "In there is—"

Before she could finish, one of the men carelessly opened the sack, and it rolled onto its side. Rats poured out in a clawing flurry as the men squealed and Visteria rolled her head back in exasperation.

Once again, men weren't letting her finish her sentences.

"Just get one. One. Here, this one *on my leg* should do fine."

"Sorry!"

"We thought there would be only one."

"Dangit, this could have been a good stew."

For a moment, the rat clinging to Visteria's leather trousers looked up at her with pleading eyes. When a guard came to pluck it away, it clung to her desperately.

Something in her tugged. "Be gentle with it. Don't hurt the thing. Just . . . put it in the pod."

The guard did so. "Funny, not even biting. Just peed."

"Close it up, and now we wait for that idiot to bring a badger."

"Did he seriously try and offer up a dead spunt?" one of the men asked.

Phigar laughed. "Yeah, we were kidding. Didn't think he'd actually do it."

"Although," one of the laborers mused. "Filling one of these with water and keeping it alive could—"

Visteria did not have time for any other curious minds than her own. "That is an experiment for another day," she interjected. "Assuming I can find a way to power more pods. Go help with the badger."

They all nodded then darted off up the stairs.

Once alone, she inspected the seals on each of the three closed pods. This entire room was populated with such pods, though the rest didn't hum with dormant power. She wondered as to their purpose, but these pods were just one of many other mysteries, some such mysteries more imposing than others.

Pulling the chain around her waist, she fidgeted with her precious tome of notes and runes. "What were you hiding, Ovallin?" she asked herself.

Shuffling came from the stairwell once again, but this time four men carried a long wooden cage. Inside was a still lump, quiet and braced against their uneven gait.

"Thing's heavy for its size," one of the men grunted.

"Here, last pod. To me," she said, standing at the head of it. The blue stone thrummed with dormant magical energy, and she dared her fingers close to it. The hairs on the back of her neck stood and her toes tingled in her sandals.

The four men hoisted the cage over the pod, turned it downward, and pulled the wooden side of it up and away.

But the badger didn't budge.

"Got its legs locked in there," Phigar said, squinting into the rear of the dark cage. "Ain't dumb."

Visteria stepped a safe distance away and crouched down next to the pod. From the angle, she could look up inside the cage. It was a black and white badger with two stripes running down its long face over both eyes. The tiny, beady eyes were alert and hard to read, but the musculature of the creature was obvious.

She never understood why men enjoyed watching animals fight. If men loved it so much, they should just be in the fighting pits themselves, because now her test subject was wary of people and any space that wasn't its cage.

"Any time this thing has been shaken out of a cage, it was to fight," she speculated. "Might need to push him from the other side with a—"

Before she could suggest a *stick* or a *bat*, the spuntman reached his hand inside and shoved the rear end of the badger with all his might. The beast spun about in a furry blur and chomped down on the man's hand.

He squealed. "It's got me! Teeth! Teeeeth!"

Two other men reached in from the open end, grabbed ahold of a little leg each, and pulled. The badger's front claws peeled at the cage's inside as it lost its grip and fell out into the pod.

"Get back!" Visteria yelled as she shoved the pod's lid shut.

Spuntman clutched what was left of his hand. "My fingers! He got two of 'em and just took 'em!"

In the stunned silence after, everyone heard a casual crunching. They all looked down and watched the silhouette of the badger inside chewing. After a moment, it swallowed, bones and all.

"I hope I was tasty, you bastard!" Spuntman cried bitterly before storming off.

Phigar shrugged. "He's got eight other perfectly good fingers. He'll be fine."

The men stood around expectantly, shifting about on their feet and glancing at Visteria. She was used to men lingering in order to flirt, but this was different.

They were curious. They wanted to see the experiment.

She decided to wait them out, make them *say* that they wanted to stay and watch.

"So, uh, m'lady." One gestured to the four closed pods. "What these going to do to them beasts?"

"I don't know, but if I translated the runes properly it should be interesting." Crossing her arms, she made it clear they weren't going to get a show.

The oldest laborer got the hint and tugged at the others to leave. "Best of luck to you, m'lady," he called. As they got to the stairs, she heard him chastise the other men. "Stick around? You daft? That's how you become part of the experiment. And curiosity is the thing that the gods kill us for."

CHAPTER

# TWO

Arvin

When Uncle's illness finally took him, they came and burned down the shack. Arvin stood outside as his neighbors—if they could be called that—kicked sand on it to contain the fire as it burst forth in wild colors. The alchemy lab and storage kegs were filled with elements and powders that converted a good-ole-fashioned act of fearful hate into a splendorous spectacle.

Everyone stopped to watch the pyre. They ignored Arvin, who had already cried at the passing of his uncle earlier that day. Now he was more curious than anything.

*What happens if everything we own gets intense thermal exposure?*

The wood of the shack clearly provided proper fuel, as did the hay on the dirt floor. It was also bone dry, as expected in the northern outskirts of the desert. Additionally, the plethora of alchemical agents and refined elements had never been burned in such large, chaotic quantities before.

*Nitrate, niter, dried slink semen, shellfish iodine, marrow phosphorus.*

"Now clear off, boy!" some man yelled at Arvin. He never cared to learn anyone's name. "Yeh ain't welcome here. Nobody here no more to stick their neck out for you."

Arvin paid him no mind. The man was heaving, tired from tossing Uncle's furniture about looking for what little gold they had. Several of his friends, or possibly his adult children from the looks of it, whooped and hollered as the shack's fire increased, turning blue as the heat intensified.

Arvin continued listing the contents of the burning shack, curiosity holding his feet firm in the sand to watch. Ever since he was a boy, when Uncle first took him in, he found joy in the inventory of alchemical wealth Uncle had accumulated over a lifetime. Arvin had grown into a young man with the smells of exothermic reactions tickling his nostrils, and as the shack burned, he knew that this would be the last, marvelous one.

*Flaked rust, snake venom, refined hydrochloride, cayenne pepper, talc, flint shards, quartz soaked in vinegar, Uncle's body.*

It wasn't that the neighbors disliked Uncle in any particular way; they were just uncomfortable about his mysterious knowledge of alchemy that now resided in Arvin's mind. Things that were strange to them also scared them, and as a collective of outcasts from other tribes, everything about Uncle and Arvin was strange—especially the unwanted child the alchemist took in without reason or warning. Some were convinced Uncle brewed malicious plague brews, but were too afraid to confront him directly because who else would concoct something for their erectile dysfunction?

Arvin didn't strike them as having the subtlety necessary to maintain the position of small town alchemist. Whereas Uncle could mollify embarrassment with a nod or a pat on the shoulder, Arvin could barely manage eye contact and more than two words.

Red sparks shot up into the dry night sky. The destructive brutes paused, compelled like toddlers to stare, open mouthed.

*There goes the bottle of strontium.*

Arvin pulled on his protective goggles—darkened glass and leather straps.

"Oh, hey!" someone called out from behind. "Might want to back away from that fire."

They did, seeing that it was self-sustaining. Their misdirected destructiveness now was peppered with mystified fear and the flames changed color and popped sporadically. They cleared back just in time as three powder kegs burst and the sides of the shack flew open. Flaming wood thumped through the air and people fled in all directions.

"See!" one angry woman yelled. "He kept evils in there!"

*Sulfur and nitrate with some pine charcoal. But sure, evil.*

A pervasive, palpable reek wafted invisibly over the crowd. All gasped and a few doubled over, vomiting. The smell of rotting eggs would likely linger here for weeks. Arvin was accustomed to it in small dosages, but even this quantity made his eyes water. He was grateful for the goggles.

*Sulfide and ammonium. Whoa. I wonder if it is interacting with the cayenne?*

Then the real show began. The phosphorus store could no longer take the heat, and a screaming hiss just at the upper edge of human hearing began. It seared into the ears, and Arvin suppressed his amusement at everyone clasping the sides of their heads.

Next the light kicked in. The center of the shack burned as if it were a small, white star. It was brighter than the desert sun on a clear day, and while they all gawked and pointed, Arvin wisely turned away. Most of them would be blind by morning unless they did the same.

But he said nothing and walked through the crowd, out of the fetid camp of tribal outcasts and thieves. They parted for him, cautioning each other that the hissing and lights might be under his control.

With only a bit of traveling rations and water, Arvin walked out into the rocky expanse of Vastard valley and turned west-south-west. Having no wagon or apparent possessions, he figured himself to be too small a fish for muggers and bandits.

He walked for the rest of the evening, through the entire night, and as dawn approached he could see others trudging the same path as he. The pre-morning light revealed other outcasts and destitutes, each dragging their feet, likely heading to Tent City, the same as him.

The sun's waning light became less blue by the minute as it melted behind the desert's distant horizon. The dunes of Yellow Sea, at least those south of Vastard, sizzled beyond the opening of Vastard Valley behind him. And ahead was rockier terrain filled with prickly bushes, watering holes, and settled mercenary tribes.

Occasionally a wagon crossed his path, or several sellswords on camelback, but none bothered him. A general call had gone out for laborers, a call from Warlord Skullhew, and Arvin saw more and more fellows answering it. Soon his walk felt more like a pilgrimage as several became dozens, and dozens became hundreds.

Shoulder to shoulder they walked, too exhausted to chat. The sun pounded them. They sipped water and nibbled dried bird or salted lizard. Arvin finished the last of his trail rations, knowing Tent City had better be what Uncle said it was.

Then the evening winds came in, roiled from the drastic environmental shift across the vast leagues of the Yellow Sea to the south. They barreled up the valley, smacking every standing horse, camel, bush, cactus, and person. After their blustery arrival, they calmed. Like a nocturnal animal finally free to come out and play in the failing light, each puff of breeze eased, yet still toyed with loose hairs and camel reins.

Such a rapid drop in temperature also caused sweat to freeze on Arvin's body, right through his thin day-time linen robes. Arvin shuddered, as he had for the thousands of other dusks he'd survived in the desert, as the back of his robe grew crisp and stiff. Pulling his bundled night coat from over his shoulder, he unfurled it in a practiced motion and slipped it on. Next, he unraveled his daytime turban from his head, flapped it in the breeze to air it out, and then stuffed it in his coat pocket.

These were the practiced gestures of the people of Vastard and the dunes beyond. His motions were echoed in some way or another by the hundreds of people now traveling with him, side-by-side, in the same direction. Dozens of tribes were represented, and while Vastard was the least hospitable place in all of Andos, it was also the location of its greatest current opportunity: work.

Uncle had died two days prior, and Arvin was following the instructions imparted to him from his deathbed. With an elderly, gnarled hand, Uncle had gripped Arvin's forearm while pushing out his final words. "Vastard. Go to Vastard, Tent City, Nephew," Uncle had said. "There is where they have found the old ones. The dead city of the dead people. Evrick Skullhew is plundering it for its riches. Find work there. Take what you can and learn what others can't."

Those were Uncle's last understandable words.

He'd cried when Uncle passed. Arvin wasn't often prone to displays of emotion. His face was latently passive. But Uncle had been a patient and attentive man, serving as a father figure when Arvin's own had abandoned the position. Uncle had opened up the world of alchemy to Arvin, given him knowledge of chemicals and compounds, and even now Arvin wore Uncle's bandolier of potted chemicals and reagents. He grabbed it when they came with torches.

The desperate pilgrimage consolidated into a line. Standing with other hopefuls, Arvin shuffled forward toward Tent City's perimeter flags erected around Skullhew's gathered tribe. He hoped that Evrick Skullhew had need of an alchemist. And Arvin felt confident that he would find paying work—work that provided food and shelter— here in Vastard.

"I hear Skullhew will kill us if he doesn't hire us," a hunched man said, several feet away.

"One can only hope." An elderly woman chuckled while checking the last of her water.

"I can smell the food from here!"

Arvin could too. The wave of spiced desert weasel and seared mushrooms wafted over them, lifting their spirits. In his tired delirium, he meditated over his reaction.

*A smell offers no nutrition but teases salivation, stomach growling. All my functions are prepared to eat, and that energizes me. Is that why I feel hopeful? A burst of energy to chase the food down and consume it? My mind knows that none of that food is for me, but my body does not.*

Arvin knew his burst of energy from such tantalizing scents was a lie. A hopeful lie. He had no money, and that food was likely being sold from barkers just inside Tent City at a premium.

Looking to his left, Arvin watched the man squashed in line next to him eagerly picking his nose. Content with snagging a plump booger, he retracted it for examination prior to slipping it into his mouth.

*Well, he gets to eat at least.*

Arvin pondered the composition and nutritional potential of crusty boogers. He meditated on their viscosity, freezing point, and boiling point so intently that he didn't even realize he had entered Tent City. The wonderful smells of fresh, dangling food went unnoticed, and he was oblivious to the barkers' siren calls for customers to step out of line.

Someone sobbing pushed by him, shoving his shoulder, from the opposite direction. It knocked him back to the present reality that he was standing at the cusp of Skullhew's command tent. The distraught soul had just been rejected.

*I hope they weren't a better alchemist than me.*

Four guards, armored in hardened leather, curated the line. They chose which petitioners were permitted to enter the command tent. If someone didn't meet the apparent standard for Skullhew, they would spin them about and kick them in the rear toward whence they came.

"Cross-eyed? Nope."

"You've got rot! Fuck off."

"Where did you get an eleventh toe from?"

As they sorted folks, Arvin examined their long-shafted halberds designed for crowd control.

*Crucible Steel with a dark wavy pattern. Tempered in the old way; micro-bubbles along the surface to give a devastating saw-toothed edge but also prone to moisture damage. Oiled daily. Expensive to maintain.*

They could easily cut down anyone causing trouble, and the victim would be looted clean before gasping their last breath. He shrank under their cruel gaze, but Arvin was surrounded by too many worthy of violent rejection to be individually noticed. Slipping through the throng, he got to the entrance of the command tent uncontested.

The booger miner went first. He stepped into the expansive tent, walked several steps forward, and stood demurely as he answered a rapid flow of questions. With a pleased and grateful nod, he disappeared deeper inside.

"You don't look sick or inbred. You're next." One of the guards nudged Arvin with his elbow.

He entered, unsure of what to do with his hands. Fidgeting, he hooked his fingers over the front of his bandolier and hoped he didn't appear as desperate as he felt.

As his eyes adjusted, the falling light of dusk gave way to the tickling light of braziers and dangling torches. The warlord's command tent was massive with oiled canvas walls that could be rearranged to suit any needs, be it a wedding or the compartmentalized hosting of travelers. Incense curled in the air and each corner of the tent held clusters of wisemen and scholars. They were studying artifacts, drawings, and glyphs excavated from the ancients. Arvin discerned several tribal dialects collaborating solutions and discoveries.

*Yes! Here! Here is where I belong!*

The carpets were nearly a half-inch thick, and as his thin-soled desert boots settled on them, his back eased and shoulders fell.

*By the gods, a true carpet!*

He glanced down to study its woolly composition and fiber density when someone called out to him.

"Boy! Stand here."

Arvin looked up to see three stern elders parked at a low wooden table. They were seated on plush cushions, inkwells open and quills ready.

He scurried over to them.

"Name?" the middle one asked.

He cleared his throat. "Arvin."

"Tribe?"

"Unknown."

All three elders cocked their left eyebrow.

He realized his need to clarify. "Mother was an outcast for conception out of wedlock. She died young. I was raised by Uncle-my uncle."

*Why would they care? I'm here for alchemy, not endowment.*

The three men returned to their parchments. The middle one asked, "Age?"

"Twenty, I think?"

They continued questioning in a mundane fashion. They wanted to know past injuries: none. Past major illnesses: none. Significant birth signs: none. Wealth worthy of mention: none.

"Has it ever burned or hurt when you piss?"

*Ah. They are worried about sexually transferred ailments. If I am accepted to work below in excavation, I am likely to cohabitate with those at the camp and they are concerned for the overall health of the population.*

"No, I have never been with a woman."

The elder on the left smirked. "You can also get 'em from animals." They burst into raucous laughter.

*Oh, I should laugh along. That's what men do.*

Arvin joined in with his own practiced laugh. It was still a bit shrill and forced, but he had rehearsed it on occasion before. It wasn't perfected yet because the three elders ceased their merriment and gazed at Arvin with a combination of bafflement and horror.

*Whoops.*

They gathered themselves from his egregious display and began asking specifics regarding his skills. The first questions were expected: can he work a bow and can he cook and the like. His mind wandered, as it invariably did, along with his eyes.

In the corner he spotted a stack of empty red clay jars. He recognized them as being the kind that can sweat moisture when temperatures shift, making them ideal for hauling powdered explosives. A white, tribal marking on their sides indicated they had come from the far eastern mountain ranges of the Yellow Sea where the best explosives were made.

*A combination of ground verpus root and dried seaweed mixed with typical blast powder. Expensive, but ideal for sundering strong stone like marble. Sandstone wouldn't need it.*

His eyes then drifted to the long strands of cord drying from the command tent's rafter. Several women were still stringing it, and from their darkened fingernails Arvin deduced they were incorporating the explosive powder into blast cords for ranged detonation.

*They are making fuses, half a man's height in length, to bind together later. They desire considerable distance from the blast.*

"I said, how far can you run without stopping?" an elder repeated, annoyed.

"Oh, uh, two leagues?" Arvin guessed, hoping he wouldn't be expected to prove it.

*They are making an explosive fuse here, but it hasn't enough yield to combust without direct flame. Otherwise the braziers nearby would have set it off already. They are merely winding cord to carry the flame to its primary explosion somewhere else. Likely underground. But the fuse might be so long that if it runs that deep, it will lose air to burn. Not enough to go out completely, but to falter.*

"Boy, are you there?"

*Perhaps keeping an additional air source would be too difficult, but wrap the fuse in a fast-burning fuel source like wool . . . Or wool soaked in japperseed oil. The fuse will release the contained oxygen in the air so if the fuse falters, it will be reinvigorated with the singed oil—*

"He's a dullard. Moon touched or dropped on the head," an elder complained. "Get him out of here and try not to let in these types!"

Two guards snatched up Arvin by the arms and lifted him clear off the glorious carpet. Panic set in, and he had only had the time to fling one sentence out as they hauled him toward the exit.

"Jappers!" he called. "Soak the fuses in japperseed oil!"

The guards hurled him into the sand outside. The entire crowd gasped. A few even laughed.

# CHAPTER
# THREE

Arvin

Arvin wandered around Tent City, dragging the tears from his eyes. He wasn't hurt and nothing in his bandolier had broken, but the rejection was a brutal reality check. Without work or food, he'd starve.

Walking from food vendor to food vendor, he evaluated them. He found one woman, elderly with shaky hands. The desert voles dangling from her cart were rotten and unevenly cooked.

"I can cook," Arvin said. "It's just alchemy. It's the same. I can cook."

"And I can tell you to fuck off and eat sand." She spat in the sand and pushed her cart onward, its tiny bells tinkling.

Arvin found her cruelty unwarranted. People made no sense. Only Uncle did, and he was gone. The tears came back.

When Uncle died, the locals finally had an excuse to seize their goods and exile Arvin. Arvin was weird, unsocial, spindly, and bad for breeding, so the intention was to get him away from the local girls before he got the most desperate of them pregnant.

He had zero prospects, no connections, and nothing to eat.

Parking in the middle of the trafficked pathways between stalls and tents, Arvin rested his head in his hands. He didn't care if anyone stepped on him. And neither did they, as people nudged into him with annoyance.

"Move, dullard."

"I'm coming back with a camel to trample you."

"Hurry up and die, if that's what you're sitting there for. My dogs need to eat."

*I did it wrong. I'm always doing it wrong.*

Arvin was sometimes prone to a deep anger, a consuming rage that took the joy out of the world. It was an anger that ended his curiosity and converted it into vicious judgment instead.

And his judgment was always toward himself.

*I did it wrong. If I did it right, I'd be cooking or working on that fuse. Or being of worth! If I did it right, I could have kept the hovel after Uncle. I wouldn't be hated.*

He began clawing at his hair, his nails digging into his scalp.

*Why did I try laughing? I can't laugh!*

His tears were hot on his face, and his racked breathing made him even more angry. He tried his best not to sob.

*And now tears! I need every drop of moisture since I have none to drink.*

It was a brief thought but he considered drinking the concentrated acid on his bandolier. Only rare glass from the Vulg could contain it, it was so strong. He could just shatter the vial in his teeth and let it melt a hole right through him and down into the earth.

Down to the sand-buried cities of the ancients below.

"Jappers? Japperseed oil?" an inquisitive voice asked, standing over him. It was radically different than the chastisement from other passersby. Arvin figured someone in line must have heard him yelling it as he was carried out. Perhaps they followed him out of curiosity. He lifted his head just enough to nod.

"Hmm, wouldn't have thought of that. I was going to try wool, but I feared the condensation from the cold stone below would be gathered by it, making the fuse just wet enough to putter out."

Someone was speaking Arvin's language. Someone capable of thought. Starvation aside, Arvin was thrilled at the possibility of actual conversation.

He wiped his reddened eyes. The man looking down at him had a long mane of graying hair despite his young, strong face. His beard was delicately trimmed, and his eyes were a pale, stony color like that of an oyster's inside shell. His simple but immaculately crafted gambeson indicated a man of military rank and wealth.

"Brilliant, honestly. Jappers. I remember reading of a tonic of japperseed ichor that, when consumed, was supposed to allow a man to breathe underwater."

Arvin scoffed. "He'd have to inhale it, like a vapor. We don't breathe with our stomachs."

The man nodded. "Might be why he drowned." He reached down a hand. "Arvin of no tribe?"

*How did he know my name? Had he been in the tent?*

Arvin nodded and accepted the man's hand. He pulled Arvin to his feet with ease. Their eyes met, and Arvin didn't dare look away. Despite being of the same height, the man was layered in weathered muscle and scars compared to Arvin's slight frame and smooth complexion.

"Arvin of no tribe, I'm Evrick." His grip on Arvin's hand turned into a friendly handshake.

"Oh!" Arvin was taken aback. "Hewer of skulls?"

"Really, just the one," he playfully conceded. "You know how it is. You do it *one time* and next thing you know—"

"You are a skull hewer for life," Arvin finished.

Evrick put a hand to Arvin's back and began guiding him around the side of the command tent. "I had a brother-in-law that fucked a camel. Guess what his name was?"

Arvin smiled. A legitimate, amused smile. "Camelfucker?"

Evrick feigned shock. "What? No. Aedan."

*Oh, a clever joke! He built up a clear expectation and then subverted it. He is trying to cheer me up from my failure.*

"You're being nice to me," Arvin blurted. "Does this mean I can work on the fuse?"

Arvin's bluntness seemed to take Evrick by surprise, but his face snapped back to the same disarming smile as before. "I do have a project that could use an attentive mind such as yours. It needs someone who thinks unlike others." Several resting guards hoisted their gloves in respect as Evrick passed. He acknowledged them with a polite nod.

Arvin buzzed from excitement. "Is there alchemy involved? I'm strong with most aspects of mixtures and solutions. But talcs are frustrating to me. I can get better."

*Gods-damned talcs. One sneeze and everything is everywhere.*

"No, nothing involving chemistry just yet. Here, let me give you a small tour." He pointed toward a wooden structure jutting from the sand. It was the opening of a descending staircase, stretching far below the ground and into the depths. Torches lit the sides of its carved stone walls and the glint of copper lining flickered the yellow light back up into Arvin's eyes.

He had never seen a man-made distance so far, let alone so deep. And there was more copper present in the stonework than he thought all of Vastard had among its limestone. The copper wove an angled pattern, mathematically perfect, all the way down beyond the range of human eyesight. Such consistent precision made Arvin dizzy at first, until he unfocused his eyes and all that existed in the world was the tunnel leading below.

Its mystery tugged at his mind, luring him forward. He stared, agape at the unseen wonders he could only imagine below.

"Come," Evrick offered. "Come see what the ancients made. And know that their secrets are for us all, even the tribeless such as yourself."

Arvin's mind swam with anticipation as he followed Evrick down the sloping tunnel. The stairs themselves sat in two narrow sets, one on each side of the copper-bound stonework, closest to the walls. Between the two sets, the stonework remained flat, polished smooth from centuries of scrapes and wear.

*It's a slide downward. I bet they had a pulley and winch system at the entrance at one point. It raised and descended a sled for supplies and large objects down the slope. The stairs were for people steadying it on either side.*

Arvin, distracted by envisioning the tunnel in operation, bonked his head on a mounted torch.

"Mind yourself," Evrick passively advised.

Rubbing his sore scalp, Arvin examined the lighting fixture. It had been mounted recently and hastily, not of the original construction. Looking about, he saw no light sources leading downward other than the ones Evrick's expedition must have installed.

*How did the ancients see down here? What light source did they have?*

They continued for a good while in silence. Arvin began to feel special to have earned a personal escort from the warlord himself.

*He knows how smart I am! And he made jokes. When will I know if we are friends?*

As the air cooled and grew more and more still, Arvin looked back at the distant entrance of the tunnel. It was like a window to the surface world, a purple sky speckled with stars beyond. The perspective shift made Arvin dizzy and he steadied himself against the stone.

His fingertips encountered several sets of deep, parallel grooves cut into the wall. They were so clean, they sliced through the copper inlay. Whatever did it cleaved the metal and stone in equal measure. Arvin probed the grooves with his fingers. It was clear they were claw marks.

Evrick pulled one of the torches from its sconce and brought it close. He pointed to the blackened discoloration dripping from the gouges. "Claws. All over from here on in. Most of the bones from the victims were ground to dust by the passing centuries, but their blood remains."

"Something invaded?"

"All the exits, at least what we've found so far, are still sealed and undisturbed. Something attacked from within. Circumvented their defenses. Didn't leave a soul alive."

Arvin froze. "And we are down here because . . .?"

"This was generations ago, sealed away."

"Not everything dies of old age," Arvin countered. His sense of awe drowned under a greater sense of doom. "And you come *down* here?"

"Well, for the night. I retire down here to sleep in the space imbued with the spirit of a brilliant civilization. And, of course, my wife."

*He's completely undisturbed by this! But it makes sense, given if they were still alive he wouldn't be.*

"But did you find the things that did this? Their bodies?" Arvin was desperate to see their physiology. Currently, to his mind, they were merely abstract claw marks that cut through anything and everything.

Evrick gave Arvin a placating smile. "I'm fairly confident as to what happened, but first I need you to help me with some folks. Come." He returned the torch to its sconce and continued his descent. "And don't worry. We're cautious about which chambers we clear and open. We listen through the stone and go slowly." He laughed. "We have to, really. The deeper chambers have no breathable air in them. Takes time for the pressure to equalize."

Arvin became distracted from his unease by thinking about the ventilation issues that the excavation must be facing.

*They could use smithy bellows to pump in air through a long tube. Not insulated. Sheep skin? Dried sheep stomachs patched together? That would require so many sheep!*

An image of hundreds of sheep being sundered by the invisible claws shook Arvin. He was afraid to touch the wall next to him, fearful of discovering more claw marks.

His fearful mind spun. "Are there traps below? I've heard that ruins under the sand are trapped."

"The 'traps' as you call them, are only defensive measures. Some chambers sealed and sucked out the air or pumped in poison. But they don't have power. Yet. But we have explosives at each major tunnel entrance in case anyone takes Tent City. I'm considering your japperseed oil solution to place similar explosives deeper inside at various junctions, as well."

"So, a lot of explosives down here?"

*Made by people I don't know, who weren't taught by Uncle.*

Evrick nodded in the affirmative, ignorant of Arvin's apprehension.

Still descending, they came to a double stone door. One half of it sat open, its heavy weight supported by a track system. Arvin figured it required a dozen men to move it.

*Clearly there is another pulley system hidden away somewhere.*

His mind began constructing the gears for such a mechanism. Before he could really get going, two guards approached Evrick and saluted.

"Lord. All is well."

Evrick nodded, pleased. "We're actively recruiting more and more up above. It will take the burden off all of you, having drifters handle the remedial tasks."

"Thank you, lord," one replied.

The other appeared wistful. "I miss sleeping topside."

Evrick clapped him on the shoulder. "The tarts miss you too!"

The three shared a laugh.

*No. I learned my lesson.*

Arvin's face remained stoically passive as the three enjoyed their knowing nudges. Their jovial conduct eventually settled down, and Evrick continued on with Arvin in tow.

Both guards examined Arvin as he passed by, their eyes searching him over.

*Threat assessment. I doubt they will worry. I'm nothing.*

Beyond was an antechamber adorned with resin mesh on the sides and ceiling. Arvin could see rotted tubing underneath, made from some sort of refined leather that had dried and cracked beyond use. It took a moment, but he finally formed his guess into a sentence.

"These are for watering plants? Vines covered this room." He wondered why such a functional tunnel and antechamber would be so aesthetic.

Evrick nodded at Arvin's guess. "Indeed. Best I can figure, the plants in here had a lethal or otherwise debilitating pollen. This was a kill chamber. In the western kingdoms, they call such chambers 'murder holes' and pour hot tar and other things in. Here, the natives of Vastard had a more elegant solution."

Arvin stepped closer to search for any signs of the plant.

Evrick discerned Arvin's interest. "No sign of the plant, I'm afraid. Either extinct or an exotic import. Whatever they pumped in through these porous tubes provoked the plants to release a deadly agent." He motioned forward. "Come. I'm going to station you down here, through the right hallway, and into a holding room."

*A holding room? What does it hold?*

He followed the warlord. The perfectly aligned walls and the glowing copper inlay reflecting the torchlight delighted him. It wasn't nearly as dark as the long descending tunnel they walked down to get here, and the artistry of the minimalist ruins came to full bloom.

The occasional guard saluted as Evrick passed them by and echoes of conversations came from each off-shooting hallway and junction. Arvin heard the chipping of pickaxes in the far distance and bundles of foodstuffs and stacked bedrolls in the corners told a story that dozens of souls had made this their home for weeks on end.

*I won't miss the sun.*

"Here is the room." Evrick turned a corner and motioned toward a massive vault door. It had multiple locks, an intricate tumbler system, and it sat with perfect balance on its hinges, swung wide open.

*They found it already open. No damage or tinkering on the locks.*

Arvin nearly pushed through Evrick. His curiosity consumed him and he *had* to see what was inside. Gone was his fear of the abstract clawed evils. The mysteries of these ruins took all of his mind's space.

Beyond the door sat an arid room with a high ceiling. Ventilation grates were mounted above and below, along the floor, giving a constant flow of air. It was clearly needed because the latent stink of the room was as if it was used as either a prison cell or a latrine.

*Perhaps both. Is there much of a difference?*

A row of levers jutted from the far wall, but the room was otherwise empty. The unusual floor caught his eye: a waxy silicate radiating out into four quadrants from the center.

*Controlled growth of salt and metal combination. Must have used electrical current or perhaps magic directly to do it. Or centuries. Either could work, if patient and attentive enough.*

Arvin knelt down to examine the silicate slabs closely. Usually thin silicate of such a waxy nature could let light dimly through. A very thin layer was nearly as translucent as glass. But this was surprisingly thick, able to support the weight of multiple grown men.

Rapping a knuckle on it, Arvin listened intently. He hoped the sound would give a clue as to its composition.

But something knocked back. From underneath.

Arvin squealed and jumped back. He would have clung to the ceiling if he could.

His alarm provoked a guffaw from Evrick. "That one is Lovely."

"Who?" Arvin asked, pressing himself against the wall in avoidance of the floor.

Evrick took a knee over the silicate quadrant and placed an open palm down on it. The dim shadow of a hand on the other side mimicked the gesture. Palm to palm and fingers to fingers.

"Lovely. She can be mean, but she's at least expressive. The other three are . . . Let me see," Evrick stood and looked about the floor, sorting out everyone's location. "That one there is Rat. He's timid. The corner there is Mama. She's huge. And the one nearest the vault door is Bastard. Because he is a complete and total *bastard*. Took a few fingers from one of his handlers. We've assigned a man, Phigar, to their feeding and care but he is taxed with other duties so you'll be doing his job when he isn't around. Luckily, we found someone sharp like you in the position who can hang onto their fingers."

*Wait. What?*

"I don't do well with people. Especially prisoners," Arvin admitted, despite never having known any prisoners.

*He doesn't understand what I'm good for. Alchemy!*

Evrick stood and began pacing the room. "Oh, they're not prisoners. Exactly. Your job is to keep them fed and not let them claim any more fingers, including your own. If you are feeling enterprising, perhaps you can teach them simple orders and tasks but right now, we have too many other daggers to juggle."

"But I'm an alchemist. My specialties are wasted here. Can't someone else feed and train the moon-touched?"

A predatory stance took over Evrick's posture. The warlord title was now more apparent. "And as I said, I'll have work like that for you in the future. For now you're going to work with these . . . people. Feed them whenever Phigar rolls in a barrel of feed, keep them as healthy as you can. And take notes. Teach them a word or two if the opportunity arises. Show me that you are competent. I'll check back in a month."

Arvin was flabbergasted. Looking down, he saw another pair of shadowy hands under the floor appear. They were from the quadrant of Bastard.

"I-I don't think I'm . . ." He could barely form his protest, let alone a thought.

Evrick's eyes narrowed. "Is this going to be an issue for me?"

*He can kill me without a single concern.*

"No, no," Arvin answered swiftly. "But, uh, what happened to these people? I need more context. What did they do to be contained."

"Well, they were part of an experiment. We used the last juice in some relics below on them."

"I need to see the machine—"

Evrick raised his palm. "No. You haven't earned that just yet. We only met, and while I'm initially impressed, I've been wrong before. Show me that you can care for those in complicated situations." Evrick thought for a moment, easing his stature back to a more friendly air. "The truth is, I'm stretched thin on people. I prize your potential as an alchemist, but I *need* someone to help Phigar feed these feral folks. Show me that you can be patient. Patient like me."

"Feral?"

*Oh god, they're going to eat me!*

"Keep them alive. Bring that innovative, japperseed-oil-thinking and see if they can learn a word or two. Maybe you can calm them down and they won't have to be in cells by month's end. Then I'll reassign you to something more entitled to your strengths."

Arvin, still pressed against the wall, was at a loss for words. He should have stayed in Tent City, peddling his alchemical knowledge to any herbalists or cooks that needed new spice recipes. There were many different levels of work to be had among the tribal denizens of Vastard, even if some of that work was deplorable.

"A guard will be stationed outside the vault door. He'll get you whatever you need, including a bedroll, food, and parchment. Phigar will be by eventually when it is feeding time." Evrick turned to leave, but as he stepped out of the vault door, he called over his shoulder. "And for the love of the gods, never *ever* close this door. We're not sure if it can be opened from the inside."

*And that's it. I can also be trapped in here forever.*

# FOUR

Evrick

Like every other day recently, Evrick was exhausted. Every morning, he climbed the ascent from the ruins' depths to his command tent. He had to deal with any crisis that had occurred overnight in Tent City, wrangle his scholars and wisemen by appeasing their egos while simultaneously commanding them, and additionally handle any contests to his position as leader.

And that was to say nothing of just how *stupid* so many of his followers behaved. Growing up in Vastard, he marveled at the emotional immaturity of his elders as they bickered over meaningless things and tossed around the word "respect" as an abstract. Too many people outsourced their wisdom to their silent gods or the present hierarchy instead of devising more efficient ways to rule and operate. It was maddening.

So Oppah, the ruler of Vastard, was the first to go. He was corrupt and lazy for a leader, let alone a leader of a half-starved mercenary collection of outcast tribes. Even his personal guard despised him. Tired of his hoarding and fencing fees, his own people aligned with

Evrick Skullhew because *anyone* was better. Oppah had no choice but to flee to Daynce and shake his tiny, corpulent fist at Vastard from the battlements.

Then came the individual tribes built from the descendants of mercenary companies. Getting each tribe to throw off the yokes of their ruling council and join him had been difficult—and bloody. Part of a tribe's initiation to join Evrick was to kill their own tribal leadership outright. Evrick refused to do it himself for fear of reprisal. After all, having followers commit the act without him physically involved was true power. They had to free themselves first then willingly submit to the Skullhew banner. If the people of Vastard wanted a better future, one dug up from the ancient ruins of their marvelous land, they had better make such sacrifices with their own hands.

Motivating the people to do so was the easiest part, really. He dressed like a common swordsman, wore his hair free to buck tradition, and kept only one wife without any concubines. Women had equal value and expectation under his banner. Half of his guards in the ruins were women. This drew not only young women to the cause but also the men said young women influenced. And thusly every fat, slovenly chieftain with a harem had become a target.

He was pleased at the progress of his followers. The tribal coalition under Evrick contained seventeen tribes, all from Vastard itself, and had swelled to nearly eight thousand souls. In six years, he had taken control of Vastard and one fifth of the Yellow Sea beyond to the south. The land was hungry for change, guidance, and modernization. The timing was perfect. If he had been born during the prior generation, he would have either been ignored as an idealist or beheaded as an upstart.

But his growing and thriving people still needed a new name. Evrick did not want to be a conqueror, but instead a *founder* of a new civilization. Identity was vital for an emerging movement to latch onto, and while Evrick was currently leading the largest coalition of tribes in recent history, he still wanted even *more* under his banner.

The best way for enthusiasm to spread for his leadership was to simplify the language of it.

"New Vastard?" he wondered aloud as he turned a corner. "Vastard Risen?" was another name that he tested out with his mouth as he descended a spiral stairwell. It was his favorite time of day—time to retire to the depths of ruins where the greatest mysteries lie. The most enticing one was his wife.

As he trotted down the spiral stairwell, a scholar ascended from the opposite direction. There wasn't room for the both of them and Evrick wasn't about to smoosh himself against the wall and rub bits with one of his researchers as they shimmied by each other, so he waved the scholar back. As the man scurried down to let Evrick pass, he kept testing out names.

"The Skullhewn Vastard? The Second Kingdom of Vastard? Children of the Ancients? No, that sounds like a cult."

The scholar looked away as Evrick spoke to himself. Leaving the stairwell behind, Evrick reached a junction of hallways. It was a domed room, tiled with black obsidian hexagons, and at its center sat two reclined chairs. They were elevated on a dais, measured specifically to collect sound from dozens of brass horns sprouting from the ceiling.

It was a listening post that extended throughout all of the ruins, even to parts they hadn't uncovered yet. Every tunnel echoed up through piping to the seats, intended for scribes, to record the days' reports. Evrick figured that the ancient intended it as a means to monitor experiments and classes below with regular progress reports shouted up through the receiving horns in each room below.

It also was an excellent way to eavesdrop.

He briefly wondered what it sounded like when the entire complex had been invaded a millennia ago. Had the listening scribes just scribbled, "Ahh, something is cutting us to ribbons?"

Currently he had two men stationed at the chairs, but they were slow scribes and their handwriting was difficult to read. Vastard did not produce scribes regularly or easily.

He approached them and whispered, "Report."

One handed over a stack of uneven parchment as the other scribbled something while listening intently with his tongue out. Evrick only heard muffled words because he wasn't in the chair himself; his ears weren't in the trajectory of the horns' produced echo.

Sifting through the papers, he saw the usual: so-and-so burned himself on some electrified copper inlay, two guards got in a fight over the affections of one of the haulers, a new tunnel had been uncovered and required light and air, and lastly his wife had called up for him.

"How old is this?" Evrick flapped the parchment scrap about his wife.

The scribe looked dimly at it.

Evrick pressed. "There is no recorded time written here. I provided you an hourglass to record time. Which turn of it was this message received on?"

Still dim.

Sometimes Evrick was tempted to rule by fear. Fear was golden, after all. Beheading this man could serve as motivation for the others. But fearful warriors only did enough to avoid punishment. Followers must *love* you. He needed his men to go to the ends of the Yellow Sea for him.

Evrick sighed, letting his disappointment show.

The scribe shrank in his seat. "I'm sorry, lord. I'm sorry. There is so much noise that figuring the important things from the unimportant is impossible! I lost track of the hourglass and realized I'd missed flipping it when—"

Raising a hand, Evrick cut him short. He didn't have time for this. "I need *you* to figure out a system of note taking that works. Can you do that for me?"

The scribe beamed with eagerness. Eagerness was what Evrick needed most. It was what fueled *change* the most.

He handed back the parchment. "From now on, if my wife wants me, send a runner."

"We need more runners, lord."

Evrick was trying his best not to chip a tooth in frustration. "Well, we are actively recruiting. We added a number of haulers today, as well as a . . ." he remembered Arvin. "Just use a hauler. So long as whatever they are hauling isn't smoking or vibrating, I'm sure it isn't as important as our lady getting ahold of me."

"Yes, lord." The scribe was clearly relieved. He knew what most chieftains would have done if they were so annoyed with him.

Evrick left and proceeded down another stairwell, this one wider. It led through the barracks for the guards and dig teams below. He continued testing out names for his new, rising empire in the sand.

"Vastard, the Next Generation? Gods, that is stupid."

He gave up, realizing he was too frazzled for anything brilliant. He needed tea, he needed to get his boots off, and he needed to see the most wonderful person on the planet. The woman that saved not only his life, but now shared his goal.

Reaching a hole blasted in the stonework, he nodded to the attentive guards surrounding it. The lower levels of the complex had the better guards. He wanted the best to not only surround and protect his wife, but also the treasured magical machines below.

Especially the mysterious Concentrix. If they were to activate it and power everything properly, it would require constant observation and protection. The Concentrix was a mystery of ancient magic, currently beyond comprehension, but Evrick felt it to be the nexus of this entire ruin. Perhaps the nexus of this entire civilization. Every copper wire, rune, glyph, and hallway led to it below.

Upon seeing their approaching master, one of the guards drew up a long rope from the hole. The floor had been blown open by Evrick's first dig team to provide a way down before they discovered a nearby available staircase. So many junctures and stairwells had been barricaded or collapsed that Evrick had his men use explosives to sunder the stone and make fresh doorways and passages. He worried about weakening the structure of the tunnels and halls, but not enough to temper his impatient urge to discover.

This particular hole was just a blackened crack in the ground with a winch over it like a well. He could walk the long way down one of those sets of stairs, but this was the fastest descent and time was always at a premium. The rope came up with a short plank dangling on its end. Evrick took the rope and waited for the guards to finish winding its length up tightly in the winch.

"Things above well, lord?"

Evrick found that the smarter, tougher guards spoke to him with more ease and initiated conversation. They also tended to be more curious and intellectually invested in their surroundings. He enjoyed their company immeasurably more since fearful people didn't provide meaningful discussion or insight.

"Well as they can be. A fair number of haulers and laborers recruited these past few days." He was getting tired of repeating it, "But one has some knowledge, at least."

The guards seemed pleased at this modicum of good news. Evrick had lost brilliant minds to cave-ins, moldy and unbreathable air, and one even managed to melt himself when he discovered a chemical storage chamber. The personnel problem Evrick faced was very much felt on all levels of the Skullhew hierarchy.

His worries about the future of the Skullhew banner reemerged. "Make kids. As many as you can," Evrick ordered his guards with a smile. "At least one of them will be smart. We need smart people."

The guards laughed. One held the rope steady as Evrick stepped on it, both his boots flanking the knot tied through the center of the plank.

"Sadly, lord," the guard began. His eye was missing, buried under a mound of scarred flesh from a burn. "My kids are all dullards like me."

Evrick took a mental note of the guard's face. He wanted to meet his kids. "Bring them down sometime."

"Back at home with my sister-in-law."

"Well, are they tough? Dullards must at least be tough." Evrick said, enjoying the repartee.

The guard shook his head. "Nope. But at least they inherited my looks."

The accompanying laughter roared loud enough for the two scribes at their listening post to likely jolt.

It was what Evrick needed. A good, hearty laugh. "All right, I'm ready. Down I go."

They nodded and began cranking the winch. Evrick was lowered slowly through the hole, the rope spinning him slightly as it settled from his weight. The descent was far enough to kill a man if he fell, so he gripped the rope tightly. This wouldn't be a dignified manner for a warlord and visionary to die.

"Vastardian Coalition? Ugh, sounds like it's from the North."

The crack expanded into a large chamber below. Massive copper tubes ran along the ceiling in dizzying clumps and the heat radiating from them glowed just enough to light the entire cavern a deep orange. Below sat two rows of silicate pods, all broken save four, designed to hold individuals or creatures. Skeletons of odd monstrosities and bipeds lined the rooms, some still intact, leaving only the imagination to complete their forms with flesh and skin.

He wondered which species had managed to escape and kill everyone a thousand years ago. Was it one apex predator that did it, or a horde of them? Evrick wondered what Vastard could do with an army of such killers.

"The Claws of Vastard?" He didn't like it. Any civilization built around its desire to intimidate was sure to fail. Inspiration was a far better direction.

The plank lowered to the alabaster floor. A guard reached for the descending rope and steadied it as Evrick stepped off. "We got some laborers recruited above," Evrick told him before he could ask. "They will be assigned here for two weeks to clean and polish the floor. Make sure they have bedding and proper warm food, yes?"

The guard hesitated. "I'd-I'd have to start a cooking fire down here."

Evrick thought for a moment. "Yes, do it. Just away from all of the"—he gestured at the silicate pods, the copper tubing, and the blue stone panels jutting from the walls—"stuff."

Seeing his wife Visteria in the distance, Evrick dropped the conversation. As he approached her, he could already feel his shoulders easing. She was a magnificent woman, slightly older than he with tightly bound hair that glowed rose gold in the orange light. Her purposeful hands adjusted several knobs on the cobbled machinery that dangled over the only occupied pod in the entire chamber. It was one of the broken ones, but it still served as an ideal hospice bed.

When he approached, Visteria must have recognized his boot steps because she unfixed her hair and shook it free in one fluid motion. It was her way of letting him know he was going to have an eventful, passionate evening.

"How fairs your *niece*, Love?" he asked, hovering over her shoulder to both smell her and watch her work. The released scent of her unfurled hair darted up his nostrils, swelled into his sinuses, and pleasantly fogged his brain.

Coyly, she pretended he had surprised her. "Oh! You are *stealthy* husbandthis evening."

But with a wink, she dropped the act. Serious things were clearly afoot. "I moved Ovallin here, closer to my research so I can watch over her. She's not well, but"—Visteria checked to make certain all other guards and nearby laborers were out of earshot—"I doubt we have to worry about her dying, since she doesn't really do that." Turning to the unconscious prepubescent girl laying in the silicate pod, Visteria pointed to the various tubes coming out of her arms. They were of flexible and ageless rubber, just one of the countless fruits found in the ruins. "We've taken as much blood as we can without risking her heart stopping, Husband. And according to the best physician we have, trepanation would buy us a few more months."

"You mean boring a hole in her skull?" Evrick seethed. He pointed at a crossbow bolt's cut shaft that jutted off-center from her forehead. "What does the idiot think that is? A horn? She's already *got* a hole in her head." He huffed in frustration. "If we let an idiot bore a skull in her head, a second one that is, she will likely die, spring up like a sun blossom wherever she's from, and come roaring back for us. I prefer her like *this*." He jabbed a downward finger at the vegetative girl.

"Well, of course. Remember, you haven't had the easiest time bringing prime physicians under the banner of Skullhew."

It was his driving desire behind rebranding the coalition of tribes under him to something more appealing. "Skullhew" scared away intellectuals and skilled artisans, but he wanted Vastard to bloom with commerce and culture. Evrick wanted a standing professional army, a tribal council with equal representation, and a swift court system. Again, his mind raced for a welcoming, inspiring name. He had promised himself several to pick from by today's end.

"I'm still working on that," he huffed. "But anyway, I know her kind is supposedly immortal." He paused, gazing at the repurposed sheeps' bladders feeding water and nutrients into her through a cauterized hole in her throat. "I'd rather not test it, though. Not with the most valuable commodity known running through her veins."

Visteria nodded. "I checked my translation of the Concentrix glyphs yet again. 'Godly blood' is the fuel for the engines. As a sorceress, she *should* fit the bill."

Evrick wracked his brain. The intact metamorphic pods were operational when found, but they appeared to only have one charge in them and that had recently been spent. To refuel them, the "blood of the gods" was required. But clearly there was something they were missing. They had bled the girl nearly dry, used her blood on the activating blue stones, and still nothing.

And that went for all of the magical machinery they had unearthed, including the Concentrix below. None of Visteria's *niece's* blood worked. If it wasn't already charged up, waiting to be activated, they couldn't get the sorcerer's blood to fire it up.

"Godly blood *indeed*." He looked at the comatose girl with disappointment. "For someone who came to kill me, I expected more. A bit insulting, really." Evrick didn't know where the young woman had come from, but when she levitated him in his tent, ready to pull him in half with unseen divine power, Visteria saved him with a surprise crossbow bolt to the skull.

Whoever sent her, or whatever her motivation was, remained a mystery. He suspected he was digging where he shouldn't, and a sorcerer's appearance confirmed to him that true power lay below the sands here. Hence his impatience.

His mind returned to the ruins surrounding them. "Did you figure out the Concentrix, yet? It *is* a power source, yes?" If only he could get everything *working*. What ancient power lingered in the halls just wasn't enough.

Visteria shook her head. "All glyphs regarding it are scratched out or burned away. I have nothing."

"Did we try just repainting the glyphs with her blood? Right from the vein? Not from a bag?"

She shook her head. "She is in limited supply, to say nothing of whatever time we have before someone *else* comes after you. I halted all such experiments until we have a better idea of how to proceed. Dragging her around and just throwing more blood at things without changing how we make the attempt is wasteful."

Evrick saw the logic, but knew he would have gone ahead with such an experiment anyhow. Visteria was always more mindful than he in such matters.

He took her hand and squeezed it in appreciation. "So the translation is correct, but her blood doesn't activate the Concentrix or the pods. Could the blood of the gods be a metaphor?"

Visteria shrugged. "Maybe? What else would be blood of the gods?"

Before he could stop himself, he just fumbled it out. "Semen?"

". . . semen."

"Well, I'm just trying to think outside the box."

"Oh, I think you're trying to get *inside* the box."

"I do so love boxes."

"Always semen with you. The girl doesn't *have* any semen."

"I was guessing just semen in general. Not a great metaphor. But hey, no ideas are bad ideas, right?"

Visteria leaned in to her husband, her hands against his chest, and gazed up at him. "A long day, I take it? Are you *over-cooked* husband?"

"Seems so," he confessed, wrapping his arms around her. "We might just have to let the mystery of the Concentrix lie for now. Do what we can with the metamorphs we managed to make. I got Phigar an assistant, at least." He sighed. "After all, there are still tunnels to excavate and depths to explore down here. Perhaps we'll find a vat of gods' blood somewhere below."

"Let's retire for now," she said with a hint of mischief. "The sauna calls. Growing your nation can wait."

# CHAPTER
# FIVE

Arvin

It felt like hours since Evrick had departed, and Arvin remained in silence with his back against the far wall. At some point he had slept, but the hunger gnawing at his gut woke him. His thirst parched his throat, and he had tried and failed several times to call into the hallway. He practiced what he would finally ask for.

*Hey there, friend. Do you have any water you don't want?*

*Is there food to be had? By me, perhaps?*

*I'm hungry and thirsty and dying and scared!*

Paralyzed by the social barrier between him and his needs, Arvin decided to distract himself. He took to examining the room more thoroughly. The four silicate slabs in the floor compelled him the most. Their grain was so uniform and their surfaces polished down so perfectly that he could hardly fathom the craft and care put into their creation. It would take a hammer and chisel hours to punch through one of them, and each had to weigh as much as several men.

The wall farthest from the vault door had an embedded winch

system with four levers in a row serving as controls. Arvin could easily see how each lever would open each individual chamber.

*But which lever opened what chamber?*

It was maddening. The four levers were in a row, yet the four chambers were arranged in the floor like a grid. The lever to the far left might be for the left chamber nearest the vault door, but it could also be for the one on the left behind it. What's more, would the levers activate the chambers in a clockwise manner, or in rows like the written word?

There was no way to know.

*Oh no. I'm going to have to talk to people.*

"Excuse me? Hallway man?" Arvin called out, his voice strained between meekness and requiring volume.

A guard peeked into the vault through the door. He had a whip curled on his belt and a cudgel dangling loosely in his meaty hand. His other hand had been recently mangled with a finger and a half missing. From the puffy red flesh, the wound appeared recent.

"What?" His voice echoed, like a bark, off the silicate.

Arvin pointed like a perplexed child. "Which lever opens which—"

"I'm not coming in there." The guard disappeared back into the hallway.

"But, um . . ."

From the hallway he responded tersely. "I'll only come in there if you're about to die."

*Oh. I'll be seeing him soon, then.*

Arvin pondered what his next move should be. He could simply get one of the bedrolls from the hall and sleep on it. His body was exhausted from traveling tirelessly and shuffling in the crowd for most of the day.

*I should just wait for this Phigar. Or try and sleep. Sleep would help me forget my hunger.*

But his curiosity had already fallen victim to the scenario. The dark hands under the silicate haunted him, and he had to see what this person looked like. He wanted to smell them, see the inside of each holding chamber, and feel the silicate from the other side. What other wonders of construction were within?

"How long will Phigar be? When is he coming to feed them?" Arvin called.

No answer from the hall.

"Will there be food leftover?"

Arvin had a month, and within that time his curiosity would be sated. He should just wait for Phigar to show up at feeding time, get some food of his own, and learn how things work. There were simple expectations to this task, and Arvin could easily excel. All he had to do was be patient and exercise self-control.

But Arvin's eyes landed on the round shape of the levers' fossilized and cracked wood. His fingers twitched. If he opened one of the slates, the guard would likely call for Phigar. And he would get food earlier. Besides, Arvin was *curious*.

*Whelp.*

With a few compulsive steps, he walked across the silicate platforms and gripped the lever on the farthest right. It was as good as any, and he figured it wasn't likely to be Bastard's.

He tugged down.

The streamlined gearwork hidden within the walls spun as one of the silicate slabs retracted. It was on a hidden track system and as it glided away, Arvin fell to worry.

*Yep. That's Bastard's.*

With nothing else to do and no way to protect himself, Arvin merely crossed his legs and sat. He'd made no preparations, had no placating offering of food or drink, and hadn't even set up soothing incense or tonics for Bastard to ingest.

*Curiosity is more lethal than arsenic.*

He closed his eyes, partly out of an attempt at dignified resignation, but also because someone named Bastard was likely going to be terrifying. He didn't want to see that.

*Maybe he's sleeping?*

From beyond his closed eyelids, something shuffled onto the floor. Then came a half snort-half snarl. Thick fingernails scratched across the silicate flooring. Then came a hot exhalation on Arvin's face.

Bastard was nose-to-nose with him.

*But he hasn't struck yet.*

With his eyes still shut, Arvin figured a gentle greeting was in order. "Hello?"

Bastard was on him, rolling Arvin onto his back. He was straddled and pinned. Arvin could no longer resist and he opened his eyes. The hairiest man he'd ever seen drooled over him. Crazy-eyed, naked, and grimacing with malice, Bastard and Arvin evaluated each other.

Bastard then rummaged clumsily through Arvin's duster, tugged at his bandolier, and messed with his alchemical bottles and bindings.

That, Arvin could not permit. His chemicals were too precious, and several like the hydrochloric acid were astoundingly dangerous if unleashed. Reacting with indignation, Arvin smacked away Bastard's hairy hands.

"No, sir!"

Bastard reeled away for a moment in shock, seemingly stunned that Arvin would dare slap at him. Then his face turned to unbridled rage.

Arvin raised his arms to protect his face from the incoming flurry of blows when the guard's cudgel clubbed Bastard on the head. The hairy man spun, angered even further instead of subdued, and pounced on the guard.

The two men fell into a savage brawl, the guard cursing all of Bastard's anonymous fathers and the gods that made them as he kicked and pummeled the escapee. They tumbled about, driving each other into the closed silicate slabs as their blows each struck true.

"The lever!" the guard gasped. "Flip it back!"

Arvin leaped to his feet and flicked it upward. The gears turned once again as the silicate platform began closing. The guard kicked Bastard in the ribs once, twice, and on the third time Bastard rolled away and folded from the impact.

*Rib cracked. Bastard will be pained to breathe for days.*

"Get him in there!" the guard yelled, pushing on Bastard's curled back with his boot. Arvin wanted to help, but he froze.

*He's stopped. And injured. The fight is over.*

But the guard kept stomping and shoving Bastard toward the closing chamber, instead of just pushing him toward it. Arvin quickly calculated that Bastard would only be halfway inside once it began to close on him.

"Stop!" he yelled, but the guard ignored him.

Bastard's front half dangled into the chamber as the silicate closed in toward his midsection. Arvin doubted that he had the strength to muscle the guard away and pull Bastard up.

*There is nothing to learn from a half-Bastard.*

So he did the absolute dumbest thing.

Racing under the guard's stomping boot, Arvin wrapped his arm around the hairy man and dove into the closing chamber, pulling Bastard with him. The two fell inside just in time for the silicate barrier, which was now a ceiling, to thump shut.

Crammed inside with a hairy madman, Arvin wondered if this was the last decision he had made. He looked to Bastard, expecting the hairy man to crash into him and tear at him.

But the hairy man's labored breathing and gritting teeth indicated the fight was out of him, at least for now.

*He is intact, thank goodness.*

Arvin rapped a knuckle against the silicate ceiling. "Hello? Mr. Guard? Could you let me out?"

He stomped back. "Fuck no!"

CHAPTER

# SIX

Evrick

Within the span of ten minutes, Evrick finally got his wish; his boots were off, and he was on his second cup of tea with Visteria splayed out next to him, completely naked. She glistened deliciously from the humid sweltering of the small chamber. A dim light radiating from a hexagonal pattern within the stone ceiling was also the source of the heat, but no one had figured out the power source to the sauna as of yet.

The dig team that discovered the sauna had figured this room was some kind of humidor or seed vault, but Visteria easily deduced it to be a sauna for recuperation and relaxation. She had even figured out how the herb dispersal vents worked.

Currently, there lingered a minty scent to the sauna's sweltering heat. It opened Evrick's lungs and paired surprisingly well with the spiced tea's aftertaste. He marveled at his wife's ability to pair sensations, be it spiced tea with mint or fellatio with tickling the fronts of his thighs.

His muscles gradually uncoiled from the day's stress as he sank into the coarse straw pillows that made up the majority of the sauna's seating. "I think we should abandon all endeavors for Vastard," he said lazily. "Let someone else do it. Give it back to Oppah. I want to stay here forever and look at you naked."

Visteria rolled on her side, intentionally showing off the curve of her hip by pulling her one knee to her stomach. "Oh? Just stay here?"

"Yep," he said, mesmerized.

"And someone else would lead the . . . Hmmm. What is our movement called again? You figure out a new name to make folk flock to the banner?" she chided.

He sighed in defeat. "I know Skullhew might not do well when it comes to trading outside Vastard, but it *is* my moniker. Fighting men and women gave me the name, after all!"

"It was just the one skull, really," she said, rolling onto her back again.

Her following silence indicated to him she expected him to have a name by now. He watched her eyes follow the glowing pattern in the ceiling for a moment before speaking.

"Love?"

"Hmm?"

"I want a new name because I don't want Vastard to belong to me. Vastard needs to be its own land. *That* is what I want people flocking to: Vastard. Skullhew is just who got it started."

She smiled. "I know. That's why I first fell in love with you. A conqueror that doesn't want to conquer, but to cultivate." Her hands settled below her belly button. "Still, would be nice to be a kingdom with heirs instead of a ruling council of tribal rivals. More stable."

He now knew *exactly* what was on her mind. They had been unable to conceive for the entirety of their brief marriage. She insisted she had to be the problem since she had had other lovers before him. But he always insisted the issue could be him. Visteria wanted a child so very badly, and she wanted it with Evrick. Not just for the security of the banner and what they had built, but because she desperately wanted the connection. He knew this because he felt it just as strongly.

He had suggested adopting children, but she countered that most of the tribes wouldn't recognize them as heirs. She proposed a concubine for him to produce heirs, but he refused the possibility because if he died she'd be likely assassinated by the surviving heirs' mothers.

Evrick decided to defuse his wife's malaise with playfulness. "I've been thinking about your concubine idea, Love," he began.

Her eyebrows shot up. "Really? You were so against it? And don't worry. I'll pick her out. I won't kill her afterward or anything."

"Oh, not like that. I was thinking . . . We should find you a young buck."

She processed where he was going instantly. With a roll of her eyes, she flopped back into her cushions. "You are such a jackass."

"No, it will work. Why must it be the men with concubines, after all?"

"You are *dumb* husband right now. I'm barren."

"Are we certain? You and I try every day, but what about truly saturating your insides?"

That one finally got her laughing. "Oh. The. Gods."

"We'll pick several virile young men, a gaggle of spindly twinks, and I'll lead them upon you like a raiding party."

She was belly laughing now and it was the most beautiful thing in the world.

"I'll ride from the front, obviously, while the others take your flank. You'll be slathered by the time we're done. Awash. You'll get *exceedingly* pregnant."

Between heaving giggles, she asked, "What makes a pregnancy exceed? Twins?"

"A battalion will pour out of you! The army we need to secure our borders."

"Oh, what the fuck!" She jumped up, climbed on top of him, and play-strangled him as her marvelous locks dangled in his face.

Evrick made exaggerated choking sounds, his tongue flopped out. "Gak! Argh! But I think I'm into this!"

She fell into him laughing. They both giggled until their lungs were spent and their hearts aflutter. "You choking me might have awakened something in me, Love," he teased.

"You are *dipshit* husband. But I love you anyway." Her face became more serious. "But I worry for the future. You want a better Vastard. Everything is just so fragile that I want something to have for stability. A future to literally sing to at night and kiss in the morning."

"We can find some random kids among the tents above for you to accost."

"I'm being serious now."

"Sorry."

He sat and listened, waiting for her to continue expressing herself. As he patiently waited, he stroked her back. She settled into him, sighing contentedly.

"This will be built, but others will come to take it. You *need* a line. What about New Ramlagha?" she asked, thoughtfully. "Ramlagha was the Darrish term for 'Jungle of Dunes' I think. It's what travelers through the ancients used to call this civilization hundreds of years ago. And of course, you are bringing it back to glory so 'new' should be there."

Evrick thought a moment. "New Ramlagha?" he tried it out. "New Ramlagha, the fourteenth kingdom of Andos." He pulled away from her and looked her deeply in the eyes. "Love, it's perfect. We are New Ramlagha. We will rise from these ruins and be the envy of the world. A land, below none, run by peers."

"From mountain to mountain."

"From mountain to mountain."

They went to kiss, and their lips had just connected when a loud rapping came at the sauna's opaque silicate door.

He gritted his teeth, but suppressed his frustrations quickly. Evrick didn't want to be flustered around Visteria.

"Yes?" he called.

From the other side of the door, the interrupter didn't sound panicked. "Lord, it's Phigar. I just came down from the metamorph's containment vault."

Evrick couldn't believe it. Was Phigar daring to complain about receiving assistance? Or did the new recruit, Arvin, already botch things? That must have been a record. Arvin seemed socially dim and unwise, but Evrick was hoping the young man's apparent brilliance would see him through.

"Gods damnit," he mumbled. "The new guy I brought on."

"Phigar? No, he's been here a while."

"No, Arvin. Alchemist. Quirky. Maybe moon-touched."

"You threw a moon-touched in with the metamorphs on his first day?" Visteria balked. "I would have told you not to. They can easily kill."

"I needed *someone*, and I . . ." he returned his focus to the door. "Phigar, clean up whatever is left of the idiot and—"

"No, sir, the new guy is in one of the chambers with one of them. We aren't sure if he's even hurt."

Evrick was stunned. "He locked himself inside with one? Which one?"

"Bastard."

"Oh, this I've got to *see*."

Evrick went for the door, but Visteria deftly snapped her legs around him. Rolling her weight, she pinned him back down. "See him in the morning. You can't impact if he lives or dies at this point. But you *can* impact me."

She kissed him deep enough to reach his soul.

CHAPTER

# SEVEN

Arvin

**B**astard glared warily at Arvin with an infinite, searing intensity.

Arvin, in turn, stared at Bastard's forehead. It was his usual way to make people think he was making eye contact. He felt he should say something, but he didn't know what. Most people eased such tension through talking, but Bastard appeared more likely to attack him.

And whenever Arvin spoke to aggressors, it typically encouraged them. Uncle once sent him for fish oil and he was beaten because people didn't like the sound of his voice. Arvin knew he was no desert songbird, but he felt that reaction was a bit extreme.

The value of his words had to carry beyond the grate of his awful voice.

*I must do it right! Helpful and relatable!*

Arvin waited patiently to see what Bastard might immediately need. The brute still clutched his side, and while Arvin thought of binding his rib, he didn't want to risk touching Bastard just yet.

Besides, Arvin hadn't ever bandaged a rib before, and he was uncertain how to do so.

*You bandage ribs, right?*

Sitting and waiting was never a strong suit of Arvin's. Within less than a minute, his terror of being beaten gave way to boredom. Then his curiosity kicked on once again and his eyes began to explore the confined space they crouched in.

The cell wasn't high enough for a person to stand upright in, and the silicate barrier above gave the constant impression of pressure. There was a slab for sleeping, a hole in the ground that acted as a commode which once had a hinged cover, and the air felt ionized as if before an electrical storm.

What light crossed the barrier above kept everything dim, and the subsequent shadows accentuated Bastard's musclework and scars. It was clear the man had led a brutal life across many seasons. His nails appeared bloody and split from endless clawing, likely at the walls, and his knuckles were bulbous with fresh scar tissue.

*No sudden moves, lest I want to feel those knuckles.*

Arvin noticed the bramble-weed mattress torn up on the slab at the side of the cell. He figured Bastard had ripped it open for some reason, but he couldn't discern what that reason was. There was also a gentle trickle of water; a drinking fountain had been cast from some kind of malleable resin into a recess of the wall.

The water itself poured from a round, soft protrusion. The protrusion very much appeared to be shaped like a single breast with a nipple. Below it jutted a half-bowl, filled with what appeared to be clear water.

*A wall boob?*

In a fluid motion, Arvin yanked a pipette from his bandolier and sucked up a sample of the water. He then eased a drop on the skin of his forearm and waited a moment.

*No irritation.*

He rubbed the water drop into his skin.

*Still good. No discernible smell or discoloration.*

He licked his skin to taste it.

*Water. From a . . . wall boob.*

As soon as he realized fresh water was available, Arvin felt an intense thirst. "You drink this? It seems okay to drink."

Arvin desperately wanted to drink from it, but Bastard was wide-eyed. His demeanor had shifted from fearful rage to wonderment. It was distracting. Arvin now seemed to fascinate him—or Arvin was doing something worthy of fascination.

*Oh. The pipette.*

"This is an alchemy tool," Arvin said as he waved it around.

Bastard snarled at it, or possibly at Arvin's motion of waving it around, just before his bearded face shifted to a grimace of pain.

*Rib. Definitely a fractured rib. Or broken.*

Without thinking, Arvin reached forward toward Bastard's midsection. He wanted to check for a 'popping' to accompany each of his cellmate's deep breaths. If that severe, he felt he should bind the rib.

*But not too tight. He has to breathe.*

Bastard chomped his teeth right at Arvin's fingers. Arvin yelped and climbed backward onto the foot of the ruined mattress. Luckily, Bastard left it at that and went back to coddling his chest with both arms.

He thought to apologize, but that would subject Bastard to hearing his voice again and he didn't want to risk it. Not without a plan of what to say.

*My message has to outshine my nasally voice.*

Thinking on the word "bastard," Arvin couldn't help but perseverate. He suddenly felt the need to bond. They could be here for a long time, after all. Who knows when the guard would finally open the cell to let him out.

"Mr. Bastard," Arvin began carefully. "I'm a bastard too. That isn't to presume that *your* bastard experience is equative to *my* bastard experience. I mean, to each bastard their own journey. But . . ."

Arvin paused to watch Bastard for signs of growing hostility, but Bastard seemed to be growing more preoccupied with his injury. Feeling encouraged that he would keep all of his fingers, Arvin continued his attempt at verbal bonding.

*Reveal a vulnerable detail about yourself. Establish trustful reciprocity!*

"So, my father didn't love my mother. I'm sure of it. Mother might have loved him, but I don't really know. Either way, I know some bastards are born out of love that doesn't fit their circumstances, but I don't have that romantic consolation."

Bastard looked distant, his eyes focusing on a landscape far beyond the solid walls of the cell. He curled his feet under himself and eased from his corner and out onto the floor a bit. With a passing glance, Bastard looked as if he was annoyed with Arvin's presence more than anything, but his hostility continued to wane.

Arvin continued, "So as one bastard to another, I feel we have more in common than not." Arvin pressed. "I mean, there are apparent differences. I have clothes, whereas you have impressive amounts of body hair to do the job. My teeth are crooked but your teeth are fantastic. Your canines are long."

*Seriously. So long!*

"And I'm not currently suffering an injury, but," he remembered to focus on their common ground, "I *do* see we are in the same cell together, both of us are bastards within the purview of the word and we indeed both appreciate the joy that is clean water from a wall boob."

With that, Arvin's thirst got the better of him. He leaned over and latched onto the drinking nipple of the soft water dispenser and took a swift suckle. The water was perfect, crisp, and spring fresh. It required immense effort for Arvin to pull himself away after only a mouthful.

*Thank goodness he isn't possessive of his wall boob. And he seems to be a really good listener. Keep him engaged!*

"May I help with your . . . hurt, there?" Arvin pointed to Bastard's clasped hands on the side of his chest where the guard kicked him.

Bastard looked at Arvin's pointed finger with a vacant expression.

*Good! He's no longer hostile.*

"Here, I'll show you what I'll do." Arvin reached out with both hands. It startled Bastard, and the hairy man jumped with a snarl that quickly devolved into a whooping cough. He wheezed and clasped at his chest, sharp misery on his face.

*Too fast! Dumb! Dumb! Dumb!*

Arvin panicked, desperate to undo his carelessness. Bastard was in pain, and each cough sounded worse.

He swiftly fumbled through his bandolier for something. A painkiller or muscle relaxant would likely work.

*Not the base. Not the ethanol. Gods, not the acid. Here!*

He pulled a small pouch of crushed alkaloids. He was pretty sure it wasn't the poisonous one. That one he kept nearer to his shoulder. Fumbling it open, he pressed his fingertips into the collected brown powder and then swiftly brushed Bastard's lips.

*For the pain.*

The man was coughing far too violently to defend himself from the slap-dash application of medicine. But when he realized Arvin was standing so close and had touched his face, he flailed his arm wide and knocked the pouch away. It flew into the air, puffing out its contents everywhere in a cloudy haze.

*Oh no.*

Arvin tried to hold his breath, wondering how much of a dosage was lingering in the air. He clasped both his hands over his nose and mouth, hoping that if he could hold his breath long enough for the powder to settle, he would avoid any effects.

The currents in the air could now be seen, and the cell was revealed to be well ventilated. Porous rocks along the floor pushed air in while similar pores pulled air out near the silicate roof.

*Good! Just wait out the ventilation.*

He leaned against the far wall, as if to avoid the air itself, while watching Bastard's cough ease. He likely got a massive dose, his pain now gone, not just the pain from his lip application but also his desperate lungs coughing and quivering.

*Oh no. I hope I didn't kill him. How much is too much?*

Bastard's arms drifted to his sides. With tearful eyes, he began examining his hands intently while gnashing his teeth.

Guilt swelled in Arvin. He had tried to save the man from being pinched in half only to drug him into oblivion. Bastard could die, his blood pressure dropping and his heart fluttering to a stop. And then all of the unicorns would no longer paint with their rainbow tails.

*What?*

Arvin's concern over the unicorn coven grew considerably. They would toss off the gremlins on their backs and take to flight around the moon. All on a quest for cheese. The runny kind of cheese that soaks proper, stone-oven baked bread. When the bread gets soaked like that, it becomes sad and begins to cry.

No unicorn likes that.

*Oh no!*

When the room shifted to the color yellow, Arvin finally grasped that he was on a psychedelic trip. He fumbled at his bandolier, certain that an antidote was somewhere to be found, but his fingers turned into noodles and his bandolier sprouted wings and soared off into the sky while crying, "Freedom!"

He wasn't even angry. The liberation of his alchemist kit was a beautiful sight to see, especially after all it had endured during its childhood. Holding back tears of solemn joy, Arvin wished it well as it soared toward the distant horizon.

CHAPTER

# EIGHT

Evrick

Evrick sat on a rickety stool, and it threatened to collapse under him. He poked at his gut, checking to see if he'd put on too much weight. The glory days of wind sailing the Yellow Sea and charging armored camels into the enemy's ranks had given way to plodding days of ponderous leadership and conflict resolution between tribal leaders and mercenary companies. It was hell on his muscle tone.

Returning his attention to the unfurled leather scroll in his lap, he continued to take stock of how many arrows and able archers he had at his current disposal. He desired a foothold on the Northern hills, nearer to the city of Daynce, to establish more secure trade lines. And to do so, he had to intimidate the local mercenary groups to bend to his banner. The prosperity that would come of it would benefit all, and he intended to subtly threaten with one hand while offering with the other.

The further from the heart of Vastard New Ramlagha spread, the more rogue the people became. A typical Vastardian was a whore with their sword and bow. It was the corrupting influence of the outside world defining the culture of the Fourteenth Kingdom. The tern 'Fourteenth Kingdom' itself was a mocking moniker, loosely applied to Vastard to both acknowledge its distinction and taunt it. Vastard was seen as never being capable of holding a stable dynasty.

If there was to be a Fourteenth Kingdom to be taken seriously, its future lay with him regardless of what his banner was called. And if people didn't see that, he would be forced to *show* them. He would deliver the revelation with unearthed mysteries, effective diplomacy, and a professional military. All from the magical ruins he now called home.

And yet somehow, he was stuck reviewing arrow counts and archer strengths categorized by tribe on an inventory scroll. His boredom provoked a despondent sigh. It was louder than intended, and he heard something stir below in the open cell at his feet.

He had been wondering when Arvin and Bastard would finally awaken. Evrick arrived at the vault first thing in the morning. When Phigar opened Bastard's silicate barrier, they nearly laughed at the sight: Arvin and Bastard snuggled up under Arvin's unfurled duster. While several guards gathered around to giggle, presuming the two to be newfound lovers, Evrick recognized the faint whiff of drugs, the fun kind from his wind sailing days.

It was brilliant. Arvin placated Bastard through chemical influence, and he did it *with* Bastard which established a bonding experience. Withholding the truth about the four test subjects had worked well in Arvin's favor. The alchemist assumed they were as human as they appeared and he treated them with compassion as equals.

Hence the cuddling and the duster and locking himself in with them.

Evrick rolled his boring scroll up and returned it to its case. He was more interested in who would rise from the cell first, Arvin or Bastard.

A hairy-fingered hand reached out, palm flat, and pushed the rest of Bastard into view. His beard jutted to the side in the shape of

Arvin's shoulder. He was groggy looking, docile, and still in the fog of half-sleep.

Evrick uncrossed his legs and leaned forward in interest.

The guards tightened their grips on their clubs, but Evrick commanded them to leave the vault with a firm gesture.

"Me too, lord?" Phigar asked.

"Yes, roll in a barrel of their feed. And something proper for Arvin. I don't know when he ate last."

Phigar hesitated a moment, as if realizing he had been regulated to serving food to a drugged-up trainee. But he quickly shrugged and stepped out.

Evrick didn't want anyone messing up such a formative moment with their potential aggression. Men were always more violent when he was around, as if their leader would somehow be impressed. Even Phigar.

As Bastard rose clear of his holding cell, Evrick saw the binding on his chest. Arvin had obviously tried to dress a cracked rib, but had done it wrong. It was too tight and would restrict both Bastard's breathing and healing. And the part of it that wrapped over his head didn't make sense at all.

Evrick reached into a pouch on his belt and drew forth some jerky. Bastard's nose caught a whiff. The hairy man focused his attention on the food. No trace of Bastard's usual rage was seen. Evrick knew that some medications caused permanent changes in personality, but this felt far too drastic. Something more profound had occurred in that cell during the course of the night. Something had been *unlocked*.

Bastard stalked toward the jerky, looking down at the seated Evrick. His mouth opened as he approached, ready to eat it right from Evrick's hand.

"Your hand," Evrick said, barely above a whisper. "Use your hand." He extended his own and wiggled his fingers. He then pulled off a strip of beef from the jerky and took it into his own mouth. "I do. I do, so now *you* do." Peeling away another strip, he waved it with his hand toward Bastard.

Bastard's mouth closed. He pondered a moment, then snagged the strip away with his fingers and gobbled it up.

"Good. Good," Evrick encouraged. "This is your new way to eat. So many new things for you. Once you've learned, you can teach the others that come after you." Offering the entire chunk of jerky, Evrick couldn't help but beam. "You'll make a *fine* Skullhew. A battalion of guards and escorts just like you, shock troops that aren't mercenary whores. You'll not need pay or validation. Only orders."

Bastard clearly didn't process the words Evrick was saying, but he did process that the jerky was his to take. He lurched with his mouth at first, then hesitated and instead chose both his hands to take the offering. Sitting on the stone floor, he chewed on it voraciously.

Evrick had already spent too much time dawdling in the vault. The tents above were likely filled with grievances and requests that he had to address. He had to get his day moving.

He stood, careful not to alarm the feasting Bastard, and walked to the open cell. Arvin remained buried under his duster.

"Alchemist," Evrick called. "Up."

Arvin's foot twitched.

Evrick crouched down. The lingering scent of their drugged evening more pronounced now that he was closer. Evrick surmised they must have been blasted out of their minds, boxed in like that all night, and it prompted him to giggle fondly while recalling his own experimental youth.

"Arvin, it is time to get up. I want to know, in detail, what happened."

A hand emerged from under the duster. Then another, and they pulled the duster away to reveal Arvin's reddened eyes.

"Good morning, alchemist. How was *your* evening?" Evrick could barely contain his growing laughter. The harder he tried to contain his amusement, the stronger it became.

Arvin saw this, and began giggling as well. It wasn't the nervous, horror-show giggle that caught Evrick's attention the day prior. It was a genuine laugh of bemusement and joy.

The two men shared the moment of glee together.

"Oh no!" Evrick managed through his giggles. "You've gotten me high, too!"

Arvin squealed with laughter, kicking his feet.

Evrick was belly laughing so hard, he could hardly stay upright. He rolled to his side and draped his legs into the cell. "Oh, oh no."

"It's weak, now." Arvin laughed. "It will be mild for you."

Evrick felt his cheeks flushing with warmth. "If it's this strong *now*, how big a dosage did you two use?"

As Arvin's laughter eased, he shrugged. "I don't know. I should ask the unicorns."

It took a moment, but Evrick caught that Arvin was referring to hallucinations and erupted in laughter anew. Both men were now in a row, flailing about with tears in their eyes as Bastard looked on passively, finishing the last of his jerky.

The guards in the hall peeked in, concerned.

Evrick pointed at them and laughed. "Look, Arvin! Look!"

Arvin jumped to his feet and peeked his head out of the cell and joined in mocking the over-serious guards.

"Got any left for them?" Evrick laughed.

Arvin shook his head. "I used it all! Whoopsie!"

Evrick waved the guards away. He didn't want them being dour when this rare moment was so enjoyable. It was like he was a young man again, celebrating a successful raid with his compatriots.

"You know, those guards aren't really the best," Evrick confided in Arvin. "Sorry I gave you dull guards."

"Eh. I think they work up Bastard, and his reaction . . ." Arvin choked on a laugh, but soon recovered. "They work up Bastard into, uh—"

"A bastard?"

They both giggled a bit more, but the exertion from laughing was burning off the drugs.

"Right," Arvin affirmed. "Honestly, once he was calm, all he wanted was his hair stroked and to be warm. He needs clothes."

"He'll have clothes."

"And what does he eat?"

"Worm gruel and the water from the fountain."

"The wall-boob?" Arvin asked.

Both men returned to gales of giggles. During their bout, Bastard returned to stand over the cell. He reached down and grunted like a toddler for Arvin's duster.

"Oh! Here you go, sir. We were just talking about getting you clothes." Arvin handed the duster up willingly.

Evrick added, "He might need help putting it on, though. I'm not sure if . . ."

Bastard slowly slipped the duster on just as Arvin had worn it earlier. It was a deliberate, concentrated movement of one arm at a time, and afterward, Bastard fiddled with the leather belt.

Evrick was agape. This was amazing progress. The pods must have imbedded co-ordination and quickened his ability to learn. That and a safe space to explore was what the four needed most.

"Arvin, you are clearly cut out for this." Evrick suspected it might be the contact high, but his affection for the awkward alchemist soared. "We'll get you started on something bigger."

"I'm all out of the proper alkaloids."

"Ha! I think with Bastard, the other three will ease into line. He used to work them up." Evrick's mind raced forward; an army of dedicated fighters, each knowing nothing but to follow Evrick, could make his vision of a stable fourteenth kingdom a reality.

But first, there were deeper mysteries in the ruins. Perhaps it was the lingering drugs, or the progress with Bastard, but Evrick felt he now had an opportunity with his newfound subordinate. "Arvin, how are you with hemomancy?"

Arvin blinked, the drug-induced playfulness draining from his face. "Blood magic?"

Evrick nodded as Bastard crouched near him to examine the buckles on his desert coat. Anything metal seemed curious to him.

"Yes," Evrick said. "Specifically, the *source* for blood magic. You ever work with blood as a direct agent before? In alchemy or otherwise?"

"Sounds like something the Desert Children would know about."

This wasn't the first time someone had mentioned the Desert Children as a source for knowledge on the topic. Visteria had mentioned them a number of times.

"They aren't available to me," Evrick answered evasively. "And I would prefer to take a more scholarly approach. No sacrifices. No rituals. Just you and some blood and an alchemy lab."

Arvin stood on the bed slab, raising his waist to floor level. "To what end? Am I to test properties? Transmutation?"

Evrick thought for a moment, but he decided to throw caution to the wind. The first assassin against him was a sorcerer, and he feared that more would follow. And once word got out that he had such a creature under control, droves of hostile factions would descend upon him for his prize. Time was not on his side, and what harm could come of having a tame man like Arvin work on the problem? Arvin might be the miracle Evrick was hoping for.

"No, nothing that severe. We have machinery below that runs on blood magic, and the sooner it operates, the better defended we are. But you must understand," Evrick paused for dramatic emphasis, "this is bigger than you, or me, or just one tribe. This is for the future of this entire region." He allowed a glimmer of a threat to sneak into his voice. "And there is nothing I won't do for our future."

Then, with a slap of his knees, Evrick stood. "Come! And leave your duster with Bastard. I'll get you a new one."

# CHAPTER
# NINE

Arvin

Arvin never felt better. He made two new friends in as many days: the feral Bastard and the charismatic Evrick Skullhew.

*Granted, drugs were a factor but still friends!*

Both seemed like powerful male icons to Arvin, and he hoped to learn more about manhood from them. Prior to this, his knowledge of the world had been limited to Uncle's one-word answers and his collection of worn books.

Uncle had been too old and reclusive, always avoiding questions about intimacy and society. Evrick, however, shared a hearty laugh with Arvin. And Bastard slept next to him. Both of these experiences had delivered more overt affection than Arvin had ever imagined he'd experience.

And now he had been promised something greater, deeper within the depths of the ruins.

*Why did Uncle hide me away so much?*

A dark thought entered his mind. Perhaps it was best that Uncle had died. This was the only way for Arvin to experience the open world and establish himself. Now he was making friends and feeling important.

Then he thought of Uncle's slow, methodical hands. He measured everything several times and he was so adept at measuring he knew exactly how many grains of salt or sand were in a pinch of his fingers. The gruff, quiet man had taken in an unwanted and awkward child like Arvin and made him an apprentice. Gave him straw to sleep on, stew to eat, books to read, ink to write with, and distilled water to drink.

*How could I think something so selfish? Uncle taught me everything. He cared for me.*

Arvin chastised himself for his awful thoughts, and felt he didn't deserve the sudden attention he was getting. This had only been a single day and nothing earned in a single day was of worth. Berating himself, he followed Evrick out through the vault door and past the curious guards.

*Focus on the present. Not new friends or old losses. Treat friends like chemical findings—requiring testing and eventual validation.*

Returning his gaze to his surroundings, Arvin began searching for patterns in the copper inlay along the walls and ceiling. All of the angles of the wirework were either at 90 or 45 degrees, and he wondered if that was an aesthetic choice or a functional one.

*Perhaps both? There's so, so much copper.*

Occasionally he would find powdery, white residue within the barely visible recesses in the stonework. He ran his fingers along them, rubbed the particles between the pads of his thumb and pointer finger, and then eventually took a cautious taste.

*Bland. Remainder of some solid that disintegrated.*

He suspected the copper carried an electrical current, and perhaps there had been a layer of something grown over the copper, much like the silicate-sealed cells.

*Translucent, hardened fat? Absorb moisture? Trap moisture! And light passes.*

Arvin was so deep in thought that when he finally realized Evrick had stopped to hover over him, he nearly jumped. The warlord was clearly perplexed.

"Will you often lag behind like this?" he asked, his eyebrow cocked.

Not sure of what to say, Arvin retreated into a diminutive stance. Then his stomach growled loud enough to echo in the hall

"Food. Right. Guessing that's why you're licking the wall." Evrick's hostility eased. "If I promise you food when we get to where we're going, will you keep walking without stopping every few steps? We are surrounded by wonders, but we also still need to walk successfully down a *hallway*." He pointed at a smidge of white on Arvin's fingertips. "And you *tasted* whatever that is?"

Like a confessing toddler, Arvin nodded. He didn't realize he had been so distracted.

"I *did* tell you about my man, yes? The one that melted in the chemical storage? I feel like that would be a parable I'd have shared."

*What kind of acid could do that? How was it contained? I have to see!*

"Just keep up. We'll get food. Focus on the next thing I have for you. Solve that, and you will have dozens more puzzles."

*Promise?*

Arvin returned his focus to following Evrick and they continued down the hallway and through the guts of the ruins. He noticed the guards progressively got older and more relaxed-looking. Several were missing fingers and their weapons had signs of longer life and regular repair.

*These guys take less time to look at my eyes. They instead check for what I'm carrying.*

Then came the crack blasted in the floor. A one-eyed guard with a mangled face stood in greeting at their approach.

"Lord," he addressed. Then his eye shifted to Arvin. "Which first."

Evrick pointed at Arvin. "He goes down first." A smile crept across the warlord's face. "If he slips and falls, there'll be no point in me going down anyhow."

They all shared a good laugh as Arvin leaned over the hole and gazed downward into the crater and the expansive alabaster chamber below.

*Over such a distance, I would accelerate fast enough to shatter my legs and break my back. An installed netting or tarp could catch anyone easily with minimal injury.*

Arvin raised his hand to interject with his idea, but a guard handed the roped piece of wood to him. "Hold on as if your life depends on it."

Reluctantly, he tugged on it. The winching system complained, but it held.

"Should handle your weight," one guard chided, drawing attention to Arvin's skinny frame.

He wanted to search for another way down, and his hands started to tremble.

"Arvin?" Evrick said with reassuring calm. "Below are wonders that few have seen, and fewer still will understand. And your lunch."

His curiosity awoke. That was all he needed to place his weathered boots on the board and clutch the rope tightly.

The ugliest of the guards nodded in approval. "Atta boy. Down you go. Look up at us if it helps."

The three burly guards, two men and a woman, handled the winch as Arvin descended. At first, he took the advice and kept his eyes upward toward the shrinking hole as he lowered.

But, as always, his curiosity won. Arvin had to look around.

First he examined the maze of reddish metal tubing covering the inside ceiling of the long chamber. The welds were so articulate that he couldn't see them, and the angles again followed the same pattern as the copper inlay along the walls.

*Piping. Brass, or something like it. Distributing heat.*

Next, his eyes shifted downward to the glorious alabaster floor. Two long rows of silicate pods filled the room along with suspended skeletons of various creatures. Crates and satchels of provisions sat scattered in the chamber's corners, most of which were empty and spent. Several guards rested on bedrolls in the corners while a pretty woman hovered over the only lit pod.

*Silicate sleeping chambers? Similar to the cell ceilings in the vault.*

A guard waited at the bottom, arms high to catch the dangling alchemist. Arvin barely noticed her, entranced by the glory of the room's design and the mysteries it held.

As his tattered boots hit stone, the pretty woman looked up from the pod and approached. Eyeing him up and down for injury, she noted, "You spent the night locked in with Bastard without a scratch." She then set her intense eyes on Arvin's. "How?"

There was something piercing and uncomfortable in her pupils. He usually would look away, but she was menacingly captivating. It wasn't her beauty since such a thing rarely impacted Arvin.

He fumbled for a moment, stupefied, before answering. "Drugs."

She spent a moment processing his answer before asking for clarification. "What kind?"

"Alkaloids from ground gourds, birdshells, and clear cave fungus."

"Black Warblers?"

"Only the spotted eggshells. Ground up, they are more potent than the pure white ones."

She nodded, accepting his information. "Have you written all of this down?"

Arvin's hands flew to his bound journal that dangled at his side. He noticed she carried a similar tome in the same manner, chained to her waist. "Yes, including the location of the shells I procured." As fast as a dualist could draw their sword, Arvin had his journal open in his hands to the appropriate page. Holding it outward, he displayed it for the woman.

His drawings were cartoonish, a stick figure representing himself as he scaled a cliff face. Tiny birds with giant, angry eyebrows had been drawn pecking at him as his caricature collected eggs.

"It seems there was some peril in getting the eggshells," she remarked, smirking.

Arvin pointed at his drawings proudly. "Yes. These two picked at my head and this one got my hand. See?" Flopping the journal about, he clumsily tried to show a tiny scar on the back of his hand. "She was especially mean. I tried explaining that I only wanted spent shells, but she was an alarmist."

"She took issue with a strange man approaching her offspring?"

*That's sarcasm! I can sarcasm too.*

"Even after I explained I only wanted to make potent psychotropics."

She reached out and steadied his journal in his hands. Off to the side of the childish drawings was the formulae for the alkaloid mix, and the woman took note of it thoughtfully. "No application of heat when mixing."

"Not even sunlight. The friction of the pestle is all the heat necessary for the proper reaction. Too much cooks out the punch of the mixture."

By now Evrick had also descended. His boots were of sterner make, and clomped onto the pale flooring loud enough to get the attention of both of them. "Good. Brilliant minds connecting. Arvin, this is Visteria. Love, this is Arvin."

As Arvin turned to see Evrick, his eyes flitted across the girl laying in the nearby lit pod. He winced, seeing the end of a crossbow bolt jutting from her bandaged forehead. Without asking permission, he stepped to the side of the pod to examine her.

The woman went to protest, but Evrick held her back. "Just don't *taste* her, Arvin," he called.

*Preteen girl. Crossbow bolt delivered to forehead from direct angle. Close range likely.*

He looked at her hands.

*Leathery fingertips and palms. Worked with hands. Knuckles scarred. Worked with either sand or some other coarse, dry material for long stretches.*

Dozens of tattooed glyphs on both her forearms caught his attention. They were seemingly faded well beyond the years of the girl's age, and he wondered how such an odd aesthetic had been accomplished.

*An entire alphabet, and even some grammatical rules. All facing the wearer. References tattooed to her. She was a scribe in this language.*

Her tan faded around the tattoos, leading Arvin to believe that they were normally covered up with wrappings or sleeves.

Finally, he looked at her face. She was peacefully at rest despite the feeding and water tubes inserted into her mouth. It was as if they never expected her to awaken.

*What is the point of keeping her alive in such an unliving manner?*

"You aren't keeping her alive! She can't die," Arvin nearly shouted, the epiphany striking him. "She's a godling! A sorcerer, elderly. You can tell by how her tattoos have been redrawn multiple times. The ink faded constantly." He then pointed at the sheep's bladders hanging on the end of the pod and followed the tubes into her arms. "You're bleeding her for her magic blood. Is that why you won't take the bolt out and let her heal?" Arvin then suddenly remembered that this was a person he was talking about. "Why do you hate her?"

He immediately regretted how brazenly he had asked the question. Evrick was *Skullhew*, after all.

"She tried to kill me," he said. "I take that personally."

Arvin's attention shifted to the pod she lay in. "Are these for healing?" he asked, running both hands along the silicate surface to confirm its likeness to the ceilings of the cells.

"No," she answered. "They are for—"

"Actually," Evrick interrupted, "Arvin, you tell *us* what they are for."

He thrilled with the sudden rush of the challenge. It was clear Evrick had confidence in Arvin's deductive abilities and he wanted a bit of a show so Visteria would be equally impressed.

*Perhaps the making of a third friend!*

Walking around the pod, Arvin began verbalizing what he would normally think to himself. "Copper lining coming through the floor. To deliver energy! A lot of energy. Connected to that blue stone there. Silicate intended to see vague shapes inside. Large enough for several people to lay in. Certainly magic, but of what arcane nature?"

As he walked around, his foot kicked a white feather. He stopped, bending down to pick it up. It was bizarre, seeing such a fresh and white feather in the depths of ancient ruins.

*Completely out of place, but doubtfully random.*

He shifted gears, given the new variable.

"Feather. White. Bird from the north. Big. Never fly into the Yellow Sea. Transported here, but was alive when this feather came out given the tip. Feather only a few days or a week old with hints of down."

He sniffed it. Then licked it. Things started to click for Arvin. The sensation of something coming together was there, even though he hadn't reached the destination yet.

Evrick gave a wily smile to Visteria.

Arvin continued, "Imported live swan. Not for eating, obviously. Or breeding or there would be many, and avian shit everywhere. Imported for experiment." His eyes rested on the dusty floor beside one of the spent pods. The fresh print of a woman's bare feet were there as if she had climbed out of one. She must have been clumsy, because her handprint was nearby where she steadied herself.

"In a bird, out a woman! Metamorphic magics on a controlled scale!" he shouted.

Looking both pod rows up and down, he continued, "Convert one life-form into another. An animal into a human! Usually flesh-shifting is a punishment, banishing a person to an animal form, but this is the opposite. Animals to people." He cocked his head at the injured girl curiously. "Your niece is clearly related to you, so she wasn't flesh-shifted unless you both are..." He gasped, pointing the feather accusingly at Visteria. "Swan!"

Evrick roared with laughter.

Visteria shook herself free of her husband, stormed to Arvin, and snatched away the feather.

"Swan!" he recoiled, in horror.

"I am no swan, dullard. Husband, you brought a brilliant idiot to us," she grumbled.

"But he did it!" Evrick cheered. "Arvin, you are largely correct. These pods all were for converting the souls of animals into human form, likely as slaves. We could only get a few of the pods working, and you've already met one of them."

"Bastard!" Arvin cried. "A swan?"

"A badger, actually. Bastard is a striped badger from Three Sisters' Wood. A mean one too. Took some fingers. We also imported a royal *swan* from Sedrios, a Gold-tip bear from Bitter Heights, and we snagged a local desert rat from these very ruins. Each of them converted into humans almost a week ago."

Arvin had spent his entire life studying the tangible, building on the knowledge of prior alchemists. He had never encountered magic beyond that of stories. It made him jitter with excitement.

*The best of both frontiers!*

Evrick continued, "These ancients merged the crafts of metallurgy and alchemy with the art of magic. And we will as well." He stepped closer. "Stick with me, and bring that big brain of yours along, and New Ramlagha will be a nation. No more 'Fourteenth Kingdom' being used as an ironic moniker, but instead in earnest. A nation of our own, where we are no longer the dumping grounds of others. Respected, with laws and commerce, for future generations comprising all of the Yellow Sea."

"To every mountain," Visteria said, returning to her niece's side. She had a haunted look on her face.

"To every mountain," Evrick echoed.

# CHAPTER
# TEN

Bastard

Something in that magical powder loosened his muscles, and Bastard was finally feeling connected to his body. The gentle man had touched his lips with it, threw it into the air, and then everything after that was blurry.

Bastard then had dreams, ones that felt as real as memories unfolding within his mind. He was a badger again, clawing at burrows for mice and digging through the dirt for worms. The world made sense again with the sky above, where it belonged. His four legs obeyed his instincts, and his jaw moved as it should.

But when he woke, he was briefly saddened. The dream wasn't real. He was caught and caged long ago. Hauled by boat and then a rickety wagon.

Then came the fighting. It took a long, painful moment, but Bastard quickly learned that when the side of his cage opened, enemies waited outside for him—scaley lizards, frothing dogs, and even other badgers.

He defended himself, fought, and learned. Different animal

opponents meant different dangers and tactics. Nothing in his life had prepared him for this, and now the agility of both his small body and mind kept him alive.

All that existed was the cage, and everything outside of it was an enemy. The air changed, as did the voices and the smells. Wagon after wagon and battle pit after battle pit, each with different smelling sand stained with the gory death throes of hundreds of animals.

Then to here. He was put into a pale pod and turned into whatever he was now: a furless thing without a protective layer of fat. His limbs were lanky, teeth stunted, and ears cold.

This was the epitome of foreign.

Bastard ran his hands down his torso. Fingers were astoundingly good at sensing how bizarre his new body was. And he was always cold, vulnerable, and his jaw moved differently than it used to. It wobbled side-to-side now, and held a tiny fraction of the power it once did. The first time he bit one of the guards with his new mouth, he was amazed they could still fight.

No claws.

No tail.

His nose was dulled.

The dark was somehow deeper.

The sludge they fed him tasted bad.

Bastard desperately wanted nothing more than to be changed back. To return to his own self, instead of his current imprisonment, a prison of fragile joints and exposed flesh.

His growing panic made his chest rise and fall and his hurting rib pop. Escape wasn't currently possible given his injury, at least an attempted escape by *himself*. He decided to wait for the gentle man with the powder to come back and rescue him. At least he gave his marvelous skin to wear in the interim.

It was interesting, which in and of itself was a new concept to Bastard, to be *interested*. Before, as a badger, he could only understand what was happening or what had happened. Concrete concepts were all that passed through his mind. A thing either was presently happening or had happened in the past.

But almost immediately after becoming this form, even before the pod had opened, he had already expanded his thinking. Bastard could speculate. No longer was the world limited to what he directly observed, but he could imagine what he *hadn't* observed.

Bastard could actually speculate. And with very little reference to pull from regarding his current physical state, he found his mental wheels spinning. The gentle man had given him a wild and new experience, and now with all those images and smells in his bank of experience, Bastard discovered the wheels of his mind to be spinning even faster. And with purpose.

Bastard hoped he, or the older man with dry meat to eat, would free him. Free him of these cells and this room and this body. He could imagine going back, and not being what he currently was. But instead, Bastard heard three guards mewling around the vault door. One had a familiar voice. He didn't understand the words they exchanged, but a new part of his mind seemed to have knowledge of the function of language. The concept of high communication was there, new, much like the pale fingers on his hands.

They walked around above, their boots shuffling lazily. He had come to recognize the gait of drunken men from his days in endless fighting pits, and these three had plenty to drink. Bastard guessed where they were headed: the sticks in the wall that opened the cells.

He waited. His new mind *anticipated* trouble. The voice he recognized belonged to the man whose finger he had eaten. Bastard imagined an impending reprisal.

The pale ceiling above him pulled away and three guards gathered to look down on him. He hated these men for their reeking hair and they never provided him enough food. There wasn't even any dirt for him to dig for worms!

This hell must end.

One of the guards stooped down with the usual wooden bowl of slop. His mouth moved as he gibbered something and the other two guards joined in. Such loud, obnoxious noises from such loud, obnoxious creatures.

But not as bad as the gentle one. The one that lent Bastard his own skin to keep warm. He smelled healthier than these men, and his touch wasn't hostile. He had kept Bastard safe, keeping watch as he rested.

If only the gentle one was the one to feed him. Or the older, calm one with the dried meat that was so tasty. Bastard liked those two far better.

As he stared at the bowl in contemplation, the guard whose flesh he had tasted prior eased his club back. He was trying to be stealthy, but it was clear that he intended to strike Bastard when he reached for the bowl. Men did this, sometimes. They played cruel tricks on animals for no reason. They dangled food out of reach and faked throwing a stick for animals to run and retrieve. Men were horrible, and here they were about to punish him for suffering the slop they forced upon him.

But he had tasted delicious jerky!

He was wearing clothes!

Someone had been nice to him!

Bastard could barely contain his heaving rage. His rib popped, but the pain just cranked his adrenaline further as he scrutinized how the guard held his club. Flexing his own fingers, Bastard was confident that he could hold it in a similar manner. He *imagined* swinging it.

The gibbering between the three of them was becoming too much. One nudged the slop bowl a bit to get Bastard's attention, but Bastard focused his eyes beyond the bowl and to the row of levers on the wall. He had seen them used before when they all first came in. It was clear that moving them up or down corresponded with the pale barriers opening or closing.

Bastard knew he shouldn't do this alone, but the gentle man was taking too long. There was no waiting. The time was *now*.

Standing in his cell at his full height, Bastard's shoulders came to floor level with the guards standing above. The one with the club faked a swing forward, trying to get Bastard to flinch. But Bastard was already launching his own attack, and he wasn't playing. He swept his long arm around the back of the nearest guard's leg and brought him tumbling down into the cell.

Their gibbering nonsense turned to howls and shouts.

Bastard pummeled the one guard with his overly long limbs, just as they had done to him. The other two above struggled to reach in, and Bastard felt a club graze his shoulder.

Anticipating further attacks, he turned just in time to dodge a second swing. He'd been hit enough by them before to gauge their typical arc of attack, so he caught the third club in his open hand just before it landed on his head. Anticipation was a welcome addition to his mind.

The guard gasped as Bastard wrenched the weapon free and brought it down on his toes. He jumped away comically, dancing about as the second guard kicked Bastard right in the face.

Everything spun. Bastard still wasn't entirely used to having his head so high up compared to his body. Being vertical just didn't seem ideal for fighting. So he stuck to what felt right and rolled away. While he preferred being in the burrow for defense, he had to get out of the cell's recess. Escape *was* the desire, after all.

Boosting off the bed slab, Bastard slid out of the cell and onto the vault floor on his belly. Scrambling away, he flopped onto another pale barrier.

The shadow of a hand reached up, palm first, on the underside.

All three guards swiftly sorted each other out then they flanked outward toward him. The one Bastard had drug into the cell was so furious he spat blood through his teeth as he gibbered.

These men, the creatures that Bastard had been turned into, had a different rage than any he had seen. It was controlled, methodical, and often without an understandable purpose. Bastard had rarely seen this behavior before in the world, but when he had, it was madness. Either from disease or starvation, these bipeds didn't act like animals when angry but instead like storms, without sense or reason, but always bent on destruction. And they had forced it onto other animals in the fighting pits.

As they closed in, Bastard spied the levers on the far side of the room. He scrambled to his legs and ran, which in itself was an awkward feat. Bipedal running was a form of controlled falling. He missed the stability and strength of four legs, but there was no denying the speed given by just two.

As he reached the first lever, they were on him. All their clubs pummeled on his back at once, but he pulled the lever downward before he fell. Deflecting blows from his head, he curled into a ball, and between their legs he saw another barrier swing open.

He desperately hoped that he had opened the best one, the one he needed.

But it was the rat man who poked out his head. He had bulging eyes, a thin mustache that was barely there, and a diminutive jaw. Everything about him appeared weak and twitchy.

He evaluated the violence before him with a loud squeal. Bounding out of his cell, he ran around the vault room in aimless circles.

One of the guards saw the new escapee and peeled away. At least there was that.

The two remaining guards were tired now, their battering fell into a slower rhythm as they huffed and puffed. But the damage they had done to Bastard's back caused his muscles to tighten and lock. He knew that such swelling bruises bloomed fast and he didn't have much time left for full mobility.

Kicking outward, he drove a heel into the knee of one of the two swinging guards. The man buckled, his club soaring wide, and he hit another lever.

Bastard couldn't believe his fortune. Another barrier slid open. Was this the one he needed?

As she stood, the swan woman's magnetic eyes locked onto Bastard. She had been a stunning swan going into the pod, and she was a stunning creature now. Bastard had seen her hissing as feathers flew. He had seen her loveliness above in Tent City at the vendor across the breezeway. She had fight in her, but that still wasn't the barrier he needed.

Bastard needed fight *and* the meat to carry it.

Dizziness was taking him. Through his blurring vision he saw one guard chasing Rat Man around the room in circles as the other two continued digging into Bastard with their sluggish heels and clubs.

But Swan Woman approached slowly from behind, her long white hair draping over her shoulders in a display of beauty that was so startling that the two guards eased their assault and turned to witness her presence. Her magnificence captured all, and they didn't react fast enough to stop her from pulling the final lever.

The last barrier retracted open.

All three guards halted, held their breath, and shared a look of dread.

A dark, round mitt of a hand emerged. Then the other. Both then hoisted the glorious girth of Bear Woman into view. She was a powerful amalgam of muscle, width, and fat with skin so dark that it matched her black hair. Only her wide, golden eyes contained anything akin to brightness, and they beamed outward until they landed on the two guards surrounding Bastard.

With pent up speed, she hoisted herself clear of her cell and charged. She smashed into them, both men squashed under her girth, and unleashed a deafening roar into their ears.

She then snatched one by the throat and drove him down to the floor with all her weight. He only managed a gasp as she pounded both balled fists down onto his sternum over and over while snarling. Snot and drool dribbled out of her face as she did so, and when she went to bite out the man's throat she found it a fruitless and frustrating exercise. Her inability to tear his head off with her blunted, wobbly jaws made her even more angry, and she pounded him some more.

The other two guards bolted for the vault door.

Swan Woman slapped one flat in the ear and sent him sideways into one of the open cells. The third was nearly to the door when he tripped on Rat Man's flailing limbs and fell onto his head.

All three guards flopped like landed fish, gasping and flailing, clutching either their bleeding ear, their bruised throat, or their battered head.

Bear Woman delivered the message to them with a final, triumphant, standing roar; no one was to mess with her or anyone else.

Bastard rolled onto his back, and pondered what the next step for freedom would be.

# ELEVEN

Evrick

The tribes of Vastard were comprised of refugees from genocide, mercenary companies fleeing reprisal, and apostates of zealot orders all throughout Andos. The world outside of the rocky desert region was unforgiving and cruel, and those who survived such cruelty gathered in clumps for safety, and eventually settled in the lands no one else would ever want: here.

As Evrick grew, fought, and suffered in Vastard, he came to understand something. He rose to prominence within his own tribe of mercenary offspring, and he saw that these clutches of desperate folk could be refined to a greater purpose: revival. They were forged of harder steel than elsewhere. He saw not a broken mashup of people, but a thriving population of leathery souls awaiting momentum.

With the right guidance, the wandering tribes could be forged anew into a true population. They could form a proper military, stabilize supply lines, trade with Daynce to the west, control their borders up to the surrounding mountains, and perhaps even tame the searing sands of the Yellow Sea itself.

No more sacking other cities or townships to make someone *else* rich.

Under their feet, the ancient extinct civilization of Ramlagha had long ago dwindled out of existence, its culture and secrets lost. But its brilliance remained, like a vein of silver, waiting to be mined and cultivated. And perhaps *weaponized*.

Evrick watched Arvin and Visteria converse over the particulars of the metamorphic pods. Arvin chomped on a baked sheep's stomach filled with beans and cheese as Visteria walked him through page after page of her discoveries.

Evrick knew that *brains* like theirs was the key. Sharp minds would restore *all* of the pods. Through careful observance, he could determine exactly how they each worked and soon Evrick could be churning out forty fighters a week. Perfect shock troops, concubines for trade, and slaves for labor. All trained from inception to obey commands and ignore personal wants. They could be his personal guard and provide security for all under the New Ramlagha banner.

From there he could establish representative councils from the various tribes, a stable currency of their own, and even schools. A land of sellswords and notch-eared thieves could be a sovereign land.

He tingled from the possibilities as he watched his marvelous wife guide the alchemist through the ancient language that she had deciphered. Visteria showed Arvin the blue stone panels where the glyphs were once written to activate each pod. The glyph had to be brushed on in blood containing the divine to activate it. Once the pod flesh-shifted any living creature into a human, the blood burned away leaving the blue stone blank for a new glyph.

For another soul to transcend.

Arvin saw the issue once Visteria explained everything to him. The divine blood from her young "niece" wasn't sufficient. He speculated it wasn't potent enough and likely required refinement.

Humans with magic in their veins contained only a droplet of divine power when compared to the greater amount found in rogue godlings.

A question bubbled to the surface for Evrick. "Refinement? How would one do that? We have but the singular mage." Evrick reeled at the thought of having to bleed several mages. If that was the foundation of Ramlagha's ancient power, he saw no solution in his lifetime.

The alchemist shrugged. "So many have experimented with divine human blood. Its properties can't be isolated since it's simply blood. And we can't infuse the divine into a regular person's blood," Arvin continued. "So samples and surviving findings from experiments are beyond rare."

"How do you even know any of that?"

"Books. Uncle had books."

Before Evrick could ask about obtaining such valuable books, Arvin continued. "They burned."

"Well, you have a subject right here!" Evrick implored, pointing at the girl's body. "Remember what you read and figure things out."

"Nothing from her works." Visteria shook her head, stepping in. "And my husband is pressured." She assured Arvin. "The worry is that if we can't get the power below working, we continue to be vulnerable. You know how Vastard can be."

Evrick felt desperate. His face was disciplined enough to hide it, but the desire to push forward clawed at the inside of his chest. "What if refinement is something they already mastered, and we just haven't found the machinery for it yet?" He tapped his mouth with a thoughtful knuckle. "Or . . ." his eyes widened. "My god, or we've already found it! The Concentrix! It could be a magic machine for blood refinement."

"The what?" Arvin's apparent curiosity went from hot to blazing.

"But . . ." Visteria interjected. "I . . ." She was stammering, and Evrick feared her incoming logical protest. "You are grasping at straws, Husband! First, you decide with little evidence that it is a power source, and now this. You are *hopeful* husband."

"At least we can have him look at it. What harm is there in that?" Evrick pleaded. "He's eased the savage Bastard; he's solved the pod's function within mere moments. Let's set him loose on the Concentrix. The worst outcome is that it just stays dormant."

A rare look of concern molded Visteria's comely visage into something frightened. Evrick had never seen her so hesitant before. "Husband, you need to *think* on this."

"What is the Concentrix?" Arvin asked, his ears and eyebrows elevated with interest.

"Nothing." Visteria waved a hand, attempting to swat Arvin's curiosity out of the air. "We will stick to the glyphs for—"

Evrick dove in, heading her off. "The Concentrix is a series of copper rings that all appear to rotate concentrically without touching each other." He spoke to Arvin as if his wife wasn't even there.

"Like an orrery?" Arvin asked, taking the bait.

"No, far more complex. Let me show you." Evrick briefly waited for Visteria to offer up another protest, but she just silently glared at him.

He dreaded her fury and knew the level of disrespect he had just subjected her to hurt. Stuffing his guilt down, he proceeded. He would pay for it later in both regret and marital strife.

But he was intent. Every night they spent without pushing forward was a night others could see him as stagnant. He needed to hold onto what he had grasped. Evrick, deep down, was terrified of just being another footnote chieftain like his predecessors with his throat slit in the night and replaced before dawn.

Arvin might once again see an approach others had not. Evrick did his best to avoid his wife's searing eyes as he guided Arvin, a hand raised to his shoulder to aim him to the end of the pod chamber toward the mechanical elevating lift.

Visteria stayed behind, her boots not even turning on the alabaster floor to watch them leave. She was as a statue.

Evrick brought Arvin to a copper grate recessed into the stone wall. It was woven like a marvelous copper basket composed of thin metal ribbons, and a guard rushed up to slide it open for his lord. Both men entered, Arvin looking around delightedly as Evrick glanced back toward his wife. He was desperate for Visteria to scowl at him, show her rage and hurt so he could estimate and anticipate his penance. But he only saw the back of her head, her lovely hair, her still form.

A guard secured the gate, sealing the two men into a tight chamber of copper. He then spun a handle in the wall and oiled gears within the stone spun and slowly lowered the chamber downward.

"Copper," Arvin said as he ran his fingers along the elevator's grated siding. "Likely the most abundant of metals they had. Everything is made of it, and it conducts electrical energy."

"Too soft for weapons," Evrick remarked. "I'd rather find a way to master their clear crystal pods. Sharp for some truly wicked arrowheads."

"Silicate," Arvin clarified.

"Silicate?" Evrick said, testing out the word. Thinking about having such projectiles loosing from his archers' bows made him temporarily forget what he had done to his wife.

"How big is the Concentrix?" Arvin could care less about weaponry, it seemed. "Is it vertical or horizontal? What is it made of?"

"We are literally a moment away from showing it to you." The thought of forgoing his wife to be stuck in a slow elevator with Arvin finally settled in. His regret bubbled in his gut. "Just wait and see."

Arvin pressed his face against the cage, trying to angle his gaze downward. "Maybe if . . . I wonder if—"

"Arvin, listen to me carefully," Evrick began. "Visteria isn't wrong. You are to determine what the Concentrix does, and tell *me*, before you do anything. Don't set anything off recklessly. Remember, people get *melted* down here. If you get melted, the knowledge and brilliance in your head melts with it."

"I won't get melted," Arvin said with surprising confidence.

Evrick wondered if he had built up Arvin's ego too much.

As the elevator crept to a slow, clanking stop, they reached the spherical Concentrix control room. The silicate floor where the elevator landed was far more refined and with internal support struts. It was nearly clear, applying only a milky film to everything in the chamber below.

Arvin dropped to one knee, his palm against the floor to examine the space below. It took a moment, but Arvin jolted when he realized they both were suspended above a massive, spherical chamber of astounding size. Hovering in its center, likely by magical means, hovered seven toothy rings of copper. Each was of similar size, but they fit within each other in a convoluted manner that Evrick couldn't discern. He hoped Arvin could provide insight, but the alchemist only starred downward agape.

"Like a wizard's ring puzzle, the kind you get for children. As for the sphere, there is no other known construction like this anywhere *ever*." Evrick pressed upon the awestruck Arvin. "If you look close enough, you can see an entry at the bottom for moisture drainage, but there are no other ways in or out. We can't get inside."

Arvin sniffed about; his fingertips explored every crevice of the flooring until he reached the cylindrical walls surrounding them. Spaced out were blue stone glyph plates with dozens of copper lines running to each in a dizzying maze.

"Visteria thinks that painting divine blood on certain glyphs activates particular stones. Which, given the number of them, means a lot of different combinations."

Arvin's head shot up as his eyes inspected the ceiling. They rummaged through an invisible space, the pupils rolling back and forth as his mind worked, before he spoke. "I'd guess, given twenty-one glyphs in their language and the number of stones, assuming more than one stone would need to be active to make the Concentrix do something, the number of possible combinations would be . . ."

Evrick eagerly waited for Arvin's impressive calculation.

". . . a bunch."

Hiding his disappointment, Evrick thought back on Visteria. The guilt inside was swelling to a point where he was desperate to see her face. "Arvin, let's head up. You can come down here on your own and have free rein of the place. I'll keep the guard by the elevator controls for you, as well."

It was clear that Arvin was lost in his explorations. His nose pressed against the floor as he gazed at the expanse below.

"Arvin," Evrick commanded. "We go up for now. I need to fix something."

CHAPTER

# TWELVE

Arvin

rvin?"

Some voice, probably Evrick's called to him from a thousand leagues away, but there was no more 'Arvin' now, only *curiosity*.

*Blood drips. No rivulets ran to the floor. Does the blood all vanish when the glyph activates? Even the droplets that hit the floor? Or did they clean it up each time?*

"We go up. Now. I'm not leaving you alone down here with your curiosity."

He could hear the annoyance in the disembodied voice calling out to him, but his curiosity wasn't done hijacking his senses and facilities.

*The hole below, in the base of the spherical chamber, is wide. The distance is great, so its size is greater. A camel could pass through it.*

"Arvin!"

This time, Evrick's voice carried danger. Arvin's curiosity began to weigh its fight or flight mechanic against the desire to explore. Did breathing matter more than learning marvelous and forbidden wonders?"

*Not much here. Silicate is a slightly different composite than the vault and pods. No blood to sample. Blue stones are all completely blank with no remaining residue to sprinkle talc on. No idea what glyph was painted on what stone.*

"Arvin, I am now genuinely considering either killing you, or just taking the elevator up without you. You'd be surprised at how close of a toss-up it is."

Arvin considered the elevator for a moment.

*Hyper complex device to only go between two floors. Likely ceremonial, but still a waste. Only two floors . . .*

Arvin spun on his knees toward Evrick so fast that he startled the warlord. "What other floors does the elevator reach?"

"The what?"

"The elevator. It elevates. The lift. Portable room of copper weave and—"

"We just took it down," Evrick's face shifted from annoyance to critical thought. "We were always going down."

"But never up. Does the elevator go up from the pod chamber? This, *here*, is down. What is up?"

Arvin's curiosity now shifted away from the spherical chamber and its cylindrical blue stone room that capped it. It made sense that a storage subchamber be kept somewhere, and the elevator was perfect for delivering replacement blue stones or even . . .

*The divine blood. If there is a place to store it, it would be immediately accessible through this elevator.*

The gears in Evrick's head had also been turning, and Arvin surmised that he was going to conclude the same possibility, just not as quickly. So Arvin sprang to his feet and zipped into the elevator. "Come. We go up and see!" he said.

Evrick paused a moment, then nodded. "Fine. But after that I spend some time patching things up with Visteria before she kills you. Or me."

"By melting?" Arvin wondered if she was a legitimate danger to his life or if Evrick was just being hyperbolic. He was more curious as to Visteria's preferred method of dispatching people than actually afraid.

*He would obviously protect me. But still. Melting would be at least interesting.*

Evrick stepped into the elevator next to Arvin. It didn't even shift from the additional weight.

*Sturdy. Perfect construction. Materials aged extremely well.*

"No, no melting. Visteria would drain you of your blood, catalog it, and use it as scribing ink or in potions."

*What is he talking about? Oh! His wife killing me. Is she a cultist?*

"Well, if she wants to melt me I can make suggestions."

"I'm sure you could," Evrick conceded. "But for now, please shut up." He threw his head back and shouted upward, "Crank us up, but keep cranking until it won't let you! We want to see how far the elevator goes up."

The elevator jolted to life as they smoothly ascended. Within moments, they could see the guard's boots. His feet flexed back and forth in place as his body worked the elevator's control crank while they traveled upward.

Visteria stood behind the cranking guard, arms crossed, with a blank look on her face.

*Why is she angry at me? I should let her look at my journal some more. She liked that.*

"Hold the elevator a moment," Evrick said as they leveled with the alabaster flooring. Tugging the gate, he swung it wide. "Love, please join us."

She stood there a moment, hanging in stoic silence. The guard fidgeted a moment and turned away as if to examine the crank more thoroughly.

"Did you not solve every mystery of the Concentrix?" she asked, voice full of barbs.

"Not without your direct help," Evrick replied smoothly. "Join us. We're going to try to take the lift upwards."

The first sign of life crossed her face; her eyebrows scrunched together in thought. "The gods. We never tried going *up*." She pointed a sharp finger at Arvin. "Your idea?"

Arvin nodded hesitantly, his eyes fixed on the finger aimed at him as if it was the means with which he were to be 'melted.'

With a reluctant sigh, she joined the two men on the elevator. "You are *troublesome* husband," she said.

Despite her angry tone, Arvin still saw a relieved smile creep onto Evrick's face when his wife wasn't looking. "Right. Up we go," he said while closing the copper-woven gate.

The guard returned to cranking. Upward they went as the elevator glided.

"Will it just stop when it has gone far enough?" Visteria asked, looking upward at the copper ceiling as if she could see beyond. "We just yell down for him to cease cranking?"

Her voice dropped away, the sentence slipping apart as the last two words tumbled from her agape mouth. She was the first one to see the next floor, and as it appeared at their eye-level, it was nothing but bones. Sundered femurs and crushed skulls littered the ground in a macabre, ancient battlefield.

Arvin and Evrick were now as attentive as Visteria; each examined the tomb before them that stretched into the darkness beyond sight.

*Deep room. Shattered remains of tables used as barricades.*

"They had a last stand here," Evrick echoed Arvin's thoughts.

The elevator, as if sensing its occupants' reservations, gave resistance and finally began acting its age. It trembled and shook, and eventually stopped when the grisly floor was waist high.

"As far as it goes!" the guard hollered from below.

Hesitantly, Visteria reached for the copper cage handle and pulled it open. Several bones rustled loose, their dust puffing about, as they tumbled to the elevator's floor. Age had made them hollow and they made the sound expected of dull wind chimes.

Arvin stooped and squinted at a pelvis in the fading light. It was misshapen somehow, and to get a better look, he pulled a small globe of thick glass from his bandolier and shook it vehemently. The luminescent seaweed within was sealed in a glob of camel mucus, and the saltwater surrounding it washed the mucus away, powered by Arvin's arm, and exposed it. The two combined quantities brought the seaweed to life, and its sudden green glow lit the elevator. Arvin used it to examine the pelvis further.

"Love? Do you see why I like him so?" Evrick asked tenderly of his wife.

She didn't answer.

*This pelvis isn't misshapen; it's cracked. No. A portion is sundered. Sliced!*

Arvin imagined the same claw that sliced the walls could have sliced this bone. And likely all of them. Arvin hoisted his light globe high and saw many telltale signs of similar violence on the human debris before them.

Being melted was one thing—so abstract that it couldn't be comprehended or truly feared. But the slices left by unseen clawed beasts found something far more primal within Arvin. His curiosity was stifled by it, smothered by the primal fear of the dark and of being eaten alive.

"Come on, then," Visteria said. "I'll have the guards clean it all out later, but I don't want them breaking anything. Let's have a look first."

Evrick was dutiful as a husband and leaned his back against the half-portion of the wall. Weaving his fingers together, he made a boot hold for Visteria to climb up and inside. She pulled her desert mask up over her mouth and nose, then climbed up her husband with practiced ease. Within a moment, she disappeared into the dark. "Hand me the light," she commanded, her hand re-emerging from the boney void.

*I can teach her how to make them. Then she'll like me again.*

Arvin handed it over right away and pulled a second one from his bandolier. He shook it the same way and it came alive. "I only have two," he said to Evrick, hoping that the warlord wouldn't want his last one.

Evrick seemed to understand. "No worries. You two should provide enough. Come. Climb up."

Arvin nearly fell over, raising his boot toward Evrick. He tried a second time, and kicked the warlord in the leg by mistake. The third time, Arvin finally found purchase and before he could find his balance, Evrick hoisted him and shoved up and backward through the opening.

Crashing through the bones and fragments of ribboned cloth, dust went everywhere. Arvin broke through, sliding on the floor, to produce an Arvin-shaped empty space for Evrick to easily climb up into on his own.

With minimal dust on him, Evrick brushed off his sleeves and looked down at Arvin expectantly. "Do you need help with the globe?"

*I have people powder in my hair. People. Powder.*

Arvin wanted to hang onto his light, so he sputtered and spat out the dry remains as he stood. Rubbing his irritated eyes, he used his tears to clear his vision. By the time he could see again, Evrick had joined his wife deeper in the room's recess.

It wasn't nearly as large as the pod chamber, and not nearly as tall. The same piping covered the ceiling, and along the walls sat dozens of stacked crates filled with food provisions rotted into oblivion, as well as tattered bedrolls and ossified leather blankets and boots.

"They were sleeping when the attack came," Evrick said. Carefully stepping around the ancient carnage, his warlord's mind went to work. "Likely a small shift on watch. They clearly knew they had been overrun, and were hiding here. Spare boots, food, even a few books. Are those books useful?" he asked his wife hopefully.

Visteria leaned her light down toward a small shelf. "Rotted into oblivion."

*The trapped moisture from mass decomposition would ruin any and all parchment and scroll work, including books.*

Arvin nudged the tip of a spear, its wooden handle long disintegrated from age. But its keen edge still gleamed enough to reflect his globe's light to something in the far, best protected corner.

All three of them saw it—five stacked glass boxes with copper corners. A man could easily haul one by himself.

"What are those?" Evrick asked. "I haven't seen those before."

Both Arvin and Visteria approached them, their globes high.

*She is curious like me.*

"There is a funneling hole on the side. Like . . ." she paused, lost in focus. Suddenly she reached for her book of glyphs.

*For liquid. These would be filled via pressure, but the rubber sealing on the funnel rotted away and air got in. Whatever liquid it had contained is now evaporated.*

Arvin pressed his globe against one. The bottom of it was covered in a thin, residual red layer.

*Sanguine. Evaporated blood.*

"Each copper corner has a glyph stamped in it. The same glyph." She found it, holding the page up for her husband to see. "The glyph for 'gods.'"

*Blood of the gods.*

Evrick nodded. "Nothing more divine than that."

Bastard

It was difficult, but Bastard finally got Bear Woman to stop sitting on one of the guards. His wheezing was irksome and Bastard didn't see killing anyone as necessary just yet. Once free of her weight, the guard cried like a newborn cub as the other two groaned on the floor, half-conscious.

But Bear Woman was still worked up, and she stomped around the room, clawing at the walls to mark her territory. The bluntness of her new hands didn't deter her, and she scratched futilely even when her fingertips bled.

Bastard nudged her away from the wall with his forehead. She jolted, reacting to him as if he was challenging her, but Bastard immediately rolled onto his back to offer his belly in submission. He needed no more enemies here.

She stood over him to display her weight and power, but then tilted back and plopped down on her ample behind. Her morose expression returned and she huffed several times while puffing her cheeks in and out.

It was vital to Bastard she understand that not only was he appreciative for what she had done to help them escape, but she might need to do more. This was a complex concept, and he was unsure of how to express it. The only thing he had to offer her in return was the chance to get back to where she was from.

Before he could sort through how to express his needs, Rat Man scurried up on all fours. He opened his mouth and one of the guard's water bladders dropped into Bear Woman's lap. It was leaking just enough for her to understand what it was. Using both her hands, she raised it to her mouth and suckled on it.

Rat man scurried off to inspect the other two subdued guards. Watching Rat Man fumble about awkwardly, Bastard realized he was far more comfortable in his body than his four compatriots. He began to suspect something more had changed about himself than just his body. Since his time with Gentle Man, he felt more attuned to it, for one. And additionally, he kept approaching things with his hands instead of his mouth. It was as if he had a new set of instincts —instructions on how to pilot this new form.

Pulling Gentle Man's coat on, he practiced binding the leather belt of it around his waist. The buckle was complicated, so he only tugged at the straps uselessly. He couldn't figure out how to tie the knot in the same manner as one of the groaning guards on the floor.

Another one of the guards coughed, the one Bear Woman had clobbered when he ran for the exit, and Rat Man crouched over him. He was far too close to the guard, his hooked nose against the guard's chest, as he examined the shiny buttons of his coat. Then, with surprising command of his fingers, he began plucking the buttons free and collecting them. Rat Man then wrestled with the guard's belt buckle, and Bastard learned how it worked by watching Rat Man figure it out.

It took two tries, but soon the hole in the belt's leather had the buckle's stem through it, and the coat was snug and secure. Bastard was elated with his new, fancy skin.

Bear Woman had tired of her tantrum, and Rat Man continued to undress the guards with growing adeptness. This gave Bastard time to think things through a bit. Which drew his attention to something else about himself that felt new—his ability to plan.

Before, as a badger, he would assess situations and problem solve using a combination of his prior experience and ingrained instincts. Digging, fighting, or fleeing were his primary tools for navigating the world around him. If something couldn't be resolved by any of those three options, he typically just weathered the events and hoped for the best.

But now he possessed the means to envision that which was not current or real. And he imagined himself free, under an open sky, while lying in tall grass. He wanted to be there, and now his mind could fashion methods and means to do it.

The first part of the plan was to leave this room and travel the hallways. He remembered what they looked like, and how people moved up and down staircases, but the other three were without fancy skins like the one he was given.

He backed up his thought process. The first part of his lay-in-tall-grass plan was to get everyone dressed in the clothes of these defeated men. Hopefully, Rat Man could be of help.

Then there were the guards beyond the vault. The hallways had them everywhere, and they would encounter more. Wearing similar skins would help them blend in, much like birds when they sneak their eggs into the nests of other birds. The nesting mothers can't seem to tell which egg is their own versus which is from a different bird.

Bastard figured the guards were just as dumb.

As he worked on his plan, his stomach clenched like a fist. This new form demanded food far more often than when he was a badger. Seeing Rat Man chewing on a boot lace, Bastard knew he wasn't the only hungry one. They needed to eat.

Bastard felt a sudden jolt of fear and realized he hadn't kept track of Swan Woman as well as he had Bear Woman and Rat Man. Spinning about, he nearly fell over from dizziness as he scanned the vault chamber for the magnificent fourth member of their troupe. It seemed his recent beating and popping rib made him woozy.

It took a moment for him to spy her long, white hair. She had climbed into the cell of the man she had smacked. Blood trickled down from his impacted ear, and he sat still with his eyes wide as he watched her sniff about the pouches on his belt and thigh.

For a moment, Bastard was distracted by her. She had a long, smooth back half covered with her delicate white mane of hair. Her hips were subtle and yet invitingly round, and her jawline was so defined and smooth that he could see the elegant lines of the swan she once was. He did not know that a creature could be as lovely as a dusk sky reflected in a still lake, but here was the proof.

Bastard shook his head a moment to regain control of himself. Why in the world did he find a bipedal form so compelling? What was wrong with him? Did he have to mate with other bipeds, now? It wasn't even mating season, and he hadn't even sniffed her anus yet.

Her hands zeroed in on a pouch on the guard's belt. She slapped at it, making him flinch. When it didn't fall clear, she hissed and tugged on it voraciously. Placing a heel under the guard's arm, she ripped it free of its leather binds and tore it open. Inside were seeds. She must have smelled them.

She went to peck them up, but smacked her head when she tried. Her face wasn't built for it, and she could no longer eat like a bird in the same tragic manner that he could no longer eat like a badger.

Bastard climbed down into the cell. The injured guard recoiled, and Bastard jolted defensively in response, but it was clear to both of them there would be no fight. Both men were too bruised and tired for it.

Swan Woman gazed at Bastard, her eyes a perfect pitch black. She hissed low, stepping over the pile of seeds on the cell floor. Sharing was not her intent, especially when she was as hungry as she was.

Bastard stood still, eyes averted, making certain she knew he wasn't a threat. He waited, waited as long as it took, for her to return her focus on the spilled seeds.

One seed had bounced off away from the opened pouch. Bastard slowly picked it up and held it in the flat of his palm and offered it to her. When she spied it, she darted her head down and plucked it from him with her lips.

Something in Bastard's chest soared, while something some-where *else* stirred. He picked up several more seeds and offered them in a similar fashion to her. She eagerly received them.

Next, he used his fingers and ate one for himself. This new body brought food to the mouth, like a crab, instead of the mouth to food. The concept was common enough in nature, he just had to get used to it for himself.

After he had eaten several seeds in the human way, she finally mimicked it. Progress, true progress, was being made. As she ate, she shivered, and Bastard remembered that he was the only one wearing clothing, and it was apparent that their delicate skin required they each acquire such removable skins. Snakes did a form of it, after all.

Looking at the guard in the cell, Bastard began imagining how to make him shed his outer skin. He meditated on how Rat's hands had moved before, and then he got to work. Everyone needed fake skin to protect their new skin.

CHAPTER

# FOURTEEN

Evrick

Evrick summoned several of his best people to create a proper workspace for Arvin and his wife. They followed the usual procedure: mist everything with water to prevent the dust from kicking up too much and then sweep all of the bones and detritus against the wall. He told them to skip the third and longest step of room recovery: removal. They just didn't have the time to clear everything out.

Arvin and Visteria would just have to work amid a silent audience of skulls. Evrick found it fitting, a visual metaphor for the dead stoically observing the fruits of their civilization long after their demise.

His people turned one of the intact tables upright and a lab kit was brought in via the elevator. Arvin set to work immediately, firing up the hot plates and wiping clean the vials and graduated cylinders he needed for measuring.

"I'm going to rehydrate this powder. And see whatever divine property it held, erm, *holds*," Arvin announced.

100

Visteria nodded in approval as she thumbed through her book of glyphs. The working guards zipped around both of them as Evrick looked on.

His heart was aflutter. He was confident the Concentrix was the key to it all. It radiated magical power, he was sure of it. And given the copper inlay in the walls, he figured it sent electrical energy all throughout the structure. If Visteria could figure the proper glyphs and Arvin could resurrect the dried divine blood, the entire facility could roar back to life. Chambers could seal again for protection. Perhaps there would be internal lighting, the water system wouldn't have to be manually pumped night and day by laborers and slaves, and most of all, the pods could continue converting fauna into fighters.

Arvin had been the boon that Skullhew, or New Ramlagha, had needed.

Evrick wondered about his "niece." Magical casters were unprecedented. Some even called those who controlled spell threads to be myths, but that girl was no myth. She just appeared in his command tent one night, Visteria sleeping in their suspended bed beyond the beaded curtain behind him.

With a gesture, the girl hoisted him into the air. Raising both her hands, she commanded invisible forces to wrench him. She was about to tear him in two when Visteria stepped through the beads, crossbow raised, and shot a bolt right into the girl's forehead.

Evrick remembered how collected Visteria was. She coolly reloaded the crossbow, naked and still lotioned for her evening sleep. What a stunning creature she was. Then and now.

Through all of the bustle, his eyes cut through the laborers and lab assistants and landed on her. She scrunched her nose as she reviewed her precious book. Arvin asked her something, and she proceeded to read to him from its pages.

Visteria had saved him, and she would save Vastard. He didn't need a monument of himself, but he felt Vastard would need one of her. The people had to know the woman that gave the Fourteenth Kingdom its legitimacy.

But first, *the ruins.*

His wife got to work, occupying the table on the opposite side of Arvin. The candles lit for them flickered dully off the piled bones in the corner as Arvin opened one of the glass boxes and took samples of the red powder within. They discussed which glyphs to experiment with on the blue stones below. Should they try entire sentences or simply isolated glyphs? And on which stones should they start?

Arvin began moisturizing the powder under pressure, and as his hand worked the tiny leather pump, he openly speculated about how far he could stretch their supply. "I wonder if there are more cache's elsewhere?"

Evrick wondered, as well. He quickly decided to pass the word along to all dig teams that locating such glass boxes was now their top priority. Turning to notify one of his nearby guards, he nearly jumped when he saw one standing directly next to him.

It was the guard with the burned face and one eye. Evrick smiled at him, embarrassed at how jumpy he was. The recent spurt of progress must have his adrenaline up. "How are the kids?" he asked. "What was your name again?"

"Good, lord. Thank you. And my name is Pista." He shifted uncomfortably. Clearly, something was distressing him. "I came to tell you of a problem."

"Oh?"

"The shifted fleshes have escaped."

Evrick spent a moment processing it. His mind raced through the ways that could have possibly happened, and he quickly concluded that it was partly due to the incompetence of the men guarding their vault.

He guided Pista over to the elevator and kept his voice low. Evrick wanted nothing to distract his two brilliant minds from their progress.

"Tell me everything you know," Evrick told him. "And stop looking nervous. Visteria can detect that shit from a league away."

"Yes, lord." He cleared his throat and hooked his thumbs into his sword belt in an effort to appear more casual. "We learned of it when a naked guard ran to us. There were three of them; one was a boxed ear with no balance, one had a cracked skull, and this one was the only one clear headed enough to run for help."

"Naked?"

"Yes. They stripped all three guards and attempted to dress themselves."

Evrick tapped a thoughtful knuckle to his lips. "Clothes would be the first thing I'd go for, too. And the bonus of being relatively disguised, but not much could fit Mama. Is that why you said 'attempted?'"

The guard nodded. "That and, apparently, they weren't entirely sure of how clothes worked. The guard said Rat is wearing pant legs over his arms and chewed a hole in the crotch for his head to poke out."

"That is a sentence."

"Mama is wearing boots on her hands."

"Uh-huh."

"Lovely is wearing clothing so loose that she was apparently tripping everywhere."

"And Bastard?"

"He is in the robe of the skinny idiot at the table there," the guard pointed to Arvin.

Evrick pushed his raised finger back down with the aim of continued discretion. "Any idea where they are now?"

"A lot of hiding places down here. I wasn't sure of how many souls to commit to the search. One of the elders demanded finding them and killing them outright, but I wanted you in the loop before anything was done that can't be undone. For now, I just ordered everyone to be on the lookout and hold positions."

The elders in Tent City had their uses: placation of the growing populous topside as well as logistic chores. But this kind of thinking was beyond them. They lacked vision, and only reacted to threats without ever seeing opportunity.

"Good. Do not kill them. Or harm them, if you can. Wrangle them up. Use food, good food that is pungent and leave it out for them."

The guard nodded. "Bester's got a sheep's stomach of spice and we can throw that in."

Evrick laughed. "They'll shit lava."

The guard nodded in agreement. "We can gather them up as they're doing it."

"Get laborers to do it. Not you guys," Evrick said. He didn't want his best taking the moral hit of being covered in reeking liquid shit. "How did they do it? Break out?"

"They worked the levers."

Evrick perked up in delight. "Problem solving. Within a week of being transformed human. I knew it. I knew those pods scratched something into their minds. It wouldn't make sense just to convert an animal to a human body without giving the human body some type of tutelage at the same time. Such wonders!"

"They still are very much animals, though, lord."

"As are we. They desire freedom and will fight for it. I'm glad for that." Evrick knew his hopes for generating obedient shock troops were dashed to pieces, but he was too amused to care at the moment.

Pista leaned in close and bit his lip as he formed his words. "They . . . sniffed asses."

Evrick paused. "I have questions."

"The naked guard alerted us to his ass being sniffed."

"You said 'asses' before so I assume all three guards got a sniffing?"

"Correct."

Evrick nodded. To him, it was the best of both worlds. They sought to understand their enemy. If Evrick could sniff an enemy's scat for information on his health and eating habits, he certainly would.

"All of them did," the guard continued.

"Yes, you said that."

"No, uh, all of them sniffed all of their asses."

"Wait, they lined up?"

"I honestly imagine not, but maybe."

"Okay, take the elevator back down and enact the plan to catch them. You're in charge. Use Bester's spicy soup or offer up your own ass for their sniffing pleasure if you must. But I want them unharmed. And don't take them to the vault since they clearly hate it and already figured out how to escape it. Just somewhere else, like the mess hall. Arvin will be by when I can spare him. Bastard likes him and maybe he can get them high again."

With that, the guard turned and wiggled into the half-waiting elevator. As he did so, Evrick pondered. He hoped the injured guards would eventually recover, and he'd be certain to send them up to Tent City for proper care with his own tribe. If one had died, that would have been more of an issue, but the shittier guards that he had assigned to the vault were typically from less reputable tribes like Barking Lizard or the Corpse Grind Mercenary Clan. Neither of which gave too much of a stink when their members died for the Skullhew cause. They just presumed their clan members were destined to die anyway.

The worst was when someone left a widow. If a dead guard had children, Evrick would need to move fast to protect and foster them before anyone exploited them. That, above all things, was the first tradition of Vastard Evrick wished to erase: the indentured trade of orphaned children to settle debts.

Visteria waved to him, and it shook him out of his thinking.

"Yes, Love?" he called, walking to her side. He took her summoning of him as a good sign she would let him touch her tonight.

"I've narrowed down these glyphs to likely be the ones to start the Concentrix. Or, at least, I've eliminated a majority of them," she said, flipping through her journal. "This glyph especially seems to be likely. And Arvin agrees."

Evrick was pleased Arvin's input proved useful to her.

"Wonderful," Evrick said, looking at the glyph. It looked the same as the others. "And, Arvin, how goes reviving that blood? Could it do what the girl's can't seem to?"

"Water won't work," Arvin said. "When heated, it doesn't integrate with the dehydrated material. It just floats around like grinds in fluid. Hardly blood, at all."

"Are you sure it won't work?" Evrick asked, dismayed.

Arvin nodded. "You certainly can't paint with it, so I assume that any special properties required would also be missing."

"What about the divine blood we already have on hand?" Visteria suggested. "From my niece? We have several pints in lizard skins, kept fresh. Use that instead of just water. Mix hers with that there."

With a shake of Arvin's head, his face soured at the thought. Arvin was about to protest, but Evrick cut him off.

"Would be interesting to see what happens if we did that."

Arvin froze, eyes locked in the distance. "Could be volatile," he whispered to himself. "Magic blood is as dangerous as those who carry it. Uncle warned me."

"Aren't you curious, Arvin? Try it, at least. If you can paint with it, then try the glyph on one of the stones below."

"Which?" Visteria asked.

"Any," he responded, sharper than he intended. Immediately, he regretted it. Since it was only Arvin within earshot and not any of his guards, Evrick felt safe enough to apologize. "Sorry, Love. I've been on edge. And pushing hard. We're so *close*."

Luckily, she didn't seem upset. "I've noticed. You will make it up to me later."

Evrick tried to share a knowing glance with Arvin, but he seemed oblivious to the sexual implications of Visteria's pleasant threat.

She placed a finger on the page of her book. "We'll try this glyph. And I'll go down and fetch a pint of my niece's blood. Arvin, it is yours to experiment with as you wish. I regret to say this, but Evrick is right. Besides"—she cocked a playful eyebrow at Arvin—"I'm curious too."

Arvin drew in his breath in a long drag, indicating an internal battle occurring between his caution and his curiosity.

"I'll grind some barley as a binding agent," he said, pulling off his bandolier to empty it more easily.

Curiosity had won.

# CHAPTER
# FIFTEEN

Arvin

When he was this focused and invested, Arvin lost complete track of time. Uncle called it time blindness and Arvin was deep into it. Hunger, thirst, and comfort all vanished when in this state. Arvin had even been known to pee himself without noticing, he was so absolute in his task.

He felt Visteria moving around on the other side of the table, the musty air swirling with her movements. From a thousand leagues away, he heard her occasionally ask him a question. A part of Arvin, the least important part, mustered to produce whatever answer was sufficient to appease her inquiry.

Additionally, Arvin was vaguely aware of guards coming and going from the elevator as it half-emerged from below. They rummaged through the ruins of bones for trinkets and precious metals, often finding something of interest to share with Evrick. Spearheads, buckles, arrowheads, and jeweled pommels got them excited.

More and more sconces were also added, and the room began to glow yellow like Uncle's shack when he was working at night. Arvin directed several of the fixtures to be in ideal locations.

"Are these pearls?" one guard asked, hoisting a necklace.

Arvin tore himself away briefly enough to evaluate them. "Those have properties. Save them."

The guard appeared annoyed, clearly prizing them for their value in trade more so than their value in alchemy. "Anything else I should set aside for you, oh lord?" she asked.

*Sarcasm. Again! I can sarcasm.*

"If you happen to find any bones, I could use some more bone-meal. For phosphorus."

The guard looked about her feet at the ocean of bones that surrounded them. She clearly was struggling to calculate if Arvin was joking or not.

*Let her calculate.*

Arvin returned to his work.

*The clotting in their mage's blood is an issue. Shake it away? No. Pour blood in dish. Scrape off and pluck out clot material to save for later.*

The barley wasn't even needed to revitalize the dried blood powder from the glass containers. Only the smallest amount of water, distilled water from Arvin's bandolier, helped unthicken it once the two bloods mixed.

*This dried blood. What is it from? Human? What if the divine blood is a mixture, or 'blood' is a metaphor entirely? This could blow up.*

The growing caution in his mind was quickly countered by his curiosity. His uncle had always said that taking one's time was ideal when faced with dangerous reactions.

*This could also be really, really amazing.*

But his curiosity trampled Uncle's advice. His mind raced with possibilities of what the Concentrix was, and what it might do. He had never heard of such a machine before, let alone something so large and complex. The sense of infinite wonder that he had been surfing on carried him through the rest of his experiment. After three different attempts, he found the exact viscosity he was searching for.

The blood was perfect.

"A partial fluidic state!" he declared, straightening from his side of the table with both arms in the air. "The friction within maintains its shape and slow movement. It's as good as I can get it."

Only then, Arvin realized that all of the guards had been asleep on the floor and Evrick was snuggled with Visteria in the corner on a bedroll.

"H-hello?" Arvin asked. "Wake up!" he shouted.

Several of them jolted awake, alarmed. Evrick was on his feet, knuckles up, ready for a fight.

"The gods, idiot. I was sleeping!" Visteria roared. She tried to continue berating Arvin, but her own body betrayed her with a yawn.

"But I got it. The blood is ready. Let's try a rune with it on a stone." Arvin needed her up since he wasn't confident enough to emulate her runework. "Get up," he demanded.

And, much to his surprise, she *did* get up. Very quickly and headed toward him with purpose.

Upon seeing her hand on the dagger in her belt, he backed away against the table. "Please don't hurt me."

"Maybe we should compare this blood to another variable, like *yours*," she snarled.

Evrick laughed, encouraging the other guards to do so as well.

*Is he trying to distract her? Defuse her? Save me?*

The dagger remained sheathed. Visteria's nostrils flared as she sniffed the air near Arvin. "Did you... piss yourself?"

"No! No, not this time. I peed next to the table. Right there."

"Where I'm standing?" she balked. The dagger was now out.

"I was working!" Arvin begged, his hands up as if he could dissuade an imminent strike. "You know how it is when you're working!"

"Clearly I don't." She looked about, spying the wet spots on the dusty ground near the table. There was part of a skull there that hadn't been swept away. "You literally pissed on the dead. On the ancestors of—" She caught herself.

"All right, everyone." Evrick patted the air above his head with both palms, as if to sooth the very atmosphere. "As good a reason as any to wake everyone up. Breakthroughs are always welcome." He turned to his wife. "Love? Would you be willing? I am desperate to see what comes of our first attempt."

"Husband, I am *tired*."

"Just one glyph. One attempt," he implored lovingly. "If it works, we can have heat and lighting of a nature you've never imagined."

She sighed, relinquishing. "You are *lucky* husband, lucky that I'm just as eager as you are." Looking to Arvin, she grimaced at the smell of him. "Bring your blood. I've a brush to paint the glyphs with." Walking away, she muttered, "Afterward, I'm going back to sleep."

Sliding on their butts, the three climbed back into the half-arrived elevator. Evrick gave the order for them to descend while he brushed off Visteria. She was too focused on her book of glyphs to be bothered with doing it herself.

"There are dozens of glyphs to use. I'm having second thoughts on which to try," she said to no one in particular. "Do we still want to stick with the one we picked out?"

Arvin nodded. "With so many variables, I doubt anything will happen anyhow. Pick any one you want. This is mostly a test to see if the blood adheres enough to the blue stone so it doesn't streak."

The elevator shifted gently, descending.

*They must have oiled the exposed gearwork. Smoother ride.*

"What glyph were you considering?" Evrick asked.

Visteria flipped to a page committed to a single rune. "Since you've always thought that the Concentrix is a power source, I'm thinking the rune that translates to 'power' most directly would suffice."

Arvin wondered. His first suggestion would have been for Visteria to select a rune that either translated to "yes" or "go" in that he felt an affirmation of some kind would be the safest option. But

Visteria seemed intent that "power" within the written language didn't translate to anything forceful. He kept his mouth shut, afraid to rile her further.

As the elevator passed by the pod chamber, Evrick looked to the guard stationed there. "We're just going to test something. Nothing should happen, but just in case, something might."

Her eyes went wide for a moment, but she swiftly recovered and nodded. Spinning on her heel, she shouted orders to several others that slept soundly on bedrolls. "To yer feet and in boots! We are up and awake!"

The elevator continued its short descent. A pensive moment passed between the three of them when they were isolated once more.

"Nothing will probably happen," Visteria said. Unable to contain a yawn, the last half of the sentence was distorted. "We'll try this once, and then I'm going back to sleep."

The dim light of the sconces below peeked through the metal grating of the floor. Apprehension welled up in Arvin, and he struggled to contain it. He was coming down from the high of discovery, and suddenly the results of his work were about to become real.

*We can wait. Make other samples and compare them. Use them on the pod blue stones instead. I don't want it to run. I don't want to have woken everyone just to embarrass myself.*

But he didn't know what to say.

Easing to a stop, the elevator leveled with the silicate floor of the blue stone chamber. Below their feet was the massive spherical chamber containing the rings of the Concentrix.

Arvin opened his mouth to express his hesitation as Evrick opened the gate, but nothing came out. He wanted to make the case for waiting. They could unearth other tunnels, find different blue stones, discover other blood samples that might not be dehydrated. Something ominous was gnawing at his nerves.

*What would Uncle do?*

It wasn't Evrick's expectant gaze that kept Arvin silent, but his own curiosity.

*Uncle wouldn't have been curious. He died in a shack, unknown. Let's just see. Just see what will happen.*

He stepped off, followed by Visteria.

Evrick gestured for them to proceed as if he were a servant in a castle, guiding his guests to their dining seats.

Unstringing a leather pouch, Arvin opened it just enough for Visteria to dip in her brush. She studied the rune one last time, then let her book hang from her waist as she smacked her brush free of any dust it might have collected.

"Badger hair," she said. "From a mutual friend," Dipping the brush in, she withdrew it with her hand cupped under it.

*Waste not?*

Curiously, she didn't move. Arvin couldn't read her, but her eyes remained unfocused. Finally, she spoke. "We should wait on this. At least a day. Just... to wait."

*Wait? Why? This is amazing!*

Arvin rapidly thought of what to say. He had to move her forward. The brush was right there, reddened with his perfected blood solution. She could just draw a rune on any of the blue stones available. All it would need to do is glow, and he'd confirm his success. It was almost maddening. His curiosity chewed on him, and he nearly pleaded. "If anything goes wrong, I'll fix it," he said.

She finally came out of her trance and looked him over. "I'll hold you to that." Almost impulsively, she randomly selected one of the blue stones and in the instant the red hairs contacted its surface, the entire world around them *groaned*. The air condensed, crushing their ears and just as quickly, it receded.

The hairs on Arvin's neck stood and a thrumming vibration ran up his legs.

*Ionization. Movement of hidden gearwork. The Concentrix!*

He nearly spilled the entire blood bag onto the silicate floor, but Visteria caught him in time. "Tie it!" she said. "Wait until this—"

Through the silicate, the three of them saw the machine moving below. First the largest, outer-most ring. Then the next, and the next, and soon all seven of them began rotating in seemingly random directions, their speeds varying and their trajectories shifting.

"It moves!" Evrick declared. "It works!"

The entire chamber below lit up as the copper inlay all along its curved surface glowed a gentle orange.

"My god," Visteria whispered, her hand to her mouth. "I haven't even finished the first stroke. It's like this thing *wants* to be awake."

The rings of the Concentrix spun faster and faster until they could no longer be seen individually. They had become a reddish metal sphere, suspended in the center of the chamber, humming so loudly that Arvin could barely hear anything else.

*Power from friction? Air ionization? How does this work?*

A light, faint at first, emanated from the sphere. Its intensity grew and grew until all three of them shielded their eyes from it.

"Why is it so bright? I couldn't finish the rune if I wanted to!" Visteria shouted. "Did their scribes go blind?"

*Thermic goggles!*

Arvin had just the thing for this. Clamping his eyes shut from the intensifying light below, he rummaged around in the pockets of his bandolier until he found his goggles. He used them for experiments that either gave off light or risked explosion.

He wore them often.

Slipping them on, he could look downward once again.

"I can see!" He informed his two companions. "I have goggles! I can see! The Concentrix is moving so fast it looks like a solid sphere."

"Why the light?" Evrick shouted back.

"Could be from heat. Because of friction?" Arvin asked out loud of himself. Kneeling, he pressed his nose against the silicate floor to see better. It was still cool. "Wait."

The sphere became solid, metal, and still. Then it rippled as if it were a shimmering liquid. It had changed its state of matter to a gleaming and perfect *metal* liquid.

"It's reflective. The light is coming from around it, not from—"

The surface of the Concentrix smoothed out, no longer splashing about. It sat still, but with tiny echoes of movement under its surface. Arvin could see the entire chamber reflected perfectly in it, even a small dot of himself looking down from above.

"Silver? Liquid silver?" he speculated.

*Too gray. Chrome? An alloy of chromium!*

"Chromium! Maybe with nickel bonded given the shine."

"Chromium?" Evrick asked, confused. "What is that?"

Arvin focused his scrutinizing eyes. He saw something long ripple across the surface. Then he saw it again, headed the other direction. It reminded him of a big fish swimming just below a pond's surface, ready to breach.

"Something . . . Something's moving like under a . . ."

*Like under a membrane.*

He didn't understand why, but his fear spiked. Something in Arvin screamed for him to run.

The Concentrix was like an egg, swollen with dozens if not hundreds of hands all reaching out. Claws pushed outward, piercing through from the inside. Long-fingered hands emerged.

"Uh-uh . . ." he stammered.

"What's wrong?" Visteria asked. "Arvin? Answer! We still can't see."

"I-uh . . ."

The hands sprung arms and then bodies. They pulled themselves free of the sphere—long-limbed shapes with horns and blank heads. Unlike baby birds or any other newborn, they made no sound but just poured out. Gravity took hold of them, dropping them down into the chamber, clumped and tangled into each other like giant, man-sized, shimmering ants.

*The claw marks.*

He saw their outstretched limbs, four limbs with a clawed hand on each end. He judged the distance between each long finger, and realized this was the doom of the Ramlagha. These were what stalked their halls and ended this civilization.

A blood-curdling, terrified scream erupted from Arvin. He clasped the sides of his head while chanting, "No, no, no, no, no!"

"Arvin! What is it?" Visteria demanded.

But Evrick wasn't as interested in answers. He grabbed Arvin by the elbow, wrapped his other arm around the waist of his wife, and hoisted them both back to the elevator in an instant.

"Up!" he shouted. "Up, gods damn it!"

The elevator immediately moved.

"Lord, what is happening?" The guard called from above.

"Arvin?" Evrick asked, squinting to see the alchemist's eyes through his goggles.

Arvin clutched the warlord. "Invasion," he gasped.

# SIXTEEN

Evrick

A toggle had flipped inside of Evrick. It was a toggle he remained familiar with. A builder of kingdoms no longer, he was now completely the man known as Skullhew.

"We pick up and go!" He roared to his wide-eyed guards. His voice thundered enough for it to carry through the polished copper sounding pipes to the listening chairs above. "Spread the word! Banner wavers of Skullhew, we are *leaving*."

Several laborers tripped over strewn bedrolls as others caught on instantly, snatching up precious supplies and crates to head for the exits. His guards all drew weapons and spread out to every entrance of the pod chamber.

"Rope!" a guard called down from the hole above. A moment later, the ascending rope with the wooden boot-hold tumbled down, nearly knocking Arvin on his head.

The poor alchemist was still in a panic. Whatever he had seen overwhelmed his senses. A part of Evrick calculated that, perhaps,

Arvin was just flipping his lid over nothing. He was seemingly moon-touched, after all, and it stood within the realm of possibility that this was all an overreaction.

That was what Evrick *hoped*, and since hope had no place on the battlefield, he ignored it entirely. They could always return when given the all-clear. Evrick could always redig collapsed tunnels. But he couldn't put his tribe back together. He couldn't risk a single hair on Visteria's head.

"You take this," Evrick said, handing her the board with the rope's end through it. "You go first." The piping in the ceiling shook and rattled with steam, sprinkling the pod chamber with dust and moisture.

It seemed to distract her, because she gazed intently at one of the walls.

"Love!" he cried.

She turned back to him. He could see her eyes calculating. "You first, not me. Lead from above."

An infinite scratching, a skittering as if giant rats the size of horses overcame the room like a wave. The invaders were within the walls, in the recesses of the Ramlaghan gearwork.

Everyone froze for a fraction of a second as the sound shredded their nerves. Arvin sank to his knees, crying, with his hands over his ears as Visteria's lovely face drained of color. Only Evrick was unaltered. He had already made the choice of flight the instant he saw Arvin's curiosity turn to horror.

He kissed his wife, then forcibly wrapped the rope around her waist, tucked it into a loose knot, and then shoved the board between her knees. Pulling her backward, he forced her to sit on it.

"Up!" he called.

Before she could protest, the three frantic guards above hoisted her. Every ounce of their bodies were behind it, because she shot up so quickly that her rune book caught on Evrick's belt and the small chain snapped free. It slipped from her waist and flopped open, face-down, on the alabaster stonework.

Evrick scooped it up, not just because of its precious knowledge, but because it was hers. "We go the long way!" he called up to her. He was not keen on waiting for the rope to come back down and ferry everyone one at a time.

"Save Arvin!" she called, ascending. She continued to shout something, but the chaos around him drowned it out.

With a forceful shake, he hoisted Arvin to his knees. "Don't slow me down or I'll leave you," he snarled. He was finally introducing Arvin to the true Evrick, the man necessary for the unification of Vastard. While Arvin was a valuable asset, and certainly likable, Evrick did not value the man more than himself. And if Arvin was to survive, that had to be clear.

Dragging on Arvin's bandolier, he hauled the quivering, stumbling alchemist behind him while shouting orders at the top of his lungs. He needed the listening chairs to hear.

"Leave all replaceables, blow the sixth-tier tunnels, and don't wait for the laborers." He needed a focal point for collecting what people he could before pushing out. "Rally at the listening post and we'll—"

Someone screamed behind them, near the elevator. It was followed by shouts as his guards dropped what they were doing and charged toward the chaos with weapons high.

If the threat was what he feared, Evrick knew every one of them was as good as dead. If only they weren't brave. If only they didn't care for each other and have each other's backs. They swept away the diced bones to clear this very pod chamber, so they *knew* what was coming. But they charged to fight alongside their fellows anyway.

He isolated the tragedy of it, stuffed it away in an emotional corner for processing later, and returned to the crisis at hand.

"Up the stairs here." He shoved Arvin ahead of him. "Keep going. Up! Up! Up!"

As they both scrambled, the sound of clashing steel, tearing leather, and wet splashes joined the chaos of yells and screams behind them. At least their deaths would buy enough time for them to get clear of the pod chamber.

Entering the maze of corridors, everything glowed orange, bathed in the light that emanated from the copper inlay. Evrick led Arvin by the bandolier, certain that if they got separated, Arvin would be lost.

The poor alchemist was still whimpering, his hands over his ears as he mumbled incoherently. Evrick heard the word "uncle" several times.

Two frantic laborers ran from the opposite direction. Both were spindly women, likely sisters.

"Lord! What is going on? We were just putting out soup to—"

For a moment, he considered directing them to the pod chamber as delaying fodder, but they were both so emaciated that what little resistance they gave wouldn't be worth their lives. "Move with us!" He gestured forward.

The two women clung to each other. Arvin's state of personal chaos accentuated their fear. It was beginning to get on Evrick's nerves.

"Around this corner, here," he said as they reached another stair-well. "Up!" He ran so frantically that he scrambled on all fours. The women kept up, but Arvin lagged behind with his hands still glued to his ears.

"What's wrong with him?" one woman shouted.

"Is he hurt?"

Evrick was at his last strand of patience. He briefly visualized kicking Arvin back down the stairs to be rid of the frustration he was causing. But Evrick reined it in, turned, and waited for Arvin to catch up. "You two go ahead. Get to the listening chairs. We meet there."

Eager to press on, the two women did so without their lord and his stumbling charge.

Arvin caught up, and while it took only a second, Evrick felt his fury rising. But his calculating mind was still working in the background, forever on. "Arvin, they are a puzzle. Solve them."

At the word "puzzle," Arvin's hands eased from his ears.

He yanked on Arvin's bandolier and continued guiding him up the stairs. "What do they look like?"

Arvin's eyes went wide as he internally reviewed what he had seen.

"Damnit, idiot. I need to know how they move!" Evrick pulled Arvin close, clasping him like he had seen the sisters' prior cling to each other. Maybe touch would help Arvin shake himself back to reality.

Arvin swallowed, preparing himself to speak. "Quadrupeds. Quadrupeds."

Evrick processed the word in his mind's eye. Thinking on the ancient slash patterns on the walls, he surmised that these things were climbers and highly agile, but not runners in open space. "You said 'chromium' earlier. What is that?"

They reached the top of the staircase and pushed on down another hall. Evrick saw the chalked directional markings. They were an ominous color in the orange light.

"Chromium is a metal. Dull gray. But mistaken for silver when polished. Tougher."

"So they wear armor?" Evrick asked. Everything wearing armor had weaknesses in the plate joints. It gave him hope.

"No. Their skin."

Since that was impossible, Evrick just assumed their armor was tailored so uniformly that Arvin couldn't see any joints in it through the silicate. Anything wearing armor did so because it was vulnerable underneath.

This was good news to him.

"Right, two more turns and then we're there. After that, stick with Visteria and she'll lead you out while I collapse the tunnels."

The clashing of a raging battle echoed from ahead. It was the listening post, and Evrick let go of Arvin to charge forward. Reaching the room, he saw a clump of guards and laborers shaking spears and throwing stools down one of the side corridors. Coming up another one, he saw Visteria surrounded with her escort. Pista stood with her, a buckler on his arm. They were at the opposite end of the chaos.

Evrick made eye contact with the disfigured guard. Raising his finger in the air, he gave the gesture to retreat and then pointed back the way they had come. The room was about to fall, and he wouldn't have Visteria in it when it did.

Without hesitation, Pista spun on his heels, hoisted up Visteria over his shoulder, and hauled off with her in the direction they had arrived from.

As he did so, she and Evrick's eyes met. "No!" she screamed, pounding at the man's hulking shoulders. "Evrick is there! Husband! Husband!" she cried, hands outstretched.

It tore through him. He might be sending her to different dangers, and gods knew what might have been chasing them, but she was not to be this close to an engaged fight with a superior enemy. There were other tunnels out.

Evrick's mind raced as a platoon of battered and bleeding guards stumbled in from another tunnel. They were clearly being pursued, as well. If this enemy was following a shock strategy, then they pushed toward the largest gathering of the victims in the hopes of breaking their ranks. Which meant the more people here, the juicier the target. To give Visteria the best chance, he had to draw the enemy *here* as long as possible.

"Give me a runner!" he roared.

No one responded, lost in the fever of holding two corridors.

From a third entrance, the Chromium broke through. Some charging in on the floor, some from the walls, and several ran along the ceiling as if gravity was merely a suggestion and not a rule. Each had four arms like Arvin had suggested, ending with a six-fingered hand. Their wicked fingers were long and ended in perfectly spiked tips. Each had a tail that split on the end into a prong, and their human-shaped heads lacked any features whatsoever. Each had a pair of perfect, forward-facing horns, like tuning forks, and the world was reflected in their unblemished, silvery hides. In their polished surface, he saw himself reflected. It was disorienting to even look at them, the world distorted in their smooth musculature.

They poured in, flanking his people on all sides. Their claws dug through leather armor, cracked open rib cages, and sliced faces clean off skulls. One nearly split a man in half, down to his spine, with a tail swipe. They were silent killers, without noise or the sounds of effort in their strikes. There was no sign of labored breathing or hesitation. They seemed to have no vision—no eyes; they just *knew* where everyone was and sought their enemy with deadly accuracy.

It was unfathomable. There was nothing like this in all of Andos.

This was it.

Evrick ran for the dais. The two listening chairs sat empty, the men likely a part of the futile defense efforts or already dead. As he approached, one of the things leaped in his path. Perfect rivulets of blood trickled down its glossy metal hide from its previous kill.

He faked left.

The thing shifted its weight to counter him.

Then he darted right.

It lashed its tail toward him. It sliced into his chest, but he could still run. His feet were still obeying. He hit the dais with his knees, craned his head upward to face each of the sound relaying horns above, and shouted, "Blow all the tunnels! Blow all the tunnels now!"

Everything rumbled like an earthquake as dust and pebbles shook from the ceiling and the orange lighting flickered for a moment. He desperately hoped that Visteria had somehow gotten out, or found another safe location.

Blood pooled around his knees. The strike hit his center, and it took a moment for him to realize his liver was sliced open.

This was very much it.

A macabre snicker escaped him. He reflected on everything, and felt gratitude first and foremost. Vastard had come farther than it ever could otherwise, thanks to him. He had married Visteria, discovered ancient secrets, and unified feuding tribes of aimless mercenaries.

He awaited the killing blow from the metal monster that had hit him, but it never turned around to pursue him. Someone had clobbered it with a stool, and it had turned on them, unspooling their intestines.

The room's shouts and sounds of battle dropped in volume and frequency. Invaders stalked around, stabbing quivering and gargling bodies with their fingers whenever they found one.

Suddenly, Arvin wriggled into sight. He had dropped to the floor at some point and crawled like a worm toward the dais. His arms were down at his side, feet together. It reminded Evrick of a toddler pretending to be a snake.

The alchemist silently reached the dais, rolled up onto its lip, and pressed himself between the two empty chairs in the center. Reaching out for Evrick, he gestured for the man to come closer.

Arvin had seemingly figured something out. He was still wide-eyed with horror, but the alchemist's mind was clearly working. There was a confidence to his movements that belied newfound knowledge.

Evrick tried to walk on his knees along the surface of the dais, to get closer to the chairs. They were only several feet away, but his body wouldn't budge. And his fingers and ears felt cold.

Arvin reached out with a grunt, gripped Evrick's belt, and pulled him in close to the chairs. Several of the stalking invaders perked up as if they had heard something, but soon resumed their patrol pattern of securing the room.

"Wh . . ." Evrick was trying to ask Arvin what was happening. He couldn't fathom how the man was still alive, and there was no reason why the things didn't just storm the dais and end them both. But his lungs didn't have the energy to push out the question.

Arvin pulled his head wrap from his trouser pocket and pressed it against the wound. It became red, soaked through, within seconds. Evrick shook his head with resolution and flopped his chin forward to rest on Arvin's shoulder. It was all he could do to remain upright.

"Arvin, solve this."

And all faded.

# CHAPTER
# SEVENTEEN

Bastard

Rat Man's head perked up from his bowl of spicy deliciousness. Bastard couldn't tell if he was alarmed or not, given that his eyes always appeared wild. But there was something in the air, a shift from below that made Bastard's curly arm hair straighten.

He took one last lick from his bowl, and then slid it over to Swan Woman. She was still struggling with hers, a splotch of soup on the tip of her nose. Not having a beak was clearly taxing for her and Bastard so desperately wanted to lick her face clean for her own sake, but he feared being hissed at and slapped.

Bear Woman stirred, her attention following Rat Man's. They all had crouched in the hallway where they had found the waiting bowls of steaming delight. Each was so hungry that they dug in immediately, desperate for the energy that the warm food would provide, that none of them had remained vigilant. Even when the world turned orange, they continued lapping their bowls, face-down on all fours.

Bastard took a long sniff and Bear Woman's nose wriggled as well. The lingering reek of human guards was present, and it likely came from the human clothing articles they were wearing, but whatever was stirring beyond their sight felt different.

A scratching echoed from the other side of the wall.

Each of them froze, Swan Woman doing so mid-lick. Her eyes darted to Bastard's. Bear Woman rolled her weight slowly to her knees, soup dripping down her massive belly that sagged from under the paltry coat she'd pulled off the guard.

Both Rat Man and Bastard had been hunted before, and they knew how to remain perfectly still to avoid detection. But Bear Woman was an apex predator, and likely only knew stealth in regard to hunting distracted prey. And Bastard had never seen a swan be attacked before unless it was on land, so he suspected Swan Woman just avoided shores as often as she could.

Bastard couldn't figure how the others were going to respond to whatever this new threat was. The scratch came again, longer and down the entire length of the hallway. Something was searching for a way in through the wall, and Bastard was reminded of hiding in the dozens of dens he'd dug and lived in prior. He knew when his habitat was being invaded, and this was a predator probing.

Hoping the others would follow his example, he stood on both feet and pressed himself into the recesses of the wall. Its structured shape gave him room to partly hide, and he held himself entirely still. Even his breathing was minimal, and his chest couldn't be seen to rise or fall.

Rat Man followed suit and Swan Woman took the hint instantly and hid in the opposite recess. Her bowl clanged to the floor, however, and Bastard feared it was loud enough to be heard by whatever was looking for them.

But Bear Woman sat there, her weight rolled onto her knees as she reared up with her arms wide. She sucked in air as her chest expanded, ready to deliver a classic bear roar. Swan Woman interrupted her with a terse hiss—a small, dissuading hiss like to misbehaving hatchlings. The hulking woman blinked at her in puzzlement but relented. Mimicking the others, she waddled to her feet and shuffled against the wall. But her girth was so substantial that she could easily be seen. That and her front being soaked in soup worried Bastard immensely. Whatever this was would certainly detect her, and he just hoped she could handle it.

The thought of escape, using her as a distraction for doing so, crossed his mind. But he found it distasteful. She wanted freedom as well, and had done much to earn it so far.

Besides, she wasn't the only one that could fight.

In silence, they waited. Distant cries of humans rang from else-where. They were calls of distress, and then Bastard recognized the distinct gurgle of a wet death. Whatever stalked the human warren was hunting the humans. And unfortunately, Bastard and the others were in the form of their prey.

Something glimmered at the end of the hallway. It shined unnat-urally in the orange light, and clung to the ceiling, as it stalked through the junction beyond. His ears heard each of its claws grip the stone above, scraping through the copper and molded rock as its long tail swished from side to side. It emanated a humming sound, higher than his ears could fully process, but it had no orifice on its face to produce such a noise.

It was a half-creature, the *idea* of a predator but not completed yet. As it passed, it hung its head downward and swung it slowly back and forth. The two horns bending forward from its head ended in such sharp points that Bastard's eyes couldn't see where they ended. Searching, it released one of its four hands from the ceiling, spread its fingers wide, and held perfectly still.

It gave off no scent from this distance, and Bastard didn't dare pull in a deep breath. All of his senses were confounded by this upside-down thing, a mere sprint away, as it performed its odd ritual. But one thing was certain: this was an anus he wouldn't dare sniff.

He shifted his eyes to check on his pack. Swan Woman had her eyes closed, still as stone. Rat Man was the same, but with his eyes open wide in terror. And Bear Woman had her hands balled, ready to pounce. Her chest heaved noticeably, and Bastard became terrified she would give them away.

Fight or flight played tug of war in his mind.

Loud gibbering erupted from down the hall as several humans of different sizes and skins poured in. They were clearly fleeing something behind them. One was missing a hand, the stump clung to his chest with specks of blood on his pale face.

The shining predator dropped from the ceiling, spun about, and within three strides it plowed into them with its claws out, tail lashing, and horns plunging. The cluster of humans screamed and cried and gargled and flailed.

Seeing the thing do its work, Bastard knew flight was the only option. He slipped from his recess, reached over, and tugged Bear Woman clear. She still appeared ready to fight, but he shoved her in the opposite direction, urging her away. She wouldn't stand a chance against that thing despite it being smaller than her.

Swan Woman joined in, pushing on her. Rat Man leaped clear of his recess and fled, inadvertently showing Bear Woman the direction she should flee in as well. Finally, she succumbed to the pressure and turned to follow.

The four fled further into the warrens, corner after corner, until the smell of opened human flesh wasn't as pungent. The air became tougher to breathe, the flooring dustier, and eventually they found a room filled with tables and wooden barrels. It had a round, metal door like the vault they had been trapped in.

Bastard hated returning to such a place, but this time he felt being trapped was preferable to being hunted. With his forehead, he pressed into the small of Bear Woman's back and directed her inside.

Rat Man required no convincing and followed, but Swan Woman hesitated.

A shout came from the distance, a clang of metal, and more

scratching. The hunt was still on, coming closer. It would soon be here.

Bastard reached out with one of his hands, fingers open. He'd seen the gesture between two of the fleeing humans before they died. Wrapping his fingers around Swan Woman's wrist slowly, he pleaded with his eyes.

Her lips curled to hiss, but she didn't fully form the sound. Instead, after a brief moment of narrow-eyed contemplation, she followed Bastard into the musky vault.

# CHAPTER
# EIGHTEEN

Arvin

While violent death was a common part of life in Vastard, Arvin had never seen it happen in front of him before. Such death was something that happened to someone else in some tribe, a parable of caution related to him through Uncle. And a bloody end was often between men enacting their grievances upon each other.

But this was a slaughter. Guards and laborers, men and women all lay with their eyes blank. The entire room was awash with blood as if the dais in the center was an island in a red, still sea. The orange light from the glimmering copper inlay brought out the brilliance of it, making the reflections on its sanguine surface even more vibrant. It was as if there were two rooms, an upside-down version to this one. In both stalked the chromium horrors, tails high and swishing rhythmically, as they patrolled in circles around Arvin.

*Why aren't they killing me?*

He had wedged himself between the chairs, still easily seen. What got him there in the first place was crawling low. While everyone else was screaming and fighting and being a target, Arvin had chosen a low profile. But it only got him to here. Trapped, with the dead Evrick leaned against his arm.

While being as still as he was able, Arvin evaluated the carnage. Evrick's words echoed within his skull.

*They are a puzzle.*

Calming himself, he remembered just how good he was at puzzles. How much he enjoyed them. How much he fed off them.

Arvin clamped his eyes closed, intent to reset his brain as best he could. When he reopened them, he was going to be an observant alchemist, a naturalist of the world around him. This would require all his resources, prior knowledge, and insight. He would solve whatever *this* was.

In the dark, he heard the things moving about.

*Chromium. Identification based on apparent composition.*

He listened to the slow patter of their flat hands on the stone as they shifted about the room. There was a slight thrumming sound in the air, like the fluttering of desert hummingbirds surrounding him. He could barely hear it, but it was there.

*Vibration. Sound. Emanating from them, but hard to discern.*

He opened his eyes. Focusing on one of them, he eventually found the pattern that it followed. It would raise its head with its horns high and slowly drift it side to side while walking. At the same time its tail would swish arrhythmically, the prongs on the end dipping about.

Next, he examined its head. It was shaped like a man's, but without any features at all. No eyes, no ears, no nose, and no mouth. Its smooth surface only reflected the orange world around it.

*No vision. No olfactory. No taste or visible consumption.*

Arvin went back to the tail. And then the horns.

*It moves the horns and tail like sensory organs. But how?*

One patrolled over several sundered bodies, the tributaries of their blood merged on the stonework between them. As it walked through it on its hands, he saw the entire puddle rippling.

*Tight ripples. Not just from impact of hands. Of course!*

That was it; they used sound to navigate. The prongs on the tail and the tips of the horns vibrated rapidly, at a high frequency ideal for distant travel through the air. The sound bounced off of their surroundings and they could 'see' shapes, navigate spaces, and hunt anything moving.

*Then why am I not dead?*

He looked about at the dais, then up at the dome of metal horns above him. It was a receiving room for messages from within the ruins. He had seen several large holes in the walls in various rooms and hallways. Those must have been designed for people to speak into to send the sound to here.

Looking at Evrick's restful face, he remembered he had yelled something here just before the walls shook. The sound must travel both ways, at least somewhat.

Arvin wondered if he could call for help, but he quickly dismissed it as an option. He didn't want to make loud noises around creatures that used sound as their location system for prey.

This made him return to the question of *why am I not dead?*

Searching the reflection of the room in the surrounding blood, he could see the outside of the dais both above and below the platform he perched on. A grooved design had been masterfully etched into it, forming a crisscross pattern, and soon he realized it was to dampen incoming sound waves.

*Sound can barely reach the dais. Which means they can barely hear me.*

That was why they were still stalking around. They knew he was there, but their reflected sound likely came back all jumbled. And any sound he made was like it came from behind a barrier.

*They are walking in circles around a sound blur, wondering how to get to me.*

Arvin shrank down between the chairs. He pulled Evrick's limp body closer, hoping the dead warlord's mass would stifle reflecting sound even further. It was time to wait, and hope they would give up and move onto other prey.

He took a moment to look at Evrick.

*I lost a friend as fast as I made one.*

Thinking back on the glyph, he wondered if Visteria had picked the wrong one. Or the wrong stone. Or if he had done something wrong with the blood when he rehydrated it.

*Did I do it wrong again?*

He was a failure as a person, but not as an alchemist. There had to be a reason for this horror and a way to push this bizarre invasion back. After all, it had happened once before, so there must be clues to find within these walls.

*A puzzle to solve.*

# CHAPTER
# NINETEEN

Visteria

As they fled, she had heard the things below, scraping away at the stone while picking off the fleeing stragglers. The guards in Tent City rolled explosive bundles down the descending ramp, their fuses flopping after them like lit rat's tails. She and Pista dodged them as they bounced by.

Visteria was finally in the light before the tunnels blew. It was a strong enough quake to unstring her knees, and the tent flaps of the nearby command tent rippled violently. A cacophony of alarmed shouts and cries rang out all over Tent City. Most of its three thousand residents likely had no idea what had happened below, but they certainly felt it.

When the tunnel behind Visteria finished collapsing, she was so out of breath from running she couldn't even cry out Evrick's name. The sun was just beginning to peek over the distant mountains east of Vastard.

Pista gathered his breath. "Lady?" He had been one of Evrick's favorites, one from the Iron Whores mercenary tribe. "Are you hurt, at all?"

She couldn't find words or runes or any sort of song to express what was happening inside her. The best man to walk under the stars was trapped below with a horror she seemingly unleashed.

But Evrick might still be alive. If anyone could survive, it would be him. Believing that, she found her voice. "Send runners to the other exits to see if—"

A red flare went up in the distance. It was the "all clear" signifying that another exit had successfully collapsed. Then another. And a third.

The fourth and final flare took off just feet away from her. All four exits to below had been collapsed.

"Maybe he escaped!" she cried. Her mind began constructing scenarios where he managed to get out one of the other exits in time.

Pista waved down a fresh soldier. "Run to the other exits. See if Lord Skullhew made it out. Report back!"

He sprinted out of sight as people, elders and half-awake laborers, began gathering to investigate the commotion.

Pista returned his attention to her. "Orders, Lady? Or do you want me to handle things?"

"What's to be done?" she asked of no one in particular, and yet to everyone who lived. It was just a matter of waiting, waiting to hear from Evrick. And if he hadn't made it out, they could dig him out. A man like him would *survive*.

A shout rang up from the buried entrance of the tunnel. A laborer covered their mouth and pointed at the freshly collapsed rocks within the exit tunnel.

Hoping that it might be Evrick digging his way free, Visteria ran to them and followed their gaze into the darkness below. It took a moment for her eyes to adjust, but soon she saw it, a single hand of perfectly polished metal. Three of its fingers were free, the rest of the creature buried. But even those three fingers clawed persistently at the stone. After a moment, they had cut tiny grooves and soon a fourth finger emerged.

Everyone surrounding Visteria murmured in terror.

"Is that one of them?"

"The gods!"

"How is it not dead?"

"Do we have more explosives?"

Visteria heard the commotion of Tent City increasing in the distance. The people, be they servants, smiths, slaves, elders, or fighters, were all in a panic as word spread. Someone had to address them. Someone had to take the mantle.

Which Visteria was trained to do, but that was never her desire, or even a part of her initial mission. The Desert Children had only tasked her with assassinating Evrick and compiling all the forgotten runes. Protecting what was theirs and reviving Ramlagha's written language of divine command was all that truly mattered to them.

And the book was now lost, as was the only man she would ever give herself permission to love. She betrayed the Children for him! Despair swelled in her, and she drifted down to her knees. All the surviving guards and laborers were too distracted to notice their lady had fallen to a state of catatonia.

She twitched, nearly fell over, and her bottom lip quivered violently. It was all too much, and so fast. They had just soaked in the sauna and made love a day ago. He laughed at one of her jokes, and she had been snuggling under his arm in the dark less than an hour ago.

Because Arvin had awoken her. His alchemy. His discovery. His ambition. He had seduced Evrick, faster than even she had, and made her husband careless.

"Arvin," she snarled the name under her breath. Her last words to Evrick had been wasted on Arvin. She implored him to keep Arvin alive, so he could help undo whatever it was he had done. She only touched the brush to the stone, so whatever went wrong was something Arvin did, knowingly or otherwise. Keeping him alive would make retracing his steps possible.

"Another one!" Someone pointed. A second shimmering hand emerged, much higher than the first, also fingering its way free.

"Lady?" Pista asked. "Lady, your orders?"

Tent City was clustered with children and families, many of which belonged to the guards. It would be chaos if she gave the call to evacuate, leading to some being trampled. Fires would likely break out and children would be lost.

But these *things* were coming.

She gathered herself to her knees and looked up at Pista.

"Evrick is down there, and until someone tells me they saw him fall, he is alive and in need."

He didn't hesitate to answer. "Of course."

"Gather the soldiers and begin corralling the families. Split up the population into relatively even groups and send them out in all directions of the compass."

His brow crinkled in confusion. "But why—"

"Because *some* of them might have a chance that way," she said. "The rest of us, those able to hold the line, will do so as long as we can for them."

Pista looked grim, even for a man with half his face melted away. But he nodded, hurled his head back, and began barking orders into the sky. Other men, some clearly having just rolled out of their cots, echoed his calls all throughout the tents.

"Hoist your iron, Whores!"

"Gather small souls, food, and water only!"

"Families stay together!"

What threads of order had kept chaos from erupting soon snapped. Women loudly lamented their buried husbands and children cried out for their mothers. Dogs barked from the excitement as camels shuffled and stomped. One tent wobbled on its posts as half-dressed men stumbled out, inquiring desperately about events.

Tears welled in her eyes as she pushed through them with her head down, in the opposite direction, and into the command tent. Several elders sat preparing for the day's interviews, when they saw her.

"Lady, where is your lord?" one said, wobbling to his knees. "Did I hear a call to evacuate to the winds?"

She ignored him. None of them mattered anymore. Skullhew was over. New Ramlagha was *over*. All that remained was Evrick somewhere below, alive or dead.

And it was Arvin's fault, not hers.

Slapping aside the hanging rug to their private quarters, she dove through her and her husband's things. She tossed aside valuable linens and jewelry to get to precious water pouches and her sand boots. After binding them on, she strung her crossbow with practiced and efficient speed.

As she fetched her quiver of precious, glass-tipped bolts, she heard a batch of camels stamping through the camp and out the main entrance. The people were heeding Pista's orders. At least some semblance of hierarchy was still in play.

When she exited, she was confronted by the gathered elders. There were eight in all—an impotent council that Evrick had suffered to give the mercenary tribes some semblance of autonomy.

Her disdain for them had never been a secret.

"Lady, where is your lord?" the bristly, tall one pressed. She forgot his name.

"Trapped below." Getting the words out hurt her tightened throat. She wiped away fresh tears. "And now you will either stay behind and fight to hold off the enemy, or you will flee."

They all blinked at her.

"Pick!" she shouted.

A fresh round of screams rang from the west side of camp. Visteria pushed through the men and out the front of the tent. The usual guards with their massive polearms were missing, likely having run off to collect their families. But many of the petitioning travelers had remained, unsure of what was going on or what to do. They had likely just arrived during the night. She craned her head over the bewildered crowd in the direction of the new screams and couldn't see anything but kicked-up dust and flapping tent cloth.

Then the ground shifted below her. The sand began to sink, a pole in the tent's awning leaning.

"What?" an elder managed to say before his own foot sank into the sand.

Pits grew all over, divots in the sand as it swirled into loose whirlpools. Several of the petitioners were dragged in, and soon they screamed as their lower halves disappeared from view, the sand around them turning red.

"Back inside!" Visteria yelled to the elders.

They instead reached for the poor souls being pulled down, only to be pulled in themselves. The petitioners scattered, some climbed poles desperately while others leaped on top of flimsy crates. A rush of them stormed the front of the command tent, but Visteria knew that was certain death.

She was proven right when the tent collapsed on them. Something moved inside the loose folds with them, several somethings, and it splashed them all over the inside of the canvas.

It was madness. The enemy came from below. Silver arms burst from the sand and snatched people by the leg. One reached for her, but she managed to dart away quickly toward a brick bread oven. She burned her leg briefly while climbing on it, but once she stood, her desert boots protected her from the heat.

People ran to and fro. Several of the metal things chased them about, slashing through them. One invader clung to a kicking horse as if to ride it.

She leveled the crossbow. The glass-tipped projectile was considered the deadliest in all of Vastard; its tip was designed to shatter after impact and tear apart sinew and arteries. Aiming at an invading creature, she pulled the trigger.

It flew true.

And shattered uselessly on impact. The thing didn't even notice as it tore open a kicking old woman.

"My lady!" a voice called. It was Pista, yelling from an armored wagon. It was for transporting gold between mercenary companies and clients. He and several men had secured it, strapped it to four *very* nervous horses, and were pushing people away as they tried to get on. "Run to us!"

Realizing she had just been standing on the oven this whole time, she bolted toward the wagon. A fire had broken out in a nearby tent, and someone ran by her as they burned and screamed. Soon one of the things slashed them into two with its tail.

The thinking part of her brain, the part that remained in control, suspected the invaders attacked the loudest targets first.

Reaching the wagon, Pista leaned down with his massive hand, grabbed her by the quiver strap, and hoisted her up onto the wagon. "Go! Go! Go!" he shouted.

Pista kicked open a hatch and shoved her down inside among a cluster of terrified children and their mothers. The driver of the wagon peeked through slits in the armor as he slapped the reins, and they jerked forward.

Claws burst up through the wooden floor, catching one of the children's legs. The mother scooped the child up, but another pair of claws pierced in. A second mother banged at the metal hands with a cast iron pan, but it did nothing.

"Get to the sides!" Visteria cried.

Pista jumped in from above. "Knock out the boards it's holding onto!"

Everyone started kicking at the bottom of the wagon, loosening the flooring. Combined with the thing tearing and tugging at it, the boards soon came loose and the thing fell off. It tried to lash its tail to cling onto something, but instead connected with one of the mothers and pulled her out with it. They both vanished under the rear axel.

Her children shrieked, arms out, as Visteria held them back.

"Ride!" she ordered the driver.

"To where?" he called back over his shoulder.

"Ride to the northern mountains! Or to the east toward an Egren outpost. Anywhere but here." Visteria had burned her bridges leading to the Children of Ramlagha when she put a crossbow bolt into their paragon's forehead. While the runes had been the primary mission, she had very much gone rogue in all other regards.

Wherever they went, she had to avoid the Desert Children. After her betrayal—loving the man she was to assassinate and lobotomizing the only sorcerer the Desert Children ever birthed—she might as well just steer the wagon back into the chrome wave of death behind them.

CHAPTER

# TWENTY

Arvin

*Time is a measurement of events, and since nothing has happened for a long time, has time stopped? If it has nothing to measure?*

The three remaining Chromium sentries had stopped, almost mid-stride, and remained. They had done so a while ago, and Arvin didn't have any accurate measurement of time. He checked his bandolier for his mercury timer but couldn't find it anywhere.

*My coat. Bastard has it.*

The horror of Bastard's situation hit him like a tumbling boulder. The poor soul had been converted from an animal merely a week ago, along with the other three flesh-shifts, and now they had likely been slaughtered by horrors from beyond the realm of under-standing.

*Another friend, gone.*

Arvin wanted to sit there and resign himself to rotting next to Evrick. He could quietly starve, or even drink the concentrated cyanogenic poison he had in his bandolier. Derived of pear and apple seeds, he wondered if it would at least taste sweet before it killed him.

*What if I have to poop?*

Chronic constipation might finally be of use. Arvin sometimes went a week without defecating and Uncle had to concoct something to loosen his bowels. And his arms, and body, and head. In fact, that special tea Uncle made was notorious and the biggest seller he produced.

He thought of Uncle again, his weathered fingers delicately measuring. Their entire shack was just a lab with two cots, and Arvin would give anything to be back there. A boy again, watching a quiet man work.

In a world of magic, Uncle had a power of his own.

*Be like Uncle.*

Arvin was certain Uncle would have remained stoically calm throughout all of this. Metal horrors stalking the halls? People fleeing or fighting fruitlessly? Uncle would have been observant through it all. He would have concocted a plan. Put together a means to . . .

*Dazzle the enemy. Sound vision. Make sound!*

Starting at his shoulder, Arvin began running his fingers down each pouch of his bandolier. He took stock of each ingredient and each instrument he presently had. Then he began cross-referencing each ingredient's interaction with everything else in an attempt to categorize what he could do with his limited supply and mobility.

*I have concentrated pink potassium. A lot of noise from that if it hits water.*

He could add droplets of water into the potassium vial, shake it, and throw it. Wherever it landed would be a light show, and the sporadic bursts from it would certainly captivate the three Chromium surrounding him.

But he had no water pouch. And after frisking Evrick's dead body, he found that he had none either.

*No water. But something watery might work.*

He had oils and extracts on his bandolier, but the most watery thing present was all over the floor at his knees: Evrick's blood.

*Ew.*

It could have been worse, like the time he needed to milk a bull for a gallon of its squeezings. That was exhausting work, and Arvin had to sing to the bull prior each time to keep it calm otherwise it would kick as it was juiced.

He unsheathed his pipette and gathered several drops of Evrick's spilled fluid. The edges of his pooled blood showed signs of congealing, so he gathered from the thicker region around his shoes. Arvin was unsure how such a thick fluid would react with pink potassium, but he hoped he'd have at least some sound coming from it to serve as a reaction.

Before Arvin tossed his clever noise decoy, he first had to plan his escape in greater detail. The Chromium had no eyes, but they obviously could "see" all around them perfectly. Their attention wasn't focalized like a typical predator with forward-facing vision. After tossing the decoy, they would likely turn back on him the moment he left the dais and appeared within their perceptions.

So when the time came, he had to *not* appear as human prey. What else could he look like? He'd have to move, after all. What moved here that didn't compel the Chromium to attack?

Arvin thought of the gear work in the walls. He had heard them clawing along inside the guts of the ruins, and they ignored the mechanisms to instead go directly for the people. It was likely that the Chromium only zeroed in on living motion.

*I need to not appear living.*

This took him back to the whole killing-oneself and that carried little appeal to Arvin. He rather enjoyed living. But he could *disguise* himself, at least, as unliving.

He leaned against the two chairs that he and Evrick were wedged between and had an idea.

*I shall be a chair!*

Confident in his solution to the current puzzle, he used his pruning knife and fingernails to pry the cushions from both chairs. They would absorb sound well, and since the Skullhew had freshly upholstered them, their coarse texture was ideal.

The three chromium creatures remained still as Arvin strung together the main four chair cushions into a square. Slipping it over his head, it altered his shape to an angular one. He wore the improvised armor at a diagonal angle so both his arms could wriggle out between the corners.

Then he bent both cushions from the headrests over his knee. Those, he wrapped around his head with his bandolier, careful to keep room for at least one eye to see through them.

Crouching down as far as he could go, Arvin waddled back and forth on his knees to test his creation. He could move forward, at half the height of a man, while using his fingers to hold up the sides so he wasn't dragging anything on the floor. Once he left the dais, the horrors would certainly perceive him and easily surmise his basic shape, but he hoped not to appear as human.

*Prey. Don't act like prey. I shall be a box.*

With one last, forlorn look at Evrick, Arvin took his first steps forward to the edge of the dais. The Chromium didn't stir, but he could hear their humming more distinctly. Their tails and horns, while appearing almost still, blurred just enough for the human eye to detect.

He was terrified, yet thrilled. This slap-dash experiment of his would determine if his observations were correct. And if so, it was the first major step in solving the Chromium puzzle.

*Be the box.*

The dais was a step above the rest of the chamber. Looking down over its lip, he saw his reflection in the settled blood below. Pressing his hands palm-down, he lifted himself and his disguise off the dais and gently lowered himself into the still, red mirror of blood.

The ripples were slight, but present.

All three Chromium shifted their weight, tails bent toward him. His head buzzed as their sonic systems narrowed in on him.

*Hearing each other's pitch, as well as their own. Three seeing as one. Thrice as effective.*

His fascination gave way to fear as their red-soaked hands, claws caked with gore, each lifted. They came closer, horns low, toward him.

*Be a box. Oh gods, be a box!*

Arvin rested his cushion box in the bloody floor briefly. Pulling the potassium vial from his teeth, he yanked the cork off.

One of them crouched down, ready to spring.

*I'm a box!*

He took the pipette from behind his ear and squirted three drops of blood inside. Flicking it away with his fingers, he landed it across the room with a gentle *tink* and closed his eyes. With quivering hope, he held his breath.

Nothing was happening. The vial wasn't popping.

*Is there a box heaven?*

The Chromium leaped, splashing as it charged across the clear surface of gore. But when the vial finally popped, it dug its claws into the flooring and halted.

*One tiny pop? That's it?*

The four of them remained still.

Then the phial popped again. And again. On the third time, it took off like a shot and began dancing about the room in sporadic bursts. The open end of the phial acted as a thruster and the chemical reaction as propellant.

*Blood is weird!*

But it worked, compelling all three creatures. They tried to follow the thing with their horns, bouncing around in an attempt to flank it like cats to a mouse. They leaped and swung their claws fruitlessly in the air as their buzzing modulated wildly.

Now was the time. Arvin hoisted the box and shuffled his feet as quickly as he could. The bloody lake surrounding his boots was already in turmoil from the bounding horrors as they jumped off every surface, so his foot falls were obscured. And since his own surface was flat and unappealing, they ignored him while chasing the far more exuberant prey.

While speedily waddling, his boot kicked something. It was Visteria's book of glyphs, half-soaked. Its waist chain strap was gone and the corner of it sheared off from the Chromium that cut through Evrick.

*He had promised to give it to her.*

Settling his box over the book, he lifted it and pinched it between his knees. Fulfilling his friend's promise was the least he could manage.

Testing his luck no further, Arvin shuffled forward and around severed limbs and sundered weapons until he reached the nearest exit. He had no idea what lay ahead in the dark, but anything was better than where he was.

CHAPTER

# TWENTY-ONE

Bastard

Having been taxed to their extremes, Bastard's exhausted nerves sporadically yanked at his fingers and arms. He had spent an immeasurable amount of time next to the vault door, palms flat against it, ready to shove it shut on a moment's notice. At the first hint of sound or approach, it had to close. The glossy predators were still out there, and he could occasionally catch the echo of their scratches from the depths beyond the tunnel.

But the hatch had to remain open. As a badger, he knew that all burrows needed ventilation. This vault was different from the one that the four of them had been held in, as it was packed with materials, canisters, and glass wares. When he did a quick search upon entering, he sensed no overt airflow.

And airflow was vital to Bastard, not just because of breathing, but because of the unnatural malodors squeaking out of the four of them. Each of the troupe had lapped up the spicy soup left in the hallway. But it now seemed that the soup was made of a volatile substance that, within their guts, had converted to a hellish vapor.

The vault reeked of their farts—an unnatural, eye-watering reek. Even with his dulled sense of smell, each time one of their posteriors puckered and vented, it punted his thought process into a ravine of fiery thorns.

Rat Man seemed to hold up the best, but both women had not only succumbed to firing out unholy fumes but also squirting liquid shit down their legs. Swan Woman was especially wobbly on her knees, clutching her gut.

He wanted so desperately to help her somehow. If they were both badgers, he'd roll her around in the dirt to soak the moisture and mask some of the smell, then escort her to a creek or stream, something with moving water. And he'd protect the bank while she washed herself off.

The distress on her face hurt him to see, but his concern was interrupted by the sudden realization that he could interpret her face. As a badger, he knew how badgers and other nearby animals expressed themselves, but he had never encountered humans prior to his capture. And yet he could understand her distressed facial expression.

He dismissed the epiphany, figuring that any creature shitting its brains out was likely in distress.

Bear Woman gasped, gripping her gut. She moved back and forth in the vault's enclosed space, as if the smell was nipping at her heels. Occasionally her massive hand clutched the wall, and as her body strained, Bastard speculated as to the volume and solidity of what was about to come out of her.

He was usually wrong. And surprised.

None of this seemed to bother Rat Man, however. His eyes, both close together and forward-focused over his nose, remained intent upon exploring. He had already toppled several glassware jars filled with powders and dusty residue. Time had dissolved whatever had once been contained in many of the containers. One crate contained long belts of leather hide, but when he moved them they crumbled.

Only the iron buckles remained, and he nibbled at their pitted surface with his buck teeth.

Bastard wanted relief from guarding the door, but he didn't trust Rat Man's attention span. Bear Woman was too restless and miserable, and he didn't want to tax Swan Woman further. So, he remained at his post, ready to shove the vault door closed on a moment's notice if danger approached.

He had escaped one vault just to flee into another. There was no long-term plan for him. No food, no cleansing water source, no airflow to sniff for distant prey or predators, and no comfy bedding to rest on. And his ribs ached.

At least he still had the soft, warm hide that the skinny human had given him. The coat had proven invaluable, and Bastard clenched his insides with determination. He would *not* soil this astounding gift.

One of the echoes sounded closer than the others.

His ears perked, and he smacked his tongue against the backs of his teeth. It was the usual badger-to-badger warning sound. Luckily, all three of his compatriots picked up on the signal and instantly froze.

The scratch came again, and Rat Man ducked down, ready to flee to nowhere.

Bastard ceased his hesitation and shoved the vault door closed with a loud *clank*. Pressing his ear against the metal, he listened intently. The sound he had heard was rapidly approaching, like a shuffling. And under it all, he heard panting. It was living, unlike the shiny things that were so scary before. But that still hardly made it a friend.

Soon Rat Man pressed against the door to listen, as well. And Swan Woman wobbled over, followed by Bear Woman. They all squeezed together, listening intently as best they could over their intestinal grumblings.

The vault door's flywheel twitched.

All four of them stared at it in bewilderment.

It turned and *thunked* into place. Then it opened toward them just a sliver.

They pressed back against it, slamming it secure. Gibbering came through the metal door, but something was unique about it. The indecipherable noise was coming from a voice that Bastard recognized.

Gentle Man!

Bastard began pulling against the other three that pushed. Bear Woman grunted in frustration, Rat Man spat in fear, and Swan Woman hissed at Bastard. He hated making her upset at him, but it was the human he liked. And he knew this human could ease their tummies the same way he had eased Bastard's ribs.

Nudging Bear Woman away from the door with his head, he tried to pry it free of her meaty grip. Swan Woman hissed louder and renewed her determination to keep it shut. Rat Man retreated, fearful of both Swan Woman's hissing rage and the threat beyond the door.

Bastard instinctively bared his teeth at her. Swan Woman reached back with her palm, ready to slap him with all the force that her body could deliver. It gave him a brief window, since her strength was redirected toward his face, so he kicked the back of Bear Woman's knee. She slipped on a trickle of her own diarrhea and stumbled away.

For an instant it was just Bastard and Swan Woman, he snapped his teeth at her. Mid-slap, she flinched and missed. He opened the vault door wide.

A boxy-appearing Gentle Man was on the other side, one eye wide through his bundled head. He quivered from delirious weariness and fell forward across the vault's threshold.

Before any of the troupe could hiss or snarl a protest, Bastard dragged Gentle Man inside and swung the vault door shut again.

# TWENTY-TWO

Arvin

Arvin saw Bastard, and easily deduced the other three with him to be Mama, Lovely, and the one that skittered away as Rat. Mama was massive, the largest person Arvin had ever seen. Rat had a hooked nose and a mild overbite with piercing eyes. And Lovley was simply the most beautiful human to grace Andos.

With the vault door secure behind them, and in the presence of other living things, Arvin felt relief and pulled off his rickety disguise of chair parts. Now, temporarily safe from the Chromium, he indulged in the luxury of sorrow. He wept, and as he did so Bastard scooted in close to him. Mama stood, from the other side, and began licking Arvin's hair.

Never, even with Uncle, had he felt so safe. When he cried as a boy, Uncle would simply stand outside their shack. Arvin allowed himself to sob it all out, chest heaving. The past month had been wretched, and it had been all he could do the entire time just to walk *forward*, let alone think. Evrick Skullhew had provided such new hope, that he had foolishly thought his days with Uncle were what held him back.

He nestled into Mama's bulky arms and cried. Bastard folded onto Arvin's back, and the three shared a soothing cuddle. It was clear to Arvin that he wasn't the only one scared and hurting. It was a relief to be cared for by people, who weren't as volatile as . . . *people.*

*They need me. We can't stay here. They need water, food, and to be cleaned of whatever that hateful smell is. Did each of them shit themselves?*

"How did you all get here? Your cells are the level above this."

Bastard responded with a blank stare. The hairy man still wore his coat, and as he examined Arvin's bruised forearm, the tip of his nose nearly touched the skin.

"I followed a trail of soup," Arvin said. "I figured guards had been eating and ran for cover. I wasn't expecting the four of you. I wish they had left you in your cells. You would have been safer there."

As Arvin spoke, Bastard's eyes settled on his mouth. Mama leaned over and rested her ear on Arvin's chest as if to hear his voice from the inside.

"Oh, are we exploring?"

Rat pulled his head out of a crate from across the room and Lovely stirred from her fetal position to hoist her head.

He now had the attention of all four.

*If they have human brains, they can learn human words. Exposure to language should be the first step.*

"You picked a good spot. To hide. This room"—he pointed, trying not to let the reek distract him—"with that door. Good. Good. *Good.*"

*Positive words first. Reinforce the positive.*

He slowly sat up. Mama rolled away, parking herself on her butt next to him. Bastard backed off only a bit, his hands out as if he needed to catch Arvin if he went limp.

*Both caring. Likely had litters as animals. Or packs. Den animals.*

Rat returned to digging through his crate, but Lovely remained up on an elbow, her wary eyes on Arvin.

*Any of their past traumas as animals can impact their reaction toward me.*

His work was going to be uphill, but he still felt far safer here than out in the hallways.

"Did the scary things chase you in here?" He knew they wouldn't answer, but he found it important they become accustomed to his voice. "It smells *really* bad in here. Are you all not feeling well?"

Never could Arvin imagine feeling comfortable around four relative strangers, but he stood slowly with confidence. He knew a shrinking posture could shake whatever authority he would need to lead them to safety.

"Thanks for the hug," he said to Mama. He felt that Bastard and he already had a rapport given their drug journey together so he put some extra effort into acknowledging her. "You're the largest human being I've ever seen."

Evrick had said she had been a Gold-tip bear, which meant even with her current girth she had lost at least two thirds of her mass.

He exercised his empathy and tried to see things from her perspective.

*Not only a different body but shrunk. Completely disarmed of claws and teeth. Must be terrifying.*

Arvin then focused on Rat's explorative ruckus. The spindly man's legs poked upward out of a crate as he grunted and rooted around. A desert rat had flexible spines, infinite energy, and natural camouflage and yet Rat was reduced to a gangly, awkward human.

*Rapidly enlarged, flexibility reduced, teeth blunted, energy and speed drastically limited.*

That alone had to be a level of trauma that would break any person.

He then looked to Lovely, who was clearly in the worst shape of the bunch.

*Was a swan. New to mammal form. Breasts and reproductive organs entirely different to say nothing of figure. No feathers.*

Arvin winced when he thought of another change she had been subjected to.

*Can't fly!*

Her hollow bones now filled, Arvin wondered at how sudden *weight* must feel.

*Alien. They all feel alien in an alien world. Travelers from another realm of existence, suddenly and cruelly dropped here.*

Sympathy soared within Arvin's chest. His throat tightened, and his eyes watered. It wasn't fair what had been done to them. The Ramlagha had built the ancient machines, revealed to be capable of great evil, and Evrick and Visteria had used them. These four might be safer as humans, but they were certainly more content as the creatures they once were.

*Converted without guidance. Thrown in cells. Kicked. Fed like animals.*

The more angry he got with Evrick, the more his guilt doubled back on him. Evrick had been kind to Arvin, recognized Arvin's worth and taken him in. And he had died for it. He shouldn't be angry with a man who cared for him, a caring which led to his demise.

All of the guilt and bitterness swirled in Arvin until his tearing eyes blurred to the point that the world became warped.

*I did it wrong. I did something wrong with the blood.*

But there were things to do, and most of all, vulnerable people to protect. He muscled through the clenching in his chest and focused on the puzzle at hand; help these people.

"Okay, so... first we get clean. Clean is good. We want to be clean." He examined the room they were in with more analytical depth. Everything was compartmentalized with runes painted on each crate. This was a storage room from before excavation, which meant the contents of each crate was thousands of years old.

Stepping carefully to not slip on any diarrhea, he moved and leaned against the wall to review Visteria's book. The bottom of it was soaked in blood, but she had used treated leather for the cover and it remained mostly bound. The pages within remained dry. He wiped it off as best he could with the leg of his trouser and then opened it. Cross referencing the runes, he compared those on the crates to those on the pages within.

*Over twenty runes. Possibly phonetic. The top tips are different. Conjugation? Bend on left means plural.*

Visteria's notes were exhausting and articulate. As Arvin read through them, he paced about while mumbling to himself. The horrors, the death, the blood, his vulnerability, all of it fell away because his curiosity feasted on Visteria's linguistic discoveries.

He lost track of time and reached the back of the book. Flipping back over it, he reviewed several sections that he was still hazy on. It was only then that he realized Mama was slouched against a crate, snoring. Lovely was curled against Mama's side, using her mammoth belly as a pillow. And Rat rested his head on Mama's opposite thigh.

Only Bastard had remained awake, his ear pressed against the closed door. His dark eyes were bloodshot from exhaustion, and he periodically smacked his lips in a sign of blistering thirst.

*They need so much right now. And I'm their best hope.*

Arvin returned to the glyphed crates. He proceeded to translate their contents. They held clay jars, glass vials, linen threading, iron winches, water bladders, leather belts and tunics, raw copper ore, coconut pulp, and scouring brushes. Eventually, he shuffled the crates to get to the ones in the back. Bastard crawled over to help, his gait limp with exhaustion.

Behind the wall of crates, in the back, was a large water tank fashioned of copper. The heating apparatus under it was long dead, devoid of fuel for burning. Arvin rapped a knuckle against the side, and it was still filled with water.

*Cold? Maybe it filled when the ruins came to life. Fresh water? From where?*

He unscrewed the copper cap on the side and took a deep sniff. Nothing. His sense of smell might be overwhelmed from the reek of dried excrement. Worrying that his human senses weren't keen enough, he decided on getting a second opinion.

Gesturing at his nose, he pantomimed sniffing deeply. He then snorted a few times at the water tank opening, hoping that Bastard would get the idea.

It took a moment, but Bastard's eyes lit up with understanding. He swiftly entered Arvin's space, inhaled and exhaled rapidly several times like an animal would, and then reached his hand inside up to his elbow. He pulled it back, and it was wet.

Before Arvin could stop him, Bastard licked his hand clean of water.

*Untested! Ancient maladies! Metal particulates! Unseen diseases!*

Bastard reached back in for another soaked-hand's worth to lap up.

*Whelp.*

Arvin checked the crate with the bladders. They were fashioned of the same flexible material that the niece's feeding and bleeding tubes were made of. He quickly fashioned a water siphon using one as a hand pump and within minutes he had five full bladders.

Arvin had concerns with rousing a sleeping bear, rat, or swan. It seemed a swift way to get hurt. He let Bastard nudge everyone awake and give each of them water.

With a belly full of water, Bastard eventually succumbed to his exhaustion. Curling against Mama for warmth, he joined the other three and slept.

*When they wake, I'll have a plan. Things will be better. I'll make this better.*

The Chromium problem was too big to tackle, currently. He feared it was his fault. But at least he could care for these four. *Someone* had to be safe through all this.

Arvin set to work performing an inventory of each crate. Most items had disintegrated from age, but some of the chemical jars were still sealed and free of air. He identified them as best he could from the runes as well as his personal knowledge. There were stores of salt, sodium, potassium, and powdered lime for water purification.

When he found a jar of gelatinous lye, he finally solved a mystery that had been bothering him.

*So that's how that one man got melted!*

CHAPTER

# TWENTY-THREE

Arvin

Firstly, he targeted the filth. Arvin carefully measured the lime out into several water pouches, shook each voraciously, and with the sudsy water he washed down each of his companions. Since Bastard was the most trusting of him, he went first.

It was an odd experience to wash under a man's fuzzy testicles, but Arvin approached the situation as he would a grooming chore, such as plucking barbs out of a camel's fur or brushing a horse's mane. Bastard was an excellent subject, and not only did he clean up well, he also seemed to learn along the way.

"Wash under here. Good. Good. You want that clean. And, uh, back between here. Trust me, you want that clean too."

Mama was next, but she wouldn't stand for her washing. She sat, slumped, with a sad look in her eyes as Arvin scrubbed her hair with his fingernails and washed the soup residue off her front.

"Madam, we are going to need to go places. Places I wouldn't normally go on a bear." After three nudges, she finally rolled on her

160

side and let him do his work. Luckily, by this time, Bastard got into the groove of how to wash with his hands and helped out.

Once they caught Rat, they did the same to him. Arvin had to jangle belt buckles in front of him to play with to keep him occupied.

Then came Lovely. She hissed ferociously at Arvin as she clutched her stomach, but she permitted Bastard approaching. The badger-man had quickly mastered how to squirt the lime-water out of the pouch and she let him wash her down.

Arvin had the idea to ease her stomach with mint leaves, but he had none. However, he did have some apple vinegar in his bandolier. Mixing it into a fresh pouch of clean water, he offered it to Bastard and pantomimed giving it to Lovely.

It was amazing how quickly Bastard interpreted gestures. And Lovely was clearly trusting of Bastard. Her stomach pains would ease within the hour.

The room smelled wonderful now. Arvin stood satisfied, his fists proudly balled on his hips.

*I did it right. We are clean!*

He declared "good" for all to hear. The next challenge he intended to solve was clothing. The crate of colorful linen had been airtight and the cloth within appeared to be preserved. Sadly, the leather belts in another crate had degenerated into dust but at least the iron buckles remained. Arvin quickly tore some cloth into strips with his knife, used the buckles on them to improvise sash-like belts, and within a half hour all of them but Bastard were clad in loose but comfortable tunics of vibrant linen. While the colors weren't complimentary, it would make each of his companions easy to spot in the dark. And since the Chromium were blind, this was an advantage.

Bastard, however, had clear affections toward Arvin's coat. The human idea of loaning was likely not something the hairy man could comprehend, so Arvin merely left what worked be.

"Hardly fashionable. But good."

He was pretty sure he had never used the word "good" this often in his life, but the phonetic structure of the word was rapidly growing on him. Each time he said it, his lips exaggerated the delivery.

"Good."

He gathered the scraps of clothing the four had stolen from their felled guards. The boots were salvageable, as well as some buckles and pouches. He also did his best strapping water pouches to each of their waists. Rat was the only one to give any trouble, constantly fidgeting with the buckles, but eventually Bastard growled at him and he calmed down long enough for Arvin to fix one on his thigh.

*Clothes. Water. Now boots.*

He easily managed to get boots on both Bastard and Rat. Lovely let him get close enough to slip her toes in, but when it came time to strap them up her calves she hissed and swiped at him with her open palm. Bastard took over, replicating what he had experienced at Arvin's hands.

*Fine motor skills. Mimicked me perfectly. Not too tight.*

Bastard was a quick study. In fact, Arvin found that each of them adjusted marvelously. The very fact that they could stand and walk indicated that the pods did more than just soul-shift them into a different form. It was likely that the Ramlagha pods implanted knowledge and skills into their heads to gradually unlock as time and experience progressed.

*Wondrous.*

Arvin considered: if he could control such pods, could he infuse certain skills and information into himself? Could he transform himself into a better, stronger human that had comprehensive knowledge of all chemical reactions?

*Or I could unleash more horror.*

His skin broke out in a cold sweat as he envisioned the Chromium once more, gliding their claws through fleeing people. Through Evrick. His curiosity had caused enough damage. He wouldn't indulge it further.

Arvin shifted gears and wondered about food. As he did so, he heard the sound of water draining away. The lime-wash pooled at their feet flowed toward the corners of the room's floor and from each side came the tell-tale noise of drainage.

Frantically, Arvin pulled crates and boxes out of the way until he found the first drain. It was big enough for someone to wriggle their shoulders through, but no wider. He wished desperately for a glow-worm or a jarred emberfly or some other means of projecting light. Both his light globes were spent.

Pulling his tinder kit from his bandolier, he swiftly struck one of his matches and dropped it in. It fell silently, revealing nothing but a narrow descent directly downward. But beyond the drain's mouth, it expanded. Possibly wide enough for himself, Rat, or Lovely to slip in and easily descend.

*Mama is too large. And we only move together.*

He wondered if he would have better luck with a different drain. Walking to the other side, he dragged the crates away and dropped to his hands and knees to investigate.

A chrome hand, claws wide, shot out of the drain and swiped at his face. Arvin shrieked, retreating backward while kicking frantically.

Lovely hissed, Mama growled, Rat hid, and Bastard bared his teeth.

"Bad! Bad!" He felt it time for his friends to learn the word. "I don't know if these things communicate or co-ordinate. We aren't safe here any—"

The Chromium's long fingers chipped away at the lip of the drain. Tiny chunks of shaped stone flew high into the air, a clear indication of the power each finger possessed.

"The door," he pointed. "We . . ." immediately, Arvin hushed himself. He knew they had to be as quiet as possible to improve their chances. Pressing a finger to his lips, he attempted to express an understandable gesture for stealth.

But the four of them just watched his failed displays in mystified silence.

*Well, that works.*

Arvin fled to the door and spun the flywheel, but before opening it, he fetched vegetable oil from his bandolier and lubricated the interior hinges. It was spent completely in the process, and he placed the empty vial back before pulling on the door.

Bastard immediately blocked Arvin from doing so. Gruffly, he pushed Arvin aside and placed his own ear on the door.

*Of course. Sound travels well through metal.*

It dawned on Arvin that the Chromium could see each other in their blind vision because of their metal skin. Chromium hide was so perfectly smooth and metallic that it likely reflected sound perfectly. Coordinated attacks and flanking maneuvers were more effective, and they could even detect each other in the middle of a melee. They would just listen for the sound waves that came back from anything moving and metal.

*We are trapped below ground with the most perfect killers conceivable.*

In another spot of the room, one of the crates jolted. The Chromium were clawing through from multiple drains. They must have heard the water running and deduced that something had to be the source of it.

After listening for a moment, Bastard appeared satisfied. He pulled the door open with impressive stealth, peeked his head out, and then opened it further for the others. Leading the way, shoulders hunched with the hair on the back of his neck bristling, he slunk out.

Lovely followed, then Rat and Mama. Arvin was the last to leave the room. As he closed the door quietly behind him, he saw a Chromium arm with its fingers spread, extending from one of the drains. A thrumming hit his ears.

*The horns. The tail. And if it suits them, their fingers. They vibrate anything pointy to see.*

They knew the door had opened and closed. They saw the five of them leave into the hallway. Arvin ran ahead and grabbed Bastard's hand, tugging at him ferociously.

"Run!" He pointed down the hall to the orange glowing depths beyond.

Bastard tugged back, resistant. Clearly, stealth had worked in his favor often when he was a badger. He didn't understand they had been spotted.

Trusting they would follow, Arvin took off. He waved them forward, occasionally pausing to look at them, in the hopes they would follow.

*This is how hunting dogs do it, right?*

He wasn't a man to offer prayers to the gods, but his panting fear and racing heart must have been heard by something *somewhere* because as he ran backward the floor vanished beneath him. He fell with a splash, sinking down into a dark depth of water. How far down it went, he couldn't tell, but it was cool and fresh.

*Explosion broke water reserve somewhere. Flooded the tank in the vault. Flooded this collapse in the hall.*

Doing his best not to breach the surface loudly, he raised his head from the water and took a breath. The four of them had raced to where he had splashed in, and stood over him. Bastard patting at Arvin's wet hair as if to check for wounds.

Rat got on his hands and knees, sunk his face in, and drank deeply.

"Get in! Good!" Arvin pleaded in a hoarse whisper. "Get under water!"

Bastard seemed puzzled, but Lovely didn't need to be told twice. She slipped in, both feet together, barely making a sound. Her linen tunic splayed for a moment, colorful and enchanting, and she twirled and it pulled tight around her.

Taking that as an invite, Bastard splashed in with them. Mama, too, followed suit but did so cautiously, patting the water's surface with her palm as if to test its solidity.

Something crashed down the hall in the storage room.

*Crates falling over. One is through.*

Arvin wondered if it was the one that saw them with its vibrating finger tips.

Grasping Rat, he pulled the lanky man in headfirst with everyone else. Rat nipped at Arvin's hands and thrashed, but Bastard growled at him and he immediately calmed down.

Lovely had already drifted deep into the hall, her white hair soaked through as she bobbed her head under to survey her new swimming space.

Another crash came from the vault. Something was moving around inside, tearing about.

Desperate, Arvin pulled Mama away from the comfort of the water's edge. She bared her teeth at Arvin, but he placed both his palms on the top of her head and pushed her under with all his weight. Then he himself went under, cheeks puffed full of air.

*The water surface will show ripples, but not us. We have to be under!*

Arvin pulled Rat under by the arm. The bug-eyed man fought back, trying to surface again. But Bastard gripped him and both men descended.

But Arvin couldn't get to Lovely. She was too far away, yet possibly within range of the Chromium's detection. Frantically, he wriggled toward her as best he could, but he had little experience with water. Swimming was not a common skill among those living in the rocky desert of Vastard.

He watched as the bottoms of her perfect, pale feet dimmed in the orange darkness beyond. His only hope was to keep the other three submerged long enough for the Chromium to leave.

*Mama wasn't given warning to hold her breath. How long can she hold it?*

Closing his eyes, Arvin resided to his fate. At least Lovely would likely escape. He waited, arms around Rat to keep him still as Bastard did the same with Mama.

Something heavy splashed in the water with them. Then it happened again twice more. Opening his eyes, he saw that his ruse had failed; three Chromium had jumped in with them. Their claws cut bubbles through the water and their tails lashed about wildly. One nipped Rat's linen tunic and the orange-lit water grew darker.

But they were sinking, like creatures of solid metal would. Within moments, they disappeared into the depths.

Arvin burst to the surface. "Out!" he cried. "Out before they cling to the sides and climb back up!"

*They don't breathe, so they can't drown. At least I don't think they breathe.*

When Rat came up, he cried out in terror and pain with an "eek eek eek!" Bastard rushed to his aid, hauling him over the lip and back up into the hallway. He searched for wounds, unsure of what to do.

Mama sputtered on the surface, splashing with rage over the recent indignity of being dunked, but when she saw Rat was bleeding from his shoulder, she shifted demeanor instantly and crawled out to be at his side.

Before she started licking, Arvin pulled open Rat's tunic and checked the wound. It was shallow, on the meat of his shoulder, and the slice appeared clean. Healing wouldn't take long, and with such a thin cut to his flesh, infection was less likely.

*Powdered sulfur would help. But I have none.*

"Come! We go back to the vault and close the door. Then slide down where they came. They made our exit by clawing to us!" He turned toward the dark waters beyond. "Lovely! Come on!"

But nothing stirred from the vague orange darkness beyond.

"Lovely!" he called again. But he couldn't wait for much longer. Placing Rat's arm over his shoulders, he lifted the whimpering man and dragged him back to the room's waiting door. Mama followed, but Bastard remained. He gazed out over the water with longing.

"Bastard! Come! Room is now good!"

But Bastard chittered. It was a low *churr* sound, repeated rapidly. The chitter echoed out into the dim void beyond.

*What?*

Lovely appeared, stroking her arms forward as she slipped through the water toward Bastard, who waited on the lip. When she was close enough, she rolled out of the water, and before she raised off her knees, Bastard offered his arm to her, his palm downward in a submissive gesture. When she saw it, she gripped him to steady herself.

"Good." Arvin praised. "Now to the storage room!"

Within moments, the five of them were back inside. Arvin pushed the door shut, but it was bent from the Chromium breaking out and wouldn't latch. Next, he examined the drains where the three Chromium had tunneled their way in. One was large enough for humans to slip in and downward, but Arvin had concerns about Mama.

*Grease. Lubricant. She goes first and we can push down on her if needed.*

He quickly scanned the runes on each crate, mind racing for a solution.

Something scratched at the vault door and Bastard flew to it. He understood that holding it in place was vital.

Arvin didn't want to test how long it took for them to cut through the warped metal door or circle back around into the drainage system from where they came. He had to move. With a swift kick, he smashed open the crate labeled "coconut pulp." Typically, coconuts from the western isles made perfect lubricant. What such a commodity was doing in the middle of the desert was not a question to be currently pondered.

But the pulp had been stored in air-tight bladders, which in turn had been sealed in clay jars with some type of rubber sealant. He smashed one open and slopped the lube all over his hands.

"Come here, Mama!" he ordered.

She just blinked at him. He rushed her, slapping lubricant all over her. Mama was alarmed, confused, but hardly hostile as Arvin did so. She lapped at one of his passing hands and smiled.

"Don't eat that! It's ancient. Now, in you go."

Arvin pushed her, his palms shoving on the small of her back, toward the recently expanded drain. She tried to hold her ground, but the coconut pulp under her feet just made her slide like a statue. Reaching the drain, Arvin drove her in.

Falling feet first, Mama disappeared with a comical 'splort' sound.

"Rat, you next!" He was too busy clutching his wound in a ball on the ground to resist. Arvin just slid him across the floor and in he splorted, as well.

*Two down. Two to go.*

The scratching on the door was getting louder, and Bastard's knuckles whitened as he held it in place. The bent corner of the door gave enough room for long claws to peek around. Lovely ran to Bastard's side and added her weight to his own.

*More weight.*

With the lube on the floor, Arvin could more easily reposition the crates. Stacking two of them against the door, he jammed them under the interior latch. Using the buckles from one of the crates, he rapidly hooked them together into an improvised chain and bound the crates to the latch. Each attempt at opening the door was blocked by the bulk attached to it. The crates pressed against the nearby wall, preventing the door from swinging in. The Chromium would now have to cut through the metal of the door or the wall itself to get inside.

"You two." Arvin pointed to their escape. "Good. Gooooood."

He then sat and slipped into the wide drain after Rat and Mama, hoping the last two would follow.

# TWENTY-FOUR

Visteria

It took two days to navigate the southern tip of Vastard, and another to travel the established roads northward along the dry riverbed to the staked territory of the Iron Whores. The destitute refugees from Tent City only took breaks for the horses to recover, and each surviving adult took turns steering the horses while the children were told lies about their friends and loved ones surviving.

With no food and little water, the journey was miserable. The hole punched in the center of the wagon's floor served as the latrine, and the top hatch remained open for the rare occurrence of a fresh breeze. Other than that, there was no conversation except the occasional listlessly whistled song.

On dusk of the third day, Visteria saw the Skullhew banner flying high from a distant ridgeline. Below it flapped the insignia of the Iron Whores—a downward dagger stabbed through a sideways heart.

Pista climbed atop the wagon as the horses huffed and puffed wearily up a dusty ramp alongside the ridge. Cupping his hands to his mouth, he called out. "Whores! Whores! Whores!"

His echo returned from the ridge face with each shout. He continued until a response, embedded in his echoing call, came back.

"Iron!"

Pista smiled for the first time in days. Poking his head down through the hatch, he ordered the current driver to slow up the horses. Soon the wagon came to a stop and the back swung open to reveal an ambush party squinting in the sunlight. They wore camouflage with thatches of brush and tan face paint and each held a crossbow or javelin.

One with a tattooed face spoke. "When we got the orvens flooding in without any messages, we knew something went bad."

"We the first ones here?" Pista asked as he climbed down.

Visteria did a quick calculation and estimated that Evrick had one hundred and thirty Iron Whores in the ruins when it collapsed. The mercenary tribe had been one of the most supportive of Skullhew's ambitions to build Vastard into an official fourteenth kingdom and they had committed all their fighters and youth to the effort.

"You are. Pass anyone on the way here?"

Pista shook his head, then reached for the first child on the lip of the wagon. The tough demeanor of the ambush scouts melted when they saw the children, and as each starved child's feet hit the ground, the mercenaries offered up their water pouches and field rations.

"You all look awful," one said as he pointed to Pista's cracked lips.

"I'm too dehydrated to bleed." He chuckled, swigging from one of the offered water pouches. "Let's get them to a hut. We'll walk the rest of the way." He then offered his hand to Visteria, to help her out of the wagon.

She considered appearing strong, and not accepting it. But something in Pista's remaining eye told her that a matter of pride was at stake for him. Perhaps he felt he failed Evrick, so at least he could see the Lady Skullhew to safety every step of the way.

Nodding gratefully, she let the guard help her down. It was clear he wasn't leaving her side.

Shuffling slowly, the small band left the horses and wagon in the care of several of the scouts. The little girl with the wounded leg, the one who lost her mother to the metal attacker, needed someone to carry her. Visteria hoisted her onto her hip and held her close.

"We'll find some place nice. To sleep," she told her. Something warm flushed in her chest holding the child. She wondered what a child of her own would feel like in her arms.

Visteria gave the child a loving squeeze as they went. The little girl's eyes seemed to shift in and out of focus, but at least she rested her chin on Visteria's shoulder.

"Yer Lady Skullhew!" One of the scouts suddenly recognized her. "Wha' happened?"

"I'm still trying to figure that out myself."

He appeared suspicious. "Well, yeh best get to figuring. Bosses are gunna wanna hear it."

The rest of the scouts' demeanors shifted from providers of aid to guarded escort. She wasn't sure if it was to protect her or to box her in. Seeing the possibility of both, she clutched the child close in the hopes of cultivating sympathy.

They proceeded past the humble walls and up to the camp's plateau.

The Iron Whore camp had no barricade or watch towers, but the ridges surrounding it acted as both. There was a single-entry point at the top of the ridge and it was narrow, easy to defend with a clutch of shield bearing fighters.

This was prime territory for both defense and shade. Evrick had once said the Iron Whores slit a lot of throats to capture it and retain it.

As the refugees from Tent City funneled in, flocking tribals plucked up the children and their mothers for caretaking. The guards, too, had brothers and wives and mothers step forward and clutch them with tearful hugs and encouraging pats on the shoulder.

A round woman with a red, cherub face appeared before Pista. The gaggle of toddlers at her legs looked up at him with both relief and anxious anticipation. He approached them, took a knee, and gathered all five of the little ones into his arms and delivered kisses. His malformed face was a joy for them to see, and Visteria bent an ear to listen.

"Papa! Did you save everyone?"

"Mama was worried."

"Uncle Pista, where is my daddy?"

She quickly deduced that half of the children belonged to his brother, who had not made it out alive. Pista was going to have to navigate tragic waters in the days ahead.

Visteria felt her stomach flip. Barely holding in her vomit, she didn't want to sully the traumatized child on her hip. Reviewing the events prior to the invasion, she didn't understand what had happened. Her brush had only touched the stone, moved less than an inch before everything sprang to life. It made no sense.

It had to have been the blood. Perhaps Arvin did something, or worse— perhaps something carried through from her. From *Ovallin*. Visteria hadn't considered the possibility before. Ovallin was alive at the time in a technical sense, but what if some part of her still functioned in the head, or the soul, and that transferred through her blood to the blue stone.

Not wanting to think of her betrayal, Visteria tried to push Ovallin out of her mind. It just wasn't possible given her vegetative state. Only her heart and lungs worked, not her brain. The soul was a vital life force, an unquantifiable one, but it couldn't enact revenge on such a scale via mysterious magics.

Visteria would never know for certain. Ovallin was beyond reach, just as Evrick was.

"This way." One of the scouts pointed. "And give me that kid."

She hesitated to hand over the child, but the limp little thing slid off easily and clung to the scout as a matter of reflex. Visteria wanted to keep a hold of her, for both warmth and a vague sense of guardianship. But any struggle over the child would be further trauma for her and Visteria wanted no further conflict for the little one.

Such compassion was considered a liability by the Children of the Desert, and it was likely the reason that Ovallin had insisted on being Visteria's handler and mentor. Ovallin was supposed to prevent Visteria from not only straying from the mission, but to forge a proper operative out of her.

Visteria did her duty. She seduced Evrick and gained access to the runic language of her direct ancestry. But when the time came for her to end him, she didn't. Each night was supposed to be his death, but instead she curled into his side and listened to his snoring with her ear against his chest.

He was nothing like the Children. Evrick wasn't a man like Visteria had known; he was bright, charming, empathetic, driven, and compassionate. He didn't want to take over Andos. Ramlagha wasn't to go from sea to sea, but instead to have its own identity.

To compare Evrick's intents against those of the Children was to compare a whisper to a shout. And when Ovallin came to finish what Visteria could not, she loosed a bolt into her mentor's skull.

Visteria couldn't help but hang her head as she followed Pista into the cave at the back of the ravine. This is what betrayal had done; Evrick had ended up locked away below. Hundreds if not thousands dead with more to follow. Would these things stop? Would they restrain their expansion like Evrick intended? Or do they hunger for nothing less than the entire world, much like the Children of the Desert themselves.

Returning to the moment, she crossed into the cold shadow of the cave ahead. It had no ornamentation and no surrounding decorum. The Iron Whores were one of the younger tribes, a mercenary company driven here from the West only a generation ago. They hadn't established their own eccentric culture like some of the other settled tribes since their focus was still on security from not only the desert, but rivals.

It was why Evrick pursued allying with them so eagerly; he felt their mercenary professionalism hadn't given way to Vastardian eccentricities yet. And now that mercenary professionalism worried her. Companies typically did not take well to such catastrophic losses as this.

The cavern itself was functional with wooden shelves anchored into the walls and braziers dangling from above. The roof was blackened from years of cooking fires and bundles of potpourri hung from suspended string. The rumbling echo of heated debate swelled from further within and as they approached, Visteria could make out specific words like "mistake" and "toll."

A hole in the roof of the cave shot a shaft of light down into one of the recesses off to the side. Arranged within lay fur-covered logs for sitting and a small audience had gathered to witness the raging exchange between the Iron Whores' leadership.

Visteria recognized all three of them.

One was Andosh, from the far north, and was known to rarely speak unless strategy was the topic. His jumbled face displayed the scars from being sliced apart and sewn together from decades of battle campaigns. He sat on his log, arms crossed, with his eyes fixed on the fire in thought. His name was Tunny Gontz.

The second one, the one talking the most and pacing in red-faced rage, was a Darrish woman with three smoking pipes affixed to her tunic. She nearly spat while ranting about Evrick's poor leadership and how the Iron Whores had been wrong to ever submit to another banner. Her name was Goozy Sands, but only her peers could get away with calling her that. Everyone else just used "Mistress" as she demanded.

The final one was trying to get a word in but doing a poor job of it. He had been born a woman, but all accepted him as the man he was: lean, bald, and tattooed all over with cyphers. Orvens and secret messages had been his profession during the Iron Whores' free-wheeling mercenary days. His name was Booker, for the book of ciphered secrets he kept chained around his waist.

"Evrick was too inexperienced to lead such a large force, let alone endeavor into the forbidden ruins of Ramlagha," Mistress Sands continued. "He tantalized us with his charm and wit, but what did he really have?"

"Ambition!" Visteria fired out from the back. All her caution evaporated when she heard Evrick's character and qualities being degraded, especially in his absence. She muscled her way through the crowd to stand across from Mistress Sands. "Mistress, instead of speaking of doubts and regrets, we need to mount a counter offensive and retake what is *ours*."

Goozy Sands's eyes nearly burst from her skull. "The audacity of this bitch!" she roared, pointing. "To come into our house and give orders."

"Do the Whores relinquish their oath to Skullhew within mere days of trouble? Or do they keep to their word?"

Frothing, Sands looked about for something—likely a weapon to swing at Visteria. When she saw Tunny's eyes on her, she eased. "Finishing oaths is the Iron Whores' stock-in-trade, but I put my people first. We have *never* suffered such losses and every single Whore is reeling from this."

"So am I!" Visteria shot back, barely holding back her tears.

"Calm, please. I beg for calm," Booker finally managed to interject. "We still do not know the full toll, the details of what went wrong, or if Evrick is still maintaining leadership from within the ruins." He stood, his book chain making no sound. "Emotional reactions are understandable, but not fruitful, Mistress. I've sent orvens out to other tribes, even those outside of Skullhew, to see what information we can gather. Give me two more days to collate. There is a good chance that other Whores fled to other tribes for aid."

Goozy shook her head with violence. "I warned of all of this, of Evrick Skullhew and his machinations. I was the voice of dissent and outvoted by you two. I will not be silenced again. We hunker down, hope for more to return to us, and seal ourselves off in these caverns until whatever this is passes."

"It won't pass," Tunny said. His eyes returned to the fire.

"Then we evacuate? Nonsense," Mistress Sands countered. "We have too many souls doing Skullhew's bidding all over Vastard and even in the Yellow Sea to the south. Orvens would take days to contact them all, days to get back to us, and then mobilizing would be . . ." she trailed off, calculating the impossibility of it all.

Tunny Gontz's eyes shifted to Visteria. "Tell us what happened, Lady Skullhew, in detail."

Visteria cleared her throat. "The ruins woke up." She didn't know exactly how much information Evrick had allowed out since most of the ruins' contents were kept secret. But she also had to concede something to appease them. "A magic coursed through it, and something swarmed from below. Metal creatures, all hands and claws with no eyes or nose or ears. They cut through everyone. Pista got me out, but Evrick is still below!" Her voice raced as her words approached the name of her beloved husband. "We need to muster and push back. They took Tent City, so everyone under Skullhew's banner has suffered the same. We won't be alone."

"I'm not certain support would be so universal," Booker said. "Evrick was delivering payment to his tribes by trading off relics, but that source is now behind an unknown, very much *magical*, danger."

"Do you not keep your word?" Visteria roared.

Tunny, unfazed, pressed on. "How did the ruins wake up? What was done?"

She didn't hesitate. "I don't know. But an alchemist named Arvin did something. He's buried below with Evrick. We need to get to them."

With a nod, Tunny closed his eyes and mumbled briefly as if to consort with himself. "Lady Skullhew, we will wait a day more for Booker to gather what information he can, but Mistress Sands speaks for how the majority of the Whores feel: frustrated and hesitant."

Mistress Sands scoffed. "Frustrated and hesitant? I'll tell you I'm more than that!"

Tunny continued, "We gather information, then seek volunteers. Build a small exploratory force. I'll head it."

That was something. Visteria was pleased that the toughest of the Iron Whores was at least willing to put his skin on the line.

"I'm in, as well," Pista offered from the crowd.

"And of course, I wish to go," Visteria insisted.

"I'm sure many souls will want to invade with the hopes of finding both answers and loved ones, but I will pick the force. It will only be comprised of souls I have fought with before, Lady Skullhew. Your husband also did the same with any small expeditionary force he mounted." He stood, his bare arms and leather vest equally cracked and scarred. "So you must divulge all that you know of what happened," Tunny spoke as his hard eyes bored into Visteria. "I need to know everything, even if it comes to you late and seems insignificant." He then tilted his head toward Booker. "Gather all you can regarding these creatures from the other survivors. Sculpt them for me in clay."

"I intend interviews," Booker replied. "Starting with Pista."

"And what of our missing and dead?" Sands seethed. "What of our losses, or as Booker says, *tolls?*"

Visteria sank as a tiny mote of reason sparked inside her. The odds of Evrick still being alive were so slim they weren't even worth considering. But she had to hope. She could not process his hands never touching her again.

"The toll?" Tunny Gontz asked. "The toll is what we Whores sometimes have to suffer when the job goes wrong."

# CHAPTER
# TWENTY-FIVE

Bastard

Gentle Man had said the word "good" so often, it was now his name.

Good made a torch made of bone and strips of cloth, lit it, and held it high. It was clear he didn't know where they were going, but Bastard understood that anywhere *else* was better than where they currently were.

After sliding down the narrow passages Bear had greased up for them, the five eventually splashed into an underground stream. Swan helped guide the others to shore, except for Bear who seemed to understand water perfectly well. It was flowing, fresh, crisp water and Bear managed to snag a blind cavefish with her hands and swallow it whole.

Good then wrangled them up with his squawking, the word "good" coming up now and again. He continued to lead them deeper and deeper into the caverns beyond. For what felt like days, they only took rests when they could barely stand. Bear sometimes hoisted Rat over her shoulder when he was too weary.

Bastard's attention drifted to Swan. He thought of her masterful smack when she cuffed the one guard on the ear and sent him reeling. The common desire for freedom had connected them all instantly, and Bastard felt the continued desire to survive would only strengthen that bond. But there was more, a warmth that he typically only felt with his cete, his pack, back in the forests. Bastard was grateful, and as scary as this was, he preferred it still over the cage and the fighting pits.

Every few minutes, Bastard turned around and checked to make certain everyone was still together. This was his cete now, and each soul in it was precious. He had seen this with human mothers as well as possums. Vigilance was a universal virtue, and Bastard understood that all creatures needed it.

"Good," the human whispered from the front, pointing. The cavern was expanding up ahead into a tall cave filled with columns of dripping siltstone. Puddles were everywhere, shallow and corrosive, and he took a knee before one. Pulling one of his tools from his chest belt, the human poked at the water and squirted some on the skin of his forearm.

After a few moments, he nodded. "Good. Good." Pulling out his water bladder, he motioned for everyone to refill their drinking supply. They all did so, having accepted that this human was, as he often said, "good."

As he filled his bladder, Bastard watched Swan from the corner of his eye. Her slim figure crouched down elegantly, and she dipped the bladder in it. He was transfixed. Her hair, still wet, shined like the evening sun over a lake in the torchlight. It draped down the side of her head, over her shoulder, and the tips of it almost touched the rippling water.

His heart beat stronger at the sight of her. Then he noticed in the reflection that she was watching him. Their eyes met through the mirrored water, and he hoped she wouldn't hiss at him. He felt he should be submissive and turn away, but he couldn't. Swan's gaze was commanding, and he thrilled at her seeing him see her.

Then Bear unleashed a loud, voracious yawn. It was long, drawn out, and as she craned her head back with her mouth wide, Good scrambled to her. He twitched and hovered around her, trying to find a way to cover her mouth without his whole hand disappearing.

Bastard knew they needed to be as quiet as possible. Those things could be anywhere behind them, following their tracks and scents. But it had been the equivalent of days since they last saw them, so he wasn't particularly worried. What kind of predator wastes days' worth of energy hunting singular prey?

Bear likely thought the same. The danger was clearly far enough away that she could express her exhaustion loudly. But she probably didn't intend for the cavern's recesses to capture sound so perfectly and echo it everywhere. Bastard had never been in a cave so big, with so much echo. Her yawn bounced about, long after she had finished it, and her eyes traveled all around searching for its invisible location as it zipped here and there off stalactites and across watery surfaces.

Everyone froze, unsure of what to do.

Something shifted in the dark. Rock scraped against rock and Good raised his torch higher to see. The side of the cavern was a wall of thick, scratchy flesh. Rippling like a giant worm, it pulled itself away and soon disappeared down a smooth tunnel it had carved for itself with what had to be a giant maw.

Bastard eased. It had no interest in them, and he didn't have to see its front. He had eaten scores of worms, and was their natural predator, but here everything was wrong. That worm was massive; *they* were likely the predators.

Relieved at the massive creature's departure, everyone slumped and returned to filling their water. Bastard sought Swan's gaze in the rippling reflection once more, but she had become preoccupied with examining her toes. Even those compelled Bastard.

It had been a long time since Bastard had mated. Growing up in his sett, with his cete, he intended to make cubs. The female that chose him was older, stronger, and she made gentle chittering sounds when she slept. He had clawed a birthing chamber for her, but before her belly began to swell, the men came.

They cracked open the ground with shovels, ripping the ceiling of their world open. He screeched for his mate to flee, and he tore into the leg of the nearest man. They pounded him with shovels until everything went black.

And then the cage, wagons, pits, screams, blood, misery. He briefly wondered if Good had ever dug open a sett with a shovel. Had he ever cheered in the dark periphery of a fighting pit?

Bastard touched his coat, the warm skin that Good had given him, and quickly found his answer.

CHAPTER

# TWENTY-SIX

Arvin

*Trundle wurm. Saliva predigests rock for both nutrient consumption and terrain alteration. Tunneling annelid. Never stop growing. Hundreds of years old.*

Whereas the other four recoiled in terror when the entire cavern wall flexed and pulled away, Arvin had been fascinated. It delighted him to see something so massive, so ancient, thriving down here in the jagged dark. He wished he could have cupped a sample of secretions from its side. They had to have been highly corrosive, but he wanted to examine their lubricative properties.

Peeking his head down the tunnel, his eyes stung from the corrosive residue clinging to the moisture particulates in the air. He wanted to follow the thing, see if it led to a way forward, but he would have to wait until the air settled.

He returned to check on the four souls in his care.

Rat picked at calcium deposits on the stalactites above. They were tiny, white slivers that intensely reflected the torchlight and his bulging eyes swelled at each vein he found.

183

Lovely knelt, transfixed by Bastard's reflection in one of the still puddles of clear water. He ran his hands over his features, poked a finger in each nostril, and then tugged on his bristly beard.

Mama had flopped onto her back. The meat around her spine cushioned her from the unpleasant cavern floor, and she yawned again but this time kept it quiet.

As for Bastard, he just stood there, examining Arvin. It was curious, and Arvin couldn't figure out what Bastard was doing or thinking. His interest would have been more compelled if not for the massive wurm they had just encountered. Such an ancient, rare sighting was worthy of poems and illustrations. It was so momentous that Arvin had to pee.

Scanning the dark expanse, Arvin searched for a corner to let loose. While being intimate enough to wash everyone was one thing, peeing in front of them was the next level that he didn't really feel ready for.

His trousers and belt would require both hands, so first he located a twisted column to wedge the torch into. Using the stark shadows from the flickering light, Arvin found a recess in the rock for privacy. Unfastening, he aimed his member into the dark. It hadn't occurred to him how long he had been holding it until just now, and it came as a great relief.

Something stirred in the dark near him.

Arvin went rigid, afraid to move. It shifted along his periphery on his right, and a flit of yellow torchlight revealed it to be Bastard. He watched Arvin with disinterest, then looked around the column, and came back. Almost restless, Bastard shifted about on his feet with his ears tilting toward any echoing, open space.

*He's securing the area, as an animal would, protecting me while I urinate.*

His eyes watered. It was such a simple, instinctive thing but Arvin had never had someone protect him while he peed before. Bastard, his back hair climbing up his neck to the base of his skull, was the hairiest and least-charismatic man Arvin could fathom. And yet, as the man's eyes drifted about, seeking threats, Arvin had never felt safer. Not even Uncle could have provided such a sense of security.

Bastard wasn't asked to keep watch. He just did.

*They are going to survive. Bastard, Mama, Rat, and Lovely are all going to make it out of here safely. I'm making sure of it.*

Arvin finished peeing, performed the customary two-shake, and buckled back up. "Good," he said, trying out his smile for Bastard.

Bastard took a deep sniff, his nostrils inspecting the urine's scent, then looked Arvin in the eye and replied, "Good."

*He can mimic speech! Perhaps even determine the meaning through reinforced context. The brain is that of a human, so his new capacity is being used.*

Swelling with excitement, Arvin grabbed Bastard's coat sleeve and dragged him over to the other three. "Good!" he cried, flapping his hand in the air.

They all looked at him, perplexed.

"Good?"

Still blank stares.

"I peed and Bastard told me it was good."

Mama returned to her resting, Rat scraped a fresh patch of calcium free of a stalactite, and Lovely poked at a shallow puddle.

*Rat likes shiny things. I should show him how to gather a sample. Get him to say "good" as well.*

Pulling out his small knife, Arvin approached Rat and dug the blade's chipped edge into the deposit. White, wet bits flaked free into his palm.

"See? Good. I could use some calcium. Good." The two worked at it a bit, but the torch light was too far away. "Be right back."

Still brimming with excitement, Arvin bounded back to the column holding the torch. Plucking it free, he raced to return but his foot caught on the uneven cavern floor. He stumbled, caught himself, but the torch slipped free of his grasp, splashed into a puddle, and sizzled to death.

All went dark. He luckily could hear Mama breathing.

"Sorry."

Groping about, Arvin quickly found the spent torch. He shook it about, hoping to get it as dry as he could. As he did so, he realized he could still see it.

*Is my imagination filling in what I can't see?*

Squinting, he scanned for the source of the dim light. Soon he found it in the carved tunnel the trundle wurm had etched. One of the ends spilled the faint, orange glow of the activated ruins.

*Have we gone in circles?*

Arvin ducked down so the glow reflected off the shallow water puddles on the floor and into his eyes. He saw more clearly, and decided anywhere was better than the empty cavernous depths. At least, if it was a buried portion of the ruins, there might be food or something else to aid their survival.

"Good," he whispered. Taking two steps toward the tunnel, he repeated himself. "Good." He said it several more times, once between every three steps, until he reached the tunnel.

The glow was more intense, and he could make out that the four had followed him closely. Sniffing the air, he was pleased to see that the caustic air of the trundle wurm's passing had largely dissipated.

"Follow." He felt it a good word to teach next.

Stepping over the exposed lip, Arvin placed his boot inside. The wurm must have been massive, having produced a tunnel large enough for them to stand in. Its circular girth and flexing locomotion muscles left ripples in the rockface where it burned its way through. Whatever its secretions were composed of, it was startlingly corrosive.

*Biological acid? Doesn't burn self. How?*

Arvin's gears of curiosity spun furiously as he led everyone into the orange mystery ahead. The wurm tunnel opened into a cylindrical, spiraled chamber stretching upward beyond sight. Copper inlay pulsed with bolts of orange energy as they leaped from spot to spot, ionizing the air. He had never seen a structure so large before. It was a wonder of human achievement, spanning vertically into a haze of moisture cloud sporadically illuminated by jolts of power.

*We know so little about electricity. They owned the lightning here.*

All five of them stared agape at the terrible beauty of it. Arvin stepped deeper inside, hoping to shift his perspective and find a pattern in the discharges, but found none.

*Containment failure? Too much power? Damaged over time? Is this normal?*

Then he saw it. The center of the chamber had once been a massive glass enclosure. It had ruptured open, the shards blown dozens of feet clear of their origin. Among the shards lay skeletal limbs and bodies desiccated within their rusted armor. He knelt to examine the wreckage more closely.

*Glass flew into these people. Shards still wedged between ribs and skulls. Clothing and armor on bones rusted from blood drying. Discoloration indicates hundreds of years.*

It could have happened when Ramlagha fell so long ago. The layers of dust hinted as much. This likely happened when the Chromium first came to end them.

Next, Arvin peeked into the shattered glass enclosure. It was massive, capable of holding a lake's worth of liquid or the largest of animals known, trundle wurm or not. Metal spikes, most bent from tremendous force, jutted toward the center of the enclosure and from them strung leagues of rubber tubing that disappeared upward into the gloom.

*Enclosure for creature. Massive, like a sea monster. Spikes pierced flesh, held it in place, and pumped something into it. Or drained it! Its own heart was the pump since no other was present.*

He imagined the glass containment intact. A massive entity, trapped and surrounded by blasts of random lightning, had been kept here. And bled, possibly at a slow rate, dry of its fluids. Arvin instantly thought of Visteria's niece.

*Divine blood. Something divine. The glyph was a translation for god's blood. Not a metaphor! They were bleeding a literal god, or godling, as their source of power. Divine fuel was their literal power.*

This was a massive cage intended for demons or some other magic entity, and the column its prison.

The final aspect of the puzzle slid into place for Arvin when he kicked a cracked skull. He had surmised that the Chromium had broken into the room, tearing into the chamber. The evidence was hundreds of bones bound in shreds of ancient armor covering the expanse. This had been another last stand, the people of Ramlagha having built barricades of clear boxes to hold off the coming swarm of metal death. The tell-tale claw marks told the story. They were defending whatever was inside the glass containment chamber.

*Double metal doors barricaded. Chromium overwhelmed hinges with force. Claw marks on the walls and flooring, high on the walls. They piled in like an avalanche.*

His eyes followed their path of destruction right to the glass chamber.

*They came for it. Broke through. To kill it? Or to free it?*

Parking himself in the dust of a centuries-old slaughter, Arvin pondered. The puzzle rotated in his mind, shifted its own facets into stubborn shapes that he couldn't fold his thoughts around. There was too much here, and he had too small of a perspective on the matter.

His curiosity exhausted him. Looking about, he figured it was as good a place as any to rest for a bit. The lightning blasts above would likely keep Chromium from climbing down to them, and the chamber was dry enough for them to rest on the floor.

Returning his attention to the four souls in his charge, he saw three of them gazing upward, hypnotized by the light show. The fourth, Rat, scavenged about the sundered bodies, plucking off buttons and digging through scraps for anything interesting.

*He's got the right idea.*

"Good," Arvin said, joining him. "Good. I'll show you what we can use."

CHAPTER
# TWENTY-SEVEN

Arvin

Once again, Arvin was so captivated in the work and exploration before him that he lost track of time. Even Rat peeled off to sleep, curling up inside an overturned crate. As for the others, Mama lay against a stack of glass cubes with Lovely under her left arm and Bastard under her right.

Arvin took a break from searching through the remains to stretch his back. He had managed, with the help of Rat, to gather up enough bits of metal armor to fashion most of a suit. Additionally, he found several straps of the marvelous rubber tubing, the same that ran in and out of Visteria's comatose niece. Its elasticity and durability gave Arvin dozens of ideas for applications, so he stuffed as many as he found under his belt.

His thoughts bent toward the open glass chamber and the creature that was once trapped here. What did it look like? What purpose did it serve? Was it a danger or something captured for study? And most of all, what happened when the Chromium breached the room?

He was reminded of Evrick and Visteria leeching the blood out of that young girl with a bolt in her forehead.

*Not much difference between what Evrick did, and what Ramlagha did. Just on a different scale.*

Arvin had been so captivated by all the new wonders, and so eager to please his new friends, that he didn't even pause to empathize with the comatose girl in the pod or the vanished captive of the glass chamber. Whatever reservations he had he ignored either for selfish socialization, or even worse, curiosity.

*Curiosity should be for good. A good thing. I had been so taken with the mysteries, the discoveries, that I moved too fast. Why did I move too fast? I charged past my curiosity and was so busy doing what I could, I wasn't paying attention to what was to be learned. I did it wrong. Again. As always.*

*Uncle never moved too fast, and he never did it wrong. His hands were always steady, and he never feared waiting until the next day to complete a task if he was tired or doubtful.*

*That is why no one knew him in life or death. What did he discover?*

As soon as he asked himself the puerile question, Arvin answered it with shame in his heart.

*Me. Uncle gave me to the world. And I gave the world Chromium.*

Arvin knew Uncle's life would have been far simpler had he not taken in an errant, unloved bastard-child. Yet he did. And Arvin repaid him with rogue, selfish thoughts and careless accidents.

But he wasn't going to cry. For someone who didn't used to, he hated how often the urge now surfaced. He held it in, tightened his throat, and wiped his watering eyes. This was still time to focus. Survival still very much hung in the balance.

The armor could at least protect from the first swipe of a Chromium's claws. At his feet were the plates he and Rat had scrounged up. The rubber tubing that the Ramlagha used didn't seem to age or lose elasticity, so he figured binding the armor with it was best. Eyeing over Bastard from a distance, he strung the chest plate to the two pauldrons. Next was a chain shirt, lightweight and made of what

Arvin guessed to be an aluminum alloy. It had an opening around the collar where a Chromium swiped off the previous owner's head, so Arvin stitched it back together with string from the suture kit on his bandolier.

None of the armor matched, and the metal of it had chips and scratches, but it was far better than nothing. He'd keep his eyes open for greaves or any other leg armor, but for now the coat Arvin had given Bastard would easily go under the chest piece.

Holding up the lightweight armor, he grinned. It was a good gift.

*I hope Bastard likes it. Will it be comfy?*

Arvin speculated on the use of dog fur and other types of padding for the inside. There were all kinds of ways he could improve the simple plate, but for now his excitement demanded he wake Bastard and gift it to him. He felt giddy, like when he was a boy and had concocted something for Uncle's approval.

Walking over to the slumbering pile of friends, Arvin saw that Lovely had slipped away at some point. Mama's one arm lay vacant, but both Bastard and Rat remained fast asleep. She must have stealthed away, the crackling of the chamber above masking her footsteps.

*She sneak off to pee? I should stand watch over her like Bastard did.*

Arvin quietly set the armor down by Bastard's foot. He peeked back into the trundle tunnel, but saw nothing. Next he went to where the chamber's entry doors had been breached and squinted, looking beyond. The bursts of energy from above still punched his ears, but in the darkness ahead Arvin could hear a more consistent sound—the rushing call of water.

*A stream. Large one.*

With the orange glow at his back, he kept a hand against the wall and cautioned his way forward. "Lovely?" he whispered, careful of causing an echo ahead. He wanted to be heard, but only to Lovely and not wurms. Or anything else, for that matter. Moving down the hall, Arvin stepped over more bones and rusted weapons.

A voice echoed from beyond.

Then another. Both men.

*Survivors!*

Arvin ran forward. As the orange light behind him lost intensity, torchlight ahead appeared. It reflected off of rippling water, and soon the tips of Arvin's boots hit soggy ground. The river itself was wide with rocky outcroppings jutting up from its center, and while one end emerged from under a rock wall, the other end simply vanished into the dark beyond.

The gathering of men at the shore of the river had struck torches into the nearby columns, and on a spit over a fire rotated what looked to be a human without a head. From the small frame and nearby discarded tunic, Arvin suspected it was a laborer that had drawn a short straw.

*Mere days and they turn cannibal!*

But his stomach still rumbled at the lovely allure of roasting meat.

They were guards, men who served in the ruins' upper levels, and Arvin recognized one of them by his missing fingers. He was the one that cracked Bastard's rib. On their belts hung clubs and daggers, and one of them sharpened two carving knives against each other.

But none of them noticed that Arvin stood mere feet away, huffing. They were too busy lusting for the linen-clad, white-haired woman standing before them.

"Fuck me, a bint!"

The one sharpening his knives missed and nicked a finger. "Gods balls!"

"Lads, we all seeing dis or we's dead?"

The one Arvin knew from the vault craned his head and shielded his vision from the fire's light. "Boys, that's the bird."

"Right you are. Good job figuring that," one laughed.

"Naw, the *bird*. The swan. She ain't human. Just in a human body."

"And what a body!"

The expanding grins on all of their faces terrified Arvin. He'd rather face the Chromium. "Gentlemen!" He tried addressing them with authority, but what came out was a croak.

But it was enough to get him noticed.

"Oi, dinner with the show, eh?"

"Making her squawk would work up an appetite," the one with the knives said, gesturing to their spit-roasted victim. "This one ain't big enough to be an appetizer."

Three of them walked toward Lovely, palms out and open as if ready to corral a volatile horse. She hissed and retreated to Arvin's side.

"Gentlemen, you leave us be," Arvin demanded, but the quivering in his voice betrayed his fear.

"Boys, I seen 'em get beat on. He ain't nothing."

*Seven of them. All armed. One has leg bound from injury.*

They closed in. Arvin wanted desperately to shout for help, but if Bastard, Mama, and Rat didn't hear him, he would only be giving away that there was more prey to be hunted. The men would catch them in their sleep.

"Run!" Arvin cried, shoving Lovely back toward the lightning chamber. She darted off, but not toward the chamber. Toward the rolling underground river.

"Bint on the run!" They laughed as they lunged for her.

Ignoring Arvin, they dismissed him as unthreatening. He shouted and threw pebbles helplessly as Lovely hissed and dipped through the groping men. Within moments, she reached the water and leaped in. Stroking wildly, she took off toward the depths of the current.

"Fuck no, get in there after her!"

"I got plate on. *You* nab the bint."

"First to get her is the first to get her!"

They piled over each other, wading waist-deep into the water toward her.

"Good!" Arvin shouted, encouraging her. "Good!" Spying one of the guard's leather shields, Arvin used it as a shovel and scooped up coals from the nearby fire. He ran to the nearest guard, the one still holding the carving knives, and shouted "Hey!" to get him to turn around.

"Wait your turn, kid. I ain't picky." He didn't even take his eyes off the chase in the river. He was that certain of Arvin's impotence.

So Arvin poured the burning coals down the back of his collar.

The cannibal was so shocked that no sound escaped his anguished face; he only gasped as he stiffened and fell backward, flat onto the cavern floor. Sparks and smoke burst from within his coat, out the sleeves, and from under his collar as he kicked frantically.

One of the wading guards noticed and pointed at Arvin. "I got the bint, you all get *him!*"

Four of them turned on Arvin, daggers out and their amusement evaporated.

Arvin ducked behind the spit, putting it between himself and them. But they split into two groups of two and charged with their blades high.

Bastard, bursting from the dark, bodied the nearest one. The hairy man wore Arvin's gifted armor, and it served him well as it deflected one of their strikes.

"The hells?"

"He's the Bastard, lads! Nip 'em!"

Bastard rolled with the man, keeping the dagger at bay with his hands. The other three had such a wealth of targets, they couldn't decide whom to kill first.

"I got her!" one of the men in the river yelled. "Think she's wet now? Ha!"

All four men decided to pile onto Bastard. "Don't kill them all. Meat will spoil," one said.

It was such a cold, calculating thing to say that Arvin felt compelled to toss another shield-full of hot coals into his face. He screeched, clutching his burning eyes and sizzling tongue. When he sank to his knees, Arvin cracked the shield over the man's skull.

The echoes of the fight bounced off of every surface, including the river itself, and reverberated up the cavern's creases into the dark beyond in every direction.

And then came the roar.

Mama arrived, reared back like a bear as she stomped forward. One of the guards disengaged from the Bastard pile and charged her, knife ready. She swatted him away, flinging him into a tiny field of stalagmites. Small and sharp like teeth, he fell into them and they broke off, impaled into his flesh as he cried and kicked.

"Good!" Arvin cried just before he threw his bent, smoking shield at another cannibal chasing him. "Where's Rat?"

Something splashed down in the river further up, near the rimstone dam that the river emerged from. The light was too obscure at that distance, but Arvin immediately knew that whatever it was, it was too large to be Rat.

"Something else is here!" he cried, hoping to get the attention of the psychotic guards. If there was a common threat, they couldn't be fighting each other.

*Wurm? Not predatory. Cave animal? Coming toward commotion?*

Even under the water, he could see the chrome. It was big and crawling along the floor of the river toward the shore.

"Chromium!" Arvin cried. "Bad!" Jumping up and down while pointing, nobody took notice. Everyone was too busy in their individual battles of survival to see the approaching doom.

It rolled onto shore. At first Arvin thought it was a new thing, a different variant of Chromium with a dozen arms and a segmented torso. But it was three Chromium together, their arms intertwined.

*Three? Could it be the same three?*

Rolling like acrobats, they used their momentum to hurl one of themselves into one of the guards stabbing at Bastard. It tore into the guard, rending the attacker apart as the two tumbled away into the dark.

*Nowhere to run.*

A second Chromium squared off with one of the guards, testing him with lashes of its tail. He deflected the first two swipes, but the third nicked his thigh and he buckled to his knee.

*The river. Moves faster than we can run.*

Arvin looked for Lovely. She was floating in the middle of the water, near a jutting rock. One of the guards was drifting away, face-down as the other one flailed between her crushing legs as she drowned him.

"Good!" Arvin cried. "Follow! Follow! Follow!" he shouted repeatedly as he high-stepped into the water.

Mama appeared ready to stay and fight the Chromium, but Bastard was already on his feet and tugging at her linen tunic. They both splashed in as Lovely shoved away the limp body of her second pursuer. Sloshing toward each other, Arvin looked back to shore and saw the last of the guards, the one writhing from the coals down his back, impaled on a Chromium's horns.

"Under!" Arvin cried. Sucking his lungs full, he ducked below. Tugging on the others to join him, they soon got the hint. It was pitch black, and Arvin had no bearings as the current washed over him, over-stimulating his sense of gravity and direction.

Lovely's hand gripped his forearm and pulled, guiding him firmly. The waters accelerated as Arvin's sinuses and ears flooded. The disorientation was so profound he didn't even know where the water's surface was anymore.

Either pulled by her, or just by the water, Arvin did not know. All he knew was that he needed air, and he didn't know where or how to get it.

# CHAPTER
# TWENTY-EIGHT



Refugees continued to pour in. At first, they came only from Tent City, in the form of the occasional fleeing family or a cluster of guards that managed to rescue a baby.

But soon refugees came from other tribes. One traveling merchant claimed that she arrived at a mercenary tribe's border only to find sundered bodies cooking in the sun. Bloody handprints, hundreds of them, swarmed all over the sand. Terrified, she fled to the strongest tribe she could think of that wouldn't kill a stranger on sight: the Iron Whores.

When the merchant breathlessly recounted her tale to the leadership in their cave, the gathered audience gasped. Tunny Gontz ordered extra guard shifts and extended scouting patrols. Mistress Sands suggested that all the elderly and infirm be moved deeper into the cave system.

The next morning, Booker quietly informed Visteria that several of his orvens had returned with their missives unopened; a dire sign.

More tribes had fallen. Gathering the other leaders, he drew a map in the sand with the Ramlagha ruins at the center. "From here, we can track the expansion of the enemy. These two tribes are destroyed for sure, and these other two have gone quiet. Given this, and how the enemy is slowing down because it is covering more ground, you can easily see that we will eventually be hit. Once it reaches the foot of the ridgeline here."

"These things can dig and tunnel through sand and loose stone," she said. "Your barricades won't slow them down at all."

He nodded, expecting as much. Spotting Mistress Sands and Tunny Gontz in the distance, he waved them over. Under Gontz's arm was a clay molded Chromium with pins sticking out of it, indicating points to target.

As they approached, Visteria gestured at it. "Arrows can't pierce them. At least, not my crossbow."

Tunny nodded. "I feared as much. I'm hoping spears with the weight of a man will do better."

Booker thought for a moment before interjecting. "Since there are no chrome bodies, we can assume spears don't work either. It is safe to assume that any melee or conventional weapons don't work." Clearing his throat, he proceeded to repeat the unfolding situation in detail and included Visteria's information about the Chromium's digging ability.

In a gesture of frustrated despair, Sands stretched her face downward with her hands. "We can hide in the caves, at least. Blow the entrance closed after us."

Tunny waved dismissively. "Sands, we already know they can dig. They'll dig their way around the rocks into any cave eventually. Besides, there is no renewable source of water in there."

"Not all the depths of these caves have been mapped," the mistress fired back. "We go deep enough and hide long enough, they will just pass us over like we were never here."

Visteria couldn't read Tunny's face, but she wondered if he was annoyed with Mistress Sands's arguments. He leaned toward Booker without taking his own eyes off the map in the sand. "Booker? Thoughts?"

"I don't have time to train any bats to help me map the depths," he said. "And my kids are all busy aiding the refugees. We would lose some in the caves, anyhow. They haven't the skill."

"Then sealing ourselves into the caves would just be entombing ourselves before we die." Tunny brushed his boot over the sand, erasing the map.

"Then what else do we do? Just die here, or die trying to outrun them. Which we clearly can't!" Mistress Sands countered. She then turned on Visteria. "Lady Skullhew, share with us your mighty wisdom. Since we're under *your* banner, deliver us!"

Visteria wanted to crack her right in the face.

So she did. A single, solid punch right into the bridge of her nose. Goozy Sands recoiled backward, but impressively kept her footing as she snorted out a speckle of blood. Her dagger was out in a flash, and she came for Visteria.

But Tunny caught her arm. "Stop. Every single body is needed." He didn't even look at Goozy the Mistress, and he didn't have to for her to submit to his instruction. She sheathed the blade, and as soon as she did so, Tunny turned and squared his shoulders toward Visteria. "And as for you, fuck off. You aren't a leader of the Iron Whores. Consider yourself demoted to guest status."

It was probably best Visteria got away from Sands for, the time being anyway. With a nod, Visteria obeyed. Tunny Gontz was close to bristling and she didn't want to see the man's blood rise. He already promised to lead an expedition for Evrick, after all.

Evrick. She imagined him in the dark, holding his breath as the things Arvin awakened stalked around him. If anyone could rally the survivors, it was him. Evrick could do it, and when Tunny finally breached the walls and liberated them, Evrick's fame would expand tenfold. The legend of Skullhew would spread across the continent, and he would return to his wife to resurrect New Ramlagha, the Fourteenth Kingdom.

Wandering off, she headed for where the refugees had piled up in the open center of the Iron Whores' land. She felt the need to be of use, and maybe she could find a wound to bind or a child to soothe.

The refugees circled their camels and wagon carts directly under the hammering sun in the center of the Whores's plateau. They had already gathered the morning dew from their canvases and were using it to brew tea. Alluring smells of searing meat and simmering stewpots woke Visteria's nostrils. It reminded her of a miniature Tent City, but the children didn't chase each other, and no one sang songs to the gods.

All was subdued and quiet, the trauma of witnessed horror prevailing. Visteria passed through the cart barrier and under the makeshift canopy of the improvised camp. Patches of intense sunlight illuminated children's vacant stares and elderly women's morning rituals. One woman poured two cups of tea, then when she realized she was alone and one cup was to be undrunk, she sobbed.

Tattoos and dangling banners indicated that the refugees came from dozens of different tribes. Some were outcasts, with no insignia at all and they offered themselves as laborers to whoever needed something hauled or threshed.

There were no takers.

Visteria explored the warren of despair until she reached the other side. One of the covered wagons caught her eye, not because of its humble construction or wide chassis, but for the tiny charm that hung on its extended canopy post; an upside-down pyramid, the point of which balanced on a flat circle. It was copper, just like any other symbol of the Children. Someone was announcing that they were from the cult. And the announcement was subtle, likely only to be seen by other members like Visteria herself.

She swallowed hard. While walking away was certainly an option, they would know she had seen it. They would come for her. Facing the music was likely best.

With a hesitant knuckle, Visteria rapped on the door. The cart swung on its suspension for a moment before the door cracked open.

Vibrant incense seeped out, the familiar scent drawing her back to the cliff dwellings that Visteria had grown up in.

"Come in, child." The voice didn't show their face, but Visteria saw the outline of a short and stout woman. "Please sit." Pulling the door wide, she stepped up inside. The wagon creaked from the new weight as she entered, and she hadn't the room to fully stand.

Visteria's eyes adjusted enough to spot two small stools flanking a tiny tea table with cheese and biscuits waiting. She had been expected, and this worried her, but the fact remained she wasn't dead yet so clearly the Children didn't know she had shot Ovallin and betrayed the cause.

Once Visteria sat, she could straighten her neck again. She picked the stool that put her back against the rear of the wagon. What little light leaked through the cracks illuminated a tiny hotplate with a vented fire under it. A kettle boiled on top.

"I apologize for the drafty walls," the woman said. It was her way of warning Visteria that they could be heard, and speaking in ambiguities was best.

When she brought two empty teacups to the table, Visteria finally saw her host's face. She was a woman just beyond her prime, but not aged out of service. Desert weather and worry had creased her face into a morose expression and her hands were leathery against the dainty teacups she set down.

"Thank you," Visteria said.

"Of course. I have good tea brewing. Perhaps hard to come by, after what has happened," she said. It was subtle, but the last sentence felt especially pregnant. "I heard rumors of a metal tide, scouring the sands for anything with a heartbeat." With a woolen mitt, she emptied the kettle into a small clay teapot. It was humble in design and the woman set it on the cheese table between them. "Please, eat. We all need our strength in these times."

Visteria felt little tolerance for the usual cloak-and-dagger discourse of the Children. "Ovallin is dead," she stated without affectation.

The woman paused, her hand hovering over a biscuit. She then redirected herself to the cheese knife and she cut off a chunk. "How?"

"The things below got her."

"She was nearly two hundred years old. Precious in . . . ability. And she succumbed?"

Visteria couldn't tell if the woman was suspicious or scared, but her voice quivered with intensity. "Casters *can* die. Even in our lifetime, they have died. And besides, have you seen what these things can do?"

The woman nodded. "I saw the remains of Bramblepoke. Even the orvens were plucked from their cages and torn open." Her eyes became glassy. "It is a cold, metal hate from old times. The first fall has returned."

"So you knew," Visteria seethed. "You knew and never warned me!"

"Ovallin knew. She was your handler. If you were to know anything, it was to be her choice. You were to get close to the rising warlord, copy the runes, and eliminate his efforts. Is he at least dead?"

She couldn't bring herself to say it, even if she felt it was a lie. Somewhere below was her love. He had to be alive. But she nodded in the affirmative.

The woman tested the side of the teapot with the back of her hand. "So he's gone, as is Ovallin. And you have a detailed record of the old language?" She gripped the pot with both hands and gently poured tea into each cup.

Visteria had confidence she could reproduce much of the Ramlagha written language, but the rules of conjugation were complex and reliant on variables within each clause that contained them. "Mostly, yes. My book is lost." An opportunity dawned on her. "But my detailed tome is below, in the ruins." If she could sell the Children of the Desert on aiding Tunny Gontz, Evrick's chances of seeing the surface again increased. "The Iron Whores are launching an expedition, and when we breech below—"

"We?"

"My mission isn't over. I need to deliver the runes." Visteria played the part of dutiful Children expertly since it was what she had been most of her life. Gontz wouldn't take her, but perhaps the Children would.

"So the book is below, lost to a force that overpowered Ovallin?"

Visteria had trapped herself in her own lie. If the most powerful sorcerer the Children had ever known couldn't handle the enemy, then who possibly could? The Children were likely to call the entire endeavor a failure and seal themselves off until the storm was over.

It was how the Children of Ramlagha, also known as the Children of the Desert, had survived since the fall of their civilization over nine centuries ago.

The woman waved her hand over the steaming tea to cool it. "I'm here to bring you back in," she said. "We can leave tonight. The call went out. All Children are to cease their operations and return for submergence. Two generations long." She lifted her tea and sipped it gently. "Once again, we vanish from the world."

A prickling sensation crawled over Visteria. The very real likelihood she would never see Evrick again chewed on her nerves. Her senses spun the wagon's interior around her as she reeled from her dismal reality.

"Child, you'll feel better with some tea."

Visteria doubled forward, holding in a lurching bout of vomit. As she did so, she noticed two tiny holes on the back of the teapot. When being poured, the user's thumb could easily cover one or the other.

She knew instantly that she sat across from an assassin. It was a teapot for delivering poison in controlled amounts to different cups while appearing to come from a single spout. One chamber had regular tea, but a smaller chamber in the pot was the same tea but poisoned. A thumb went over the holes in the back to control which would come out when poured.

Rage swelled in her, chasing away her sorrow. The Children of the Desert had ordered this woman to learn what could be learned, then clean up the mess.

Visteria's face must have reddened, indicating her revelation. The woman lunged for the cup in front of Visteria and flung its tea toward her face.

She turned away just in time as it soaked the side of her head.

The wagon rocked as both women squared off, the tiny tea table between them. As the assassin drew a hidden blade from the wagon's low ceiling, Visteria gripped the teapot with her bare hands and lunged. It burned her palms, but she shoved it into the killer's mouth with white-knuckle determination. Leaning in, she poured the contents of the teapot's dual chambers down her enemy's throat.

The woman stabbed about frantically. The boiling tea burned her insides, and she likely knew she was as good as dead, but like any loyal Child she was going to finish the job.

Visteria blocked the knife with her elbow, twice. But then the killer changed grip and came under. The blade nicked the back of Visteria's shoulder. She chipped a tooth while containing a scream, drew the empty teapot free of the woman's mouth, and then smashed it against her head.

It shattered. Visteria picked up the broken spout and jammed the jagged end into the woman's throat. Blood pulsed out of the tip, pouring down her front and pooling into the lap of her dress.

As her heart weakened, the intensity of the gushing spout eased.

Visteria knelt beside the failed assassin and looked her in the eye. "When you get to the other side, make room for any more Children that come my way."

# CHAPTER
# TWENTY-NINE

Bastard

The river had bent back and around, to and fro. Sometimes they could come up for air, and other times not. Bioluminescent algae dangled from the rocks flanking the waters, and they used the blue light to steer clear of sharp hazards.

But the underground river rolled with frothing purpose, and it eventually eased into a lake. Weary, they waded toward the nearest shore. Bastard pulled himself up onto an outcropping of thin rock. The others joined him, with Swan clinging to their limp human friend. He was still.

Bastard pounded his fists against the wet ground as Swan paced back and forth behind him, her arms flapping in worry. Rat had stayed behind, presumably to hide. The other four had submerged into the river, been taken by its fast current, and arrived here. But only three of them were breathing.

Good, who fought to protect them, lay still. Bastard whimpered and seethed, but through his raging grief and fear he noticed Bear remained surprisingly calm. She hoisted the gentle man up by one leg and dangled him upside down. Swinging him side to side, water poured out of his mouth and nose. Adding a little shake here and there, the water finally finished with only a few trickling drops.

But he still wasn't stirring. Bear lay him down on his side and rubbed his back with as much abrasive force as possible. Bastard had seen this before among badger cubs and joined in, focusing on Good's legs.

A cough. A spasming cough rasped out of Good and his lungs sucked in air. Upon exhaling, he gurgled and twitched and coughed again, this time in a full voice.

"Good!" Bastard bellowed. He was overjoyed, his forehead resting on Good's legs as he chittered in delight. Swan stopped flapping her arms, kept perfectly still for a moment as if to process the miracle, and then let out a bellowing honk from her human body. It should have echoed across the massive cavern they were in, but the sound of it never returned from the ceiling.

Bear let Good cough a bit longer until his breathing found a rhythm. She then scooped him up in her arms and carried him clear of the water, deeper into the recess of their current cavern. There was a wealth of tunnels shunting off from the central chamber, and she found herself overwhelmed with choices.

Bastard and Swan eagerly followed. There was something different about this place. The typical features of dangling rock drapes and stalactites weren't present, and it felt more like the ruins they had escaped than a traditional cave.

Bastard didn't know caves of this size, but he could easily detect the unnatural symmetry of it. It had been sculpted, and the river narrowed unnaturally toward the back. And there, turning rapidly, was a giant wheel. He had seen such structures on grain mills along rivers, and often they had tasty bags of grain piled outside from time to time.

Bastard's stomach grumbled. It was a shame they had to leave that glorious smelling meat behind, but when the three metal dogs attacked, he knew their best option was to flee. Even in the fighting pits, nothing like that had ever appeared. He couldn't fathom such a creature. And three trained together was certain death, to say nothing of the dogs being made of *metal*.

With Good in Bear's arms, they strolled from tunnel entrance to tunnel entrance. Sniffing the air, Bastard hoped to catch a whiff of something tasty. They could all use food, and sadly Bear didn't have the chance to nab any fish in this lake.

Bastard had only sniffed three tunnels when Swan gasped. She and Bastard ducked down, and Bear wisely followed suit. He squinted hard in the bioluminescence to see what she had detected: the three metal dogs were here.

Normally dogs had masters that cheered them on from outside the pit, but these three seemed self-motivated. They perplexed him. No smell, they didn't breathe, no scat, and never did they get cut or bruised.

They even lacked mouths for eating! What could they possibly want other than to just kill?

The three dogs untangled themselves once on the opposite shore of the lake. Standing up on their hind arms, their horns aimed toward the ceiling of the sculpted cavern. Whatever sensory abilities they had, they were employing them to hunt.

But they stayed put, paused perfectly, and didn't move.

Swan turned her head slowly to Bear and Bastard. She craned her neck toward the nearest tunnel opening. Bastard understood. Anywhere was better than out in the open. Line of sight with one's hunters was not ideal.

The three of them crept in a line. Bear clutched Good to her chest, careful not to let his arms swing. Soon they reached the tunnel and pressed themselves against the wall.

Bastard figured they could blindly head deeper, but a badger had certain ways to explore tunnels. He didn't want them to be caught or find themselves in an unstable area prone to cave ins or flooding. His instincts told him that simply running down a random tunnel was not the way to escape. Too much could go wrong.

Bear settled Good down gently. She tried to peek up to see the metal dogs again, but Bastard put a hand against her face and kept her down. He felt he could be more subtle.

He peeked out of the tunnel but saw only one standing still. The other two had separated. Waving their horns about, they disappeared into different tunnels across the far side of the lake.

This fanning out was a procedure Bastard had seen hunting packs do before. Usually, they performed it because their quarry was somewhere hidden within a large territory, and these metal dogs were just as smart as those of flesh and bone.

Bear's head peeked under Bastard's arm, followed by Swan's. Everyone wanted a look. They all regarded each other briefly, judging their body language and breathing for tension and combat readiness.

The conclusion was that each of them were tired, uncertain, and terrified. Good might know what to do, but he wasn't going to be able to do much for a while, perhaps days. It was up to them to make this work.

Bear jerked her head toward their current tunnel's depths. It was risky, but they had to chance it. Swan and Bastard understood and followed suit with her leading the way, Swan behind her, and Bastard in the rear.

Bastard had resolved that Swan, Rat, Bear, and Good were all a part of his cete now, so his thoughts turned to Rat. He hoped he had found a corner to hide in, and if the three metal dogs had pursued them through the river, odds are Rat was safe and sound somewhere behind them. He was a rat, after all, and rats were good at evading trouble and taking care of themselves.

The way forward swerved and dipped. They found the tunnel surprisingly easy to navigate. Something was unnatural about its height and width. At first Bastard thought one of the giant worms had carved it, but the lingering smell of its passage wasn't present.

A rhythmic clunking sound echoed from ahead. The blue glow of the dangling moss increased in density, and finally the tunnel opened to a room full of rotating gearwork, some of which were taller than Bear.

Bastard knew the safest place for him to drink was where the river was loudest. It covered any sound he might make. The downside was that it would also mask the sound of approaching predators and Bastard had yet to get a whiff of these things so sound and sight was all he had for detection. It was double-edged, but still the best option available.

Bear seemed to silently agree, leading them cautiously through the gearwork and deeper into the room. The teeth of each gear was worn smooth, but they interlocked so tightly and fluidly that not even light could peek in. Since she was the largest of the troupe, any space she could navigate, they could navigate.

Near a back corner turned a gear so large that half of it disappeared in a slot below the cave floor. It rotated on a thick axle, and Bear stepped over it to set Good's limp form down behind it. She tucked him away, behind multiple sound-producing barriers. All they could do now was wait and hope the metal dogs overlooked them and moved on.

Bear found a spot for herself to hide, and with expectant eyes, made it clear that Bastard and Swan should do the same. They each picked a tiny alcove between vertical rotating shafts, one across from another, and nestled in. Bastard and Swan's eyes met, this time without the proxy of reflective water. They shared an intense, unwavering gaze.

It was a nice moment of pulsing life, even in such circumstances as these.

CHAPTER

# THIRTY

Bastard

Bastard had drifted asleep, and somewhere in his sleep he smelled the most wonderful smell. It was a full, thick plume of vibrant strength and it curled all around him.

Something nudged him gently, just a bit, as it pressed against his ribs. The sharp bite of pain from his injury woke him. Swan had crawled across to him and nuzzled into his alcove. She curled into his body, and now he didn't mind his rib hurting at all.

She smelled amazing. Every inch of her was perfect, smooth, yet firm. Two humans had chased her into the water, and she drowned them both. Bastard couldn't fathom finding her more compelling, but the fact that she handled herself so well did it.

He wanted her. *Now.*

But he didn't dare make a move. She liked him. He knew she did, but mates had shown interest before and clawed his eyes out when he made the first move. Besides, those things were still in the tunnels behind them, slinking about. Being ready to defend her at a moment's notice was most important.

210

She curled her head under his chin and listened to his heart.

He silently chittered, stroking her hair.

She gave a long exhale from between her teeth.

He felt himself starting to drift asleep. No food, inconsistent water, and sporadic and uncomfortable sleep continued to take a toll. Bastard jolted his eyes wide, but each time they sagged even further. And when Swan began to gently snore against his chest, he knew sleep was inevitable.

So he closed his eyes again, only for a moment, to recharge. The clanking gears were his lullaby and their vibrating hum his cradle. The weight of his head rolled back onto the wall, and the thunk of it jolted him awake just enough for him to notice that Bear was missing. He could still see Good's feet peeking out from his resting spot, but there was no sign of her.

First Rat and now Bear. Bastard didn't like seeing their numbers dwindle like this. Four sets of senses were best for vigilance in any cete. Individually they were certain to die once cornered by the three monsters that hunted them. As much as Bastard didn't want to leave Swan alone to sleep, he felt it more important to protect Bear while she foraged or defecated given the risk of moving about.

Stretching his neck, he did his best to expand his vision over the gearwork without waking Swan. When he saw nothing, he wriggled a bit to see even more, but his eyes only observed the constant rolling motion of the surrounding gearwork, and it made him dizzy. Never had he seen so much motion in opposing directions before, and while there was a rhythmic order to it, his head hurt trying to decipher it.

Calling out subtly to Bear seemed like the next option. He made a churring sound first, then he attempted a kecker with his throat but it popped and collapsed in his vocal cords. He was frustrated to find that some of his badger lexicon had diminished.

Now it was time for him to search. Slipping from under Swan, her limp arm slid off his chest and flopped into his lap. Cradling her marvelous head in his hands, he settled her into the warm corner of the cavern wall that he had inhabited and pulled himself up to his feet. He almost smacked his head into a spinning flywheel as he did so. It took a full moment for Bastard to coordinate himself. He had briefly forgotten that he was now a man and not a badger, one wearing clothing and patchwork armor, and the fluidity of motion he once possessed as a quadruped was long gone. Sparing a moment, he corrected himself to his new form once again. Then he continued his search.

Still, no Bear in sight.

Sniffing about, the room had an oily stench. It smelled like an intense tar pit with a hint of sulfur, and even if he could zero in on Bear's smell it would be so smothered in other scents, he couldn't possibly track it.

Ducking down, careful of his head and coat corners, Bastard wormed his way through the gearwork in search of footprints, desperate to find scat or urine instead of blood. The gears nipped at the edges of the coat Good gave him, and the sense of being crushed in a giant mouth was inescapable.

It was maddening, but the added anxiety just increased his desire to find her. He wanted them all together, at all times, in such a wretched place while being hunted.

Among all the gears was a different movement. One of the monsters had found the room and dangled from the ceiling. Claws deep in the rock, its head and tail weaved about in a predatory fashion, like a snake trying to mesmerize its prey.

Bastard needed to lead it away from the sleeping Swan and vulnerable Good. He looked about for a loose stone, or anything to throw, but the cave floor was clean of everything including dust. Patting the coat, he felt around for anything in the pockets that he could hurl.

He found a small hourglass. It was mysterious to him, but it had heft. Returning his eye toward the monster to take aim, he saw that it was gone.

Bastard hated this room. It was so disorienting that things could appear and vanish easily among all the motion and sound. He reminded himself that he, a badger, was *also* a hunter. This enemy was without its other two counterparts, and he was confident he could do some proper damage to it one-on-one despite its invulnerabilities.

Afterall, anything can be *crushed*.

On all fours, he stealthily wriggled between the hungry teeth of the surrounding gears. Once close enough to where he had seen the metal predator hanging from the cave ceiling, he looked up and studied its claw marks. They left a pattern of four gouges, one for each finger, in a crescent semicircle.

He knew what to look for, and it left a trail. With his head craned upward, he followed the marks above. Judging by the length of its arms, he surmised where it paused to listen, and where it moved more quickly. It was circling around the room almost aimlessly, and Bastard wondered if it had been addled somehow in the previous fight. Rarely had he seen tracks this sporadic.

Bastard was so busy looking up, tracking his enemy, that he only noticed it on the ground, directly in front of him, just as it struck. All four clawed fingers raked through his ramshackle chestplate and rings of the chain shirt underneath snipped off and danced across the floor. He fell backward onto his hands and scampered like a crab as it struck the ground directly between his feet.

The hourglass rolled from his hand and the horror's tail curled around and stabbed it into pieces. Its tail reared back again, aiming for his stomach, when Bear plowed into it from the side. She slammed it against the side of a massive, slow gear and when it tried to right itself, she gripped it by the wrists and pulled its arms outward.

Its bottom two arms stabbed into her round belly.

Bear gasped to cry out, but her muscles were too tightly strung to deliver her intended scream of pain.

Bastard saw its tail lashing about, trying to control the balance of both of them, and he saw an opportunity. Leaping to his feet, he darted around both struggling bodies and caught the thing's tail. It was smooth and strong, like a thick snake.

Badgers eat snakes.

His hands clutched the tail's vibrating end tightly and he ran away from Bear with it, directly across the nearest gear. Pulling the tail into the teeth, the tail's bladed fork crunched and disappeared. It released her and instead clawed at the ground for purchase. Its motions were desperate as it understood something *strong* had it now, and the ground peeled up in slivers under its cloying fingers.

Bastard ran back around, pushed the staggering Bear aside to relative safety, and then caught one of the horror's digging hands. Its clawed fingers flicked wildly at him and it jabbed its horns toward his legs, but he had the advantage and pulled its arm into another, opposing gear.

A grinding echoed through the cavern floor. Smoke puffed from the slits above and below. The horror's horns gave off a high-pitched resonance, strong enough to rattle Bastard's teeth. Then its midsection ripped open and strings of metal muscle and metal liquid poured out.

Twitching and flailing, its free claws took chunks of stone out of everything around it, but each strike was slower than the previous and soon it succumbed to the gearwork's infinite hunger and simply tore in half. Both ends crunched and squirted metal blood until the bottom half disappeared into the turning, crushing, mechanisms that surrounded everything.

The nearby gears ground to a stuttering halt.

Looking to Bear, Bastard saw her linens had changed color to red, and her breathing was shallow. He knelt beside her, whimpering, knowing that no amount of licking would seal these wounds. Bears were hardy creatures and could survive lacerations like this. But she was no longer a true bear.

He pressed his forehead against hers lovingly, then ran to rouse Good to make everything better.

CHAPTER
# THIRTY-ONE

Arvin

Arvin's dreams were filled with clanking. Everything had been a submerged current, a cold drift through the dark. And now his lucid dream shifted to a thumping cacophony.

Then everything shook. Then again. He heard the distant word "good" chanted over and over again from somewhere in the ethereal landscape that exists between sleep and wakefulness.

He remembered he had eyes and opened them. Bastard leaned over him, nose to nose, shoving on his chest. "Good!" he cried. "Good!"

*Does he think 'good' is my name?*

Never proficient in reading facial expressions, Arvin could tell that Bastard was excited about something but he couldn't discern if it was a happy excitement or a distressed excitement.

Arvin went to repeat the word "good" back to Bastard, but his lungs gave a wet spasm, and he gargled a prickling cough instead.

Water came up, and he flopped onto his hands and knees to hack it out.

*I drowned. Partly.*

The events leading up to now ordered themselves consecutively in his mind. Catching up quickly, he then took a moment to study the smoky room around him.

*Gearwork. Various sizes. Two massive vertical axles and one in the ceiling horizontal. Polished and smooth. Recent locking. No buildup of calcium or corrosion or moisture. Maintained. Not of Ramlagha ruins.*

Bastard shoved Arvin again, harder. His intensity growing as he shouted, "Good!"

*He has something good for me.*

"Yes! Good. Show me the good," Arvin rasped. Head low, he shook off his dizziness and weathered his pulsing headache in order to find his feet. "I follow," he gestured to his chest.

With a firm grip on his sleeve, Bastard hauled Arvin through the still gearwork toward the center of the room. As they moved, Arvin got a better look at everything including the pattern carved into the room's ceiling.

*Same pattern around the dais. Absorbs sound. All along ceiling and walls.*

His mind was awash with possibilities as he wondered if someone had recently copied the sound-dampening technology of Ramlagha or if the room had the pattern for centuries prior to the gear work being installed.

The curious fury of his mind was shaken when he saw Mama on a patch of floor clear of gears, on her side with Lovely cradling her head. The girth of her belly and breasts sagged and the slashes in her linen dress revealed lacerations underneath. She had multiple stab wounds flanking her belly button, and the right side of her shoulder was slashed to the muscle.

*Oh, we need to review the meaning of "good."*

Arvin could easily see that Mama's breathing was steady, but her stillness reminded him of Uncle's last painful days. He dropped to all fours and did his best to check the wounds without touching them.

While he had read a number of anatomy books and seen horses and other animals be sutured, Arvin had no first-hand experience in it. His fingers trembled as he fumbled around his bandolier for something of use.

*Salt? No. Laudanum would slow the heart, so no.*

Suddenly he remembered his backup stitching kit in his coat's inner pocket. He used it to patch holes and tears in clothing. Tugging on Bastard's leg, he pulled him in close and rifled through the coat until he found it.

Pulling a needle and thread, he hoped his fingers were dexterous enough to keep from hurting Mama too much. If she twitched as a reaction to his clumsy work, she might expand one of her lacerations further.

The punctures were easiest, since they were small. He worried about their depth, but when he peeked at them all he saw was the fatty tissue that closed in around the wound.

*Okay. Just sewing. Steady.*

Her skin was tough, and since the Chromium were so polished and smooth, each slash was astoundingly clean. Lining up and closing each wound was easy.

By the third claw puncture, two things occurred to him.

The first was that Rat wasn't present. Arvin assumed he had stayed behind, and he didn't even know how to ask what happened. Maybe Rat died and he didn't see. Perhaps now wasn't the time anyway. Uncle always told Arvin to hold his tongue when inquiring about tragedies.

The second thing to occur to Arvin was that if a Chromium had done this to Mama, which it obviously did, where was it now? Indestructible creatures don't just vanish, and he had seen them rend people to pieces so long as their lungs drew breath. These things did not leave survivors.

"Where is bad?" Arvin asked Bastard. "Bad? Baaaaad? Where?"

Bastard just crouched and scanned about frantically as if "bad" were a mist lingering in the air.

Arvin glanced over his shoulders warily. The room's sound dampening likely kept the Chromium from having accurate "vision" and if the gears worked they would generate a lot of masking noise. They couldn't have dragged him to a safer place.

*Maybe safe for now. But Mama can't be moved without closing these.*

When Arvin returned to his stitching, Bastard appeared to calm a bit. Just like when Arvin had to pee, the hairy badger-man returned to his state of vigilance as Lovely continued to cradle Mama's head. She stroked her cheek lovingly, making a low 'ooo' sound that was likely felt more than heard to the injured woman.

Saving the shoulder for last, Arvin guided Lovely's hands to where she could help best; clamping the wound closed. Arvin feared Lovely would tire out before he was done sewing the wound, but the white-haired woman didn't quiver once. Blood pooled between her pale fingers as she continued cooing to Mama.

And most impressive of all was Mama's absolute lack of reaction. She was clearly in pain, but the pain never owned her.

*I once cried from an infected hangnail.*

He had done what he could. Only a few minutes had passed, but Arvin was already exhausted, likely from the near-drowning and lack of food. They were in a bad way, especially with Rat gone, and Arvin worried further about the inevitable infection that Mama's wounds would catch.

*Chromium claws slashed dozens of men. They carried diseases Mama now has. And cave ailments. And pus and suppuration.*

Smelling a hint of sulfur, Arvin checked his bandolier again. He didn't remember carrying any in powder form, but it typically was perfect for sterilizing a wound and preventing infection. It would be a strike of good fortune if he happened to have some he had forgotten about. Maybe it was in a pouch that was torn, hence him smelling it.

But nothing. Perplexed, he sniffed the air. The smell was nearby, wafting through the geared room.

*Is it in the smoke? Gears burned out recently. Why?*

Arvin explored a bit, never leaving the sight of Mama, and craned his head around a few corners. He quickly found the Chromium, ripped apart, with a puddle of perfectly reflective mercury gathered below the remaining upper half. It was such an unusual sight, as if a portal to a mirror universe had opened in the ground.

*They killed one! Opposing forces. Opposite grinding gears. Brilliant!*

He marveled at how effectively they had dispatched the Chromium menace. Mama had gotten hurt, and since it clogged several gears, different gears would have to be used. but the thing was very much deceased.

Taking a knee, Arvin inspected the upper half. Strings of silken metal dangled out of it and the occasional drip of mercury splotched into the pool below. Its head had also been pulled into the gear's teeth and was crushed, leaving both of its cruel horns to stick out the side at a skewed angle.

*Mercury circulatory system. Closed system. No ingestion or excretion, so it is for cooling? Are there organs? Don't touch the mercury!*

Arvin pulled his pipette free and used it like a probe. Poking around the Chromium's torso, he identified springy aluminum ribs and cobalt strands acting as sinew. Everything was metal, in both pure elemental forms as well as unidentifiable alloys. The creature was an absolute marvel of magical construction.

*Homunculus. Fashioned en masse for a single function. Minimal sensory organs make it hard to confound. Can't blind an already blind creature.*

The split seams of the Chromium's hide caught his attention. He wanted to split it open further, look deeper, but his pipette was dull and when he tried with his knife, it wasn't strong enough.

Thinking quickly, he had an idea. Gripping one of the dangling arms, he curled its wicked fingers together into a fist except for one;

the middle finger. He then bent its limp arm around and used the middle finger to slice deeper into its own hide.

It glided upward through the skin and more mercury gushed out. Coils of muscle cable followed as Arvin searched for a heart of any kind. It was cumbersome, but the Chromium's arm was astoundingly flexible and with the pipette in his other hand, he soon found a narrow vacuole among the cobalt sinew for pumping the mercury.

*Lubricant pump. Mercury instead of oil or fat. Still a thing of magic.*

He wondered why mercury was used instead of oil or anything else, but forgot the line of thinking when he realized the Chromium's dagger-like finger could cut the two horns free.

Slicing up the side of its neck, more mercury spilled out. He could see the segmented spine deeper within the muscle strands, but moved on up the side of the head. Underneath sat a metal skull, but it lacked any distinct aspects one would expect. The Chromium had no eyes, mouth, or nose and its skull reflected that.

Arvin's clumsy cutting tools reached the forehead. Slicing around each horn carefully, he was dismayed to find they were part of the skull. But one was askew, and his hope bore fruit; the gear had broken it free.

After a few cuts, he shook it free of any mercury and wiped it down on his trousers. It was a simple, narrow spike. Geometrically perfect. A marvel.

He wanted the other one. A pair would be twice as good. He could experiment on one of them more freely while preserving the other. Continuing his surgery, he found where the gear had cracked the metal skull. Gripping the still-attached horn, he wiggled it back and forth until it came free from under the remaining flaps of metal hide.

Pulling it free, he now held a horn in each hand. One perfect and the other with a small wedge of Chromium skull on the end.

*Beyond sharp. How do I carry these?*

Pulling his turban from his pocket, he wrapped them up and tied them to his belt. If he fell wrong while carrying them, they would impale his gut, but he felt the risk was worth it.

Still riding his high of exploration and discovery, Arvin stood with a smile. "Good!" he shouted, arms wide.

Bastard jumped in alarm at the noise and Lovely, her eyes red from worry, looked at Arvin in bewilderment. Mama was asleep, her breathing steady. The anguish in her face was still present, though.

*Did it wrong. Again.*

"Sorry."

Perplexed, Bastard corrected Arvin. "*Good.*"

# THIRTY-TWO

Visteria

For the entire day, she waited in the wagon with the assassin's knife at the ready. Her shoulder had stopped bleeding, but the injury made it stiffen. She soaked a rag in hot water and bundled it as best she could, but Visteria knew if she fell into any kind of physical struggle, victory was unlikely.

Waiting for nighttime was her best option, so she remained vigilant with the blade just in case the assassin had a handler of her own. Visteria had always been told that the Children of the Desert are everywhere, and while she doubted it to be a literal sentiment, her nerves were strung tight.

In an effort to make the most of her time, she dug through the assassin's belongings. She found various teas and crushed powders that appeared to be stock kitchen ingredients, but Visteria didn't dare touch or sniff them. There were several knives hidden about and even a razor-thin garrote wire. A dark cloak for nighttime reconnaissance sat bundled into a rolled mattress and within a hollow drawer handle she found another icon of the cult.

But there wasn't a single scrap of writing anywhere to be found. No notes, instructions, missives, or maps. Whatever information could have been gathered died with the would-be killer.

Sitting on the tea stool, feet astride the bloody corpse, Visteria wished desperately for Evrick. She had been raised as one of the Children of Ramlagha, a child of a mighty mother and her three dutiful husbands. Everything demanded of her, she accomplished. Visteria learned small blades and poisons, learned of the lost mastery below the sands, sang the songs of forgotten words, and killed her rival cousins when contested.

She had earned the right to marry and bear children. She was trusted with a vital mission, and given the most powerful mentor in their history for security.

But then she met Evrick, *knew* him, and everything else had fallen away. Ovallin came to kill him, to spare her the tragedy of doing so herself, so Visteria put a crossbow bolt into her head. Legends claim that sorceresses aren't so easily killed, and some legends apparently were true.

Visteria wondered if the Chromium had finished off the job, or if Ovallin would just wither away into nothingness while entombed in the ruins, entombed with Evrick.

She folded her hands together and imagined his fingers in hers, but nothing could replace them. Sausage-fingered husband is what she would call him.

The sunlight through the shades finally dimmed. The hustle and bustle of dinner preparation and evening haggling commenced outside the wagon from all sides. Visteria peeked out of the tiny windows and viewports where she could. The horse or horses had to be quartered somewhere nearby, and the wagon was going nowhere without them.

Fetching the long, dark cloak, Visteria bundled herself up. It was lumpy enough to hide her figure, and she experimented with a modified gait so no one would recognize her.

Folks outside quieted down as they ate and drank by their fires.

Now was the time. Hitching up the cloak to step clear of the corpse, she exited the wagon and latched the door properly behind her. Looking about, she found most nearby souls either too distracted by their own crisis to notice her or simply staring off into traumatized landscapes.

She needed a horse. Two, if she wanted the speed she desired. Visteria didn't know where to go, but it didn't matter. Anywhere but here. Maybe she could hide in Daynce, behind its high walls and well-equipped garrison.

Slinking through the tents and toeing around their roping, she reached the wooden stables on the eastern side of the Iron Whores' ravine. It was rickety, half-built into the rocky face of the soaring ridgeline to shield it from the brutal midday sun.

Refugees, mercenaries, and stable hands filed in and out. Some carried spent sacks of feed and others conversed over shared bowls of stew. Iron Whores often spoke with animated enthusiasm, but not as of late. Dread pervaded their every gesture.

"Oi. Lass," a blustery guard said, waving a dripping ladle. He dropped it in for the next man and wandered over to her. "Stables ain't open. Let 'em eat. Give it a turn of the glass."

Visteria was briefly impressed that he saw her for her age accurately, and not as the elderly woman she intended to be. Obviously, she wasn't as good at this as she had hoped.

"I desperately need my horses." Her sincere need came through.

He sighed with exasperation, looking back to the stew that he longed for, then back at her. "They gonna eat it all."

"Then just let me through?"

"Which animal is yers?"

She didn't have time to craft a vague description. "The one with four legs," she said. It was the kind of thing that Evrick would have found funny.

And so did the guard. He chuckled gently. "Right, but lemme see them when you leave. And if yeh get kicked, I'm not to blame."

"Right. Thank you."

He gave a dismissive nod and returned to claim his turn on the ladle.

Visteria slipped into the stables. It was well lit by closed oil lamps and each animal was busy in its own stall with its face in a bucket. Several children worked as stable hands throughout the feeding to make sure the horses and camels didn't antagonize each other over food or space. A few glanced her way, but their duties preoccupied them. The Iron Whores made sure that as soon as a member could toddle, they had a task. No matter how small the task, it was considered vital.

But they never asked their children to slit their cousins' throats after beating them in a fight. They never ordered their operatives to pull out their uteruses so honeypot missions didn't become complicated.

A child, no older than seven, nodded to her. "Which is yers?" he inquired with a wet lisp. He had been born with a split lip right up to the nostril, and the sewing job on it was hardly perfect. But he had lovely eyes and was surprisingly dutiful.

"I don't know. I'm getting them for an old lady who has to leave. She was bigger in the shoulders and waist, with—"

The boy reached out and felt Visteria's cloak. He seemed to recognize it. "She lent you her velvety cloak?" he tested, likely suspicious that it was stolen. "She yer friend?"

"We just had tea," she said in her sweetest voice. Visteria counted her blessings that her assassin had worn this very cloak when dropping the ponies off. "In thanks, I told her I'd hitch her horse."

He bought it and his smile taxed his scared lip. Releasing her cloak, he coyly continued. "I'm smart. I wanna run this stable one day."

A part of Visteria lamented, wondering if that day would ever come with what Arvin had unleashed below.

"Indeed, you are. Can you lead me?" She was careful not to indicate how many animals the assassin had stored.

The boy waved her on, deeper into the stable. The wooden walls gave way to chiseled sandstone and when he brought her to a stall, her heart sank: a single, ragged mule. It was squat like its owner, chomping away at the rope handle of its empty feed bucket.

She looked about, evaluating the other animals. Nearly anything was bigger and stronger than this.

"Um, do you have anything for sale? Or trade?"

He shook his head. "Not until daytime. Boss comes back and he makes the deals."

Seeing no other option, she extended her hand. The boy slipped on the animal's bridle and placed the reins into Visteria's hands. He then cleared his throat and looked at her expectantly. It was clear he wanted a tip.

Visteria had no coinage on her person, and feeling about she only found the dagger from the wagon. "I'm so poor," she said. "But I do have this humble blade."

Humble was a good word for it. While the blade was certainly sharpened and maintained, it was on its third or fourth handle and the nicks and scratches meant a fifth was soon needed. Her only worry was that it would excite him so much, getting a blade of his own, that he might brag about it to the men outside and blow her cover.

He evaluated it with critical eyes. "No, lady. Yeh need that more dan me." With a pitying smile, he trotted off to tend a nearby camel.

It wasn't the turn of events she expected, but the mule's reins were in hand, and she was free to leave. She eagerly did so, waving to the soup-sipping guard as she left.

The stars began to wink into existence above. Someone stroked a stringed instrument with a lazy hand while humming. A baby cried while an old man in the opposite direction complained.

She just wanted to get out of here.

The mule was easy enough to hitch to the wagon. Removing the blocks, she didn't hesitate to climb up to the driver's perch but before she could snatch the reins a man appeared as if from thin air. He held the bridal of the mule, his turban obscuring his face.

As she reached for her knife, he spoke.

"Easy, Lady Skullhew."

It was Booker.

"I'm doing what Tunny said. I'm a guest and guests can leave."

He stroked the mule's neck. Something about his bracers drew her eye. "To every sea?" he asked, dangerously.

Booker knew the Children's mantra. He knew she was a Child of the Desert. Visteria had changed it for Evrick to use. "To every mountain" indicated the boarders of the Yellow Sea and Vastard. It was to be the Fourteenth Kingdom.

Visteria was unsure how long Booker had known. "What do you want?" Fear rose in her as she inspected his bracers. They both had folded blades on them, likely poisoned.

"What I always want. Information. What really happened below Tent City?"

"I don't know. But the man who was there is named Arvin. He can tell you, if he made it out alive."

"From what tribe?"

"No tribe. One of Evrick's many lost causes."

Booker smiled. "That how you sold yourself to him? A lost cause?"

"Evrick learned I was a Child, and still loved me. I'm not the enemy." It was technically true, but she never told Evrick that the Children were the hidden remnants of Ramlagha. She never told him that *her* mission was to kill him, not just acquire the language.

"In times of chaotic crisis, anyone who is not us is the enemy," he replied.

It startled Visteria just how different Booker's mannerisms were when he was without his two counterparts. She was meeting the real him, and she suspected few lived to tell such a tale.

"Why did the Children send you to Evrick?"

"They didn't, I just—"

"Children don't wander, or drift, or join causes. There is zero freedom in the cult. You were assigned. Why?"

She had to give him something. "To monitor. That's all."

"And your niece?"

"My trainee. We operate in twos."

He tilted his head, examining the wagon. "Not always."

Booker must have searched the wagon when she left for the mule. He likely found the assassin's body, and then searched the entire tribe for a possible accomplice. Or he knew about her before, and already knew she came alone.

Visteria had enough with the games. It was one of the many reasons why she hated being a Child in the first place. "Just let me go."

"Where to?"

"I don't know, just . . . Damnit, let me go!" She jerked the reins, but he held firm. His blades could come out at any moment and dig into her leg.

"Daynce has giants," he said, ignoring her protest. "Salt-blooded. They've never been this far south before. They are typically mercenaries, and I feel they would do well against our invaders. Hiring them would go a long way to helping Tunny and you."

He was giving her a lead, likely to save himself the trouble and expense of hiring mercenaries himself. She knew little of the giants. They were beings from an older civilization in the North, reputed to have been pounded into rubble by their angry god.

But it was also clear that Booker's spy network covered Daynce.

Her silent ponderings left her open for Booker to continue his interrogation.

"Answer me this one question, then I'll let you go. Do the Children want you dead because of a job you failed, or a job you fulfilled?"

"Riddles? What the hells does that mean? Why would I be killed for being successful?"

Booker gave a conciliatory smile. "You're new to the spying gig, eh?" He let go of the bridle. "You can go, but keep an ear out for me. I might have more questions for you, wherever you land." With a gentle pat on the mule's rump, he stepped back to make room for the wagon to peel away from the refugee cluster.

Visteria slapped at the reins a few times, eyes ahead toward the mouth of the ravine. She'd feel better in the wider desert hills and rocks of Vastard, but her mind was awash with questions. Why was Booker letting her go when he clearly wanted more information from her? How much about the Children did he know? And his network extends all the way to Daynce. Did he also have assassins of his own there?

She didn't dare look back over her shoulder to see if he watched her leave.

Mistress was the most flamboyant of the Iron Whores' leadership.

Tunny the most prudent.

But Booker, by far, was the most lethal.

CHAPTER

# THIRTY-THREE

Arvin

*Solve the puzzle.*

Arvin evaluated the smoky gear room. Most still rotated at their laborious pace and he found their infinite *clunk* soothing. Approaching the situation in a manner that gave him the least anxiety, he considered this as a puzzle.

First, he solidified his goals. Mama, Bastard, and Lovely must survive. They were his priority above all other things. Too much had been lost already, including dozens of guards and laborers, Rat, Evrick, and when he permitted himself to think about it, Arvin still ached for Uncle. He was done with the world taking. It would take no more. Mama, Bastard, and Lovely were to survive.

*It's not fair that just anyone can die whenever.*

Second, Arvin realistically considered the elements impeding this goal. They were hungry. Additionally, Mama couldn't be moved for days given her injuries and when she could be moved, she weighed well over three hundred pounds. Arvin felt hunger now, which meant his three friends did as well. In a day, perhaps two, they would feel faint as they entered the true stages of starvation. Hunger was rough, but starvation was deadly.

*And a grumbling tummy gives off noise.*

Another impediment to their survival were the two remaining Chromium. Arvin had no notion of their whereabouts but given how the three had attacked them in such a coordinated fashion at the cannibal camp, he was confident that the two survivors would come around eventually in search of their missing third.

His observations and brief experience gave him a substantial amount of information regarding the metal beings of magic, and it would come in handy. Their blindsight gave them advantages, but the ceiling of the defunct gear room where they hid made it clear that those advantages could be circumvented. Someone *made* that ceiling, and it provoked the question: what else have they made?

*No chairs around for me to hide myself in.*

He understood his goal and that which challenged it.

*Take note of resources.*

The bandolier remained partially stocked with a number of useful elements and compositions including peel shavings for clearing the sinuses, cactus oil, bird-bone paste, refined urine powder from a camel, the usual semen, shavings of magnetized iron, collected calcium residue, chunks of lead, chunks of gold, porous calcite that was unrefined, four types of salt, dried cloves of garlic, and several drips of potent acid that, while strong, still couldn't melt through the glass vial that held it.

Then there was his alchemist's toolkit with pipette, probes, and tinder set. Several unageing rubber strands still hung from his belt, as well as the two collected Chromium horns. He also had a mostly spent suture kit, a handful of empty vials, and a bladder still filled with fresh spring water.

*Think like Uncle.*

A whiff of sulfur hit his nose again. It wafted from somewhere beyond the smoky gear room in the opposite direction in which the Chromium clawed its way in on the ceiling.

Turning to Bastard, he raised both his palms up. "Stay here. Stay. Good." With a hopeful heart, he dashed away further into the tunnel, minding his head for low-hanging gears. Reaching the small exit, he noticed the flooring wasn't as worn as it was in the gear room. The ceiling's protective sound-dampening pattern also tapered off the further he traveled.

But the light changed color. It went from the bioluminescent blue to a purple, and then to a yellow. Heat pushed against him like a barrier and the smell of sulfur became so intense that Arvin choked on it. He pulled his undershirt above his nose and coughed into it as he went.

His eyes burned as the tunnel expanded, prompting him to wet his fingers with the bladder and rub his eyes clean before fixing his goggles. The surrounding rock turned to jagged mafic and appeared untraveled. Then the tunnel ended abruptly, and he saw why.

It released into leagues and leagues of cavern, hundreds of feet deep, with a burning stream of liquid rock below. The lava, in all of its roiling magnificence, traveled at considerable speed. Within its hazy steam floated isles of blackened stone as puffs of fire burped from the dripping burnt shores.

*That could certainly melt anything.*

Arvin examined the rock formations surrounding him. Any new compound or chemical, especially sulfur, could be of use. As he scanned, he spotted something lurking behind him.

He squealed and nearly leaped off the ledge into the chasm below. But it was only Bastard, who had followed him.

"Good gods! No, not good. But not bad." The adrenaline shook his hands and he gripped his knees to remain steady. "So, so many ways to die here."

Bastard was oblivious to his faux pas and approached curiously. Peering over Arvin, he became mesmerized with the lava flow below.

"Been a heck of a time for you," Arvin said, sitting down. "So, that's lava. Lava, this is Bastard." He pulled his small knife from his belt and scraped away at the yellow buildup of sulfur that had solidi-fied along the lip of the drop.

The sound of scraping drew Bastard's attention.

It occurred to Arvin that his original duty, the one Evrick had given him, had never been satisfied. He was to care for and teach the four prisoners, Bastard being one of them.

"You look good in your armor," Arvin said, tapping his own chest while gesturing to Bastard's breastplate. "What remains of it anyway."

"Good," Bastard echoed.

Arvin added an exaggerated nod. "Good," he repeated. It was best to assign the gesture to the word for the sake of future commu-nication.

Bastard returned the nod. "Good."

*Faster learner than me.*

He handed the small knife to Bastard, handle first. "Here. You scrape. Like this. *This.*" Arvin forced the handle into Bastard's hands and held them together as he performed the motion with him. It was odd holding another man's hands. It was odd holding *anyone's* hands.

*I don't think I've ever touched anyone more than Bastard.*

Bastard wasn't the only one having a difficult time. Arvin had lost his guardian, made and lost friends, went on a heavy drug trip, summoned metal evils from beyond, and was now standing over a lava chasm.

*Should have stayed in Uncle's shack when they burned it down.*

But he was grateful not to be alone, and as he watched Bastard focus on the motion of the dagger, the seed of hope in him grew. Each scrape came easier to Bastard, and soon a faint smile emerged. Progress, tiny but measurable progress, was happening right under Bastard's nose and he was clearly pleased.

*What is pleasure if not measurable progress?*

Arvin meditated on the thought. There had been three Chromium chasing them and now there were only two. *Progress.*

But his mind countered immediately with the loss of Rat. Arvin would not accept the trading of lives, if the Chromium could be considered such.

*The goal. Mama, Bastard, and Lovely survive. And hope the best for Rat.*

Rejuvenated by Bastard's enthusiastic scraping, Arvin returned to examining the rock formations around them. He located some yellow quartz, colored by sulfur, which was interesting but little else. There were also wavy patterns in the mafic tunnel, indicating that this had once been liquified prior to cooling.

*Poured in from elsewhere. All of the tunnel, and gear room, is mafic but that was ground down and polished. This isn't.*

Staring at the pattern for too long made him dizzy. He took a knee to steady himself. As he did so, the rubber straps in his belt dangled free and it gave him an idea.

"Oh. Ooooooooh."

Bastard looked over to see Arvin grinning.

"Oh, that is good. Bastard, how tired are you getting with that sulfur? We're going to need a lot of it. A sock full."

Once Bastard started to slow down, Arvin took a turn grinding away. The blade became dull, and eventually chipped to the point of uselessness, but Arvin was pleased with the pile of yellow powder at their feet.

*Uncle used to talk me through his experiments to teach me.*

"So, Bastard, this yellow stuff we put into these two empty glass vials. Like this, see? Your hands are dry, so you can touch it. While you do that, I'm splitting the urine powder into two separate vials. It has a lot of nitrate in it, which tends to get 'angry' with sulfur. So let's not mix them, right?"

Bastard nodded. "Good." He was thriving from the interaction.

"Good," Arvin then unlaced his boots and slipped off his socks. "Next I'm going to use my tinder kit. The flint shards, here"—he showed them in his open palm—"along with the black powder from the kit with the boiled, refined camel nitrate. All of that goes into these two."

Bastard appeared overwhelmed with the information but watched, wide-eyed with interest.

"We don't shake these. Shake bad. I'm going to rip some pages out of my journal to stuff in there to keep things from moving around too much like that, see? Nice and dry and flammable. Can you say flammable? Flaaammmaaaableee."

"Flamm?"

"Yep, flam. Very flam. Able." Arvin slipped one vial into each of his threadbare socks. "Are those sulfur vials full to the top? All the way?"

They were.

"Good! Now, we put one of each of *those* in each sock. The less cloth binding together the two vials, the better. Then we cut the extra sock off with my wreck of a knife like . . ." Arvin struggled with the dull blade, but he couldn't get it through the sock's ankle.

Bastard waited a moment, watching Arvin's struggle, then abruptly took the knife and sock out of his hands. He muscled through it, tearing the sock in half with the dull knife and then handed everything back.

"Good!" Arvin shouted with excitement. "Now, I use the remainder of my suture kit to sew the foot part of the sock into a tight, little ball. For both. See? And now we have a favorite concoction of the alchemist: explosives!"

Bastard returned Arvin's enthusiastic smile, even if he didn't understand the outcome.

"Good!" he shouted. "Now, the other sock. Please."

With confidence, Bastard performed the task a second time. Then Arvin sewed them both up tightly into two roundish projectiles.

*Is this how Uncle felt? Teaching me?*

Arvin felt like everything was, for once, going right. He was communicating correctly and effectively with another person. The thrill of it warmed his soul.

After he put his boots back on, Arvin stood and brushed himself off. "Now we dig into the one you killed, pull out two rib bones, and wipe them clean of mercury."

Bastard followed, listening intently. Arvin wasn't sure if Bastard was just mimicking the act of paying attention or focusing on the phonemes, but it was a wonderful feeling to be listened to.

"And that is important. Never touch mercury. It's really bad. Super bad. It makes you dumb, and too much of it can drive you crazy."

The two men walked side by side, as if on a stroll, back toward the gear room.

"Which will happen to every alchemist eventually. Except Uncle. *He* told me that measuring with your mouth was what drove alchemists mad so he used glass spoons and cups to measure everything, but it was so expensive it kept us in a shack. The best glass we can't afford, because it comes from the Vulg to the north. Have you heard of the Vulg?"

*He obviously hasn't. Tell him!*

"They are stone giants with blood that burns the air on contact. I'd love to get ahold of their blood. I mean, not like *that*. But could you imagine a vellum cut burning down a library?"

Arvin hadn't felt this good in days. When they reached the entrance of the gear room, Bastard stopped following so Arvin turned and continued talking to him.

*He's wide-eyed with interest!*

"I've heard that the Vulg have a new war chief who is establishing trade. I only know because Uncle told me they have the best glass and maybe we could get some."

*Wait. Bastard looks afraid. Why is he afraid?*

Following his line of sight, Arvin looked into the haze of the quiet gear room. The Chromium corpse was still there, torn asunder, but a second Chromium was present. It poked the open body with its claws as its horns hummed audibly.

*Greater intensity to compensate. Because of the ceiling. Adaption.*

Arvin rolled the projectiles in his hands. He could throw them, but he knew his arm likely couldn't deliver the force to break the vials. There was no time to quickly craft a slingshot of worth, and the only thing he could use to do so would be the horns and they might slash right through the bands of rubber on contact.

*The horns.*

Arvin knelt and placed the two explosives on the ground, next to each other, against the wall, and out of the way. They would be no use to him in this fight. He had to figure something else out.

The Chromium froze, sensing his motion.

Unfastening the dangling turban-wrapped horns, Arvin retrieved them from his belt. With one in each hand, he held out his arms. In his periphery, he saw Bastard looking at him. And in the far corner, huddled and vulnerable, crouched Mama and Lovely.

*Nobody else. No one else lost.*

Arvin struck the horns together over his head. Their resonance was as piercing as their shape, causing Bastard to jolt and the Chromium to dart up to the ceiling, claws out, to dangle.

It lowered its tail and swept it through the air in agitation.

*Confused. It's confused.*

He struck them again.

The Chromium reached out a cautious hand in his direction, like a blind man seeking light.

Bastard tried to wedge himself between it and Arvin, but he elbowed Bastard away with determined force.

*Nobody else dies.*

Bastard got the hint and slipped behind one of the still gears. The Chromium's tail followed him, so Arvin rapidly tinged the horns while walking backward.

*Overload its senses. Make everything move, so he has no target.*

It followed, slow at first, then with more confidence. All of its dangerous ends focused on Arvin's hands, and as he retreated steadily it followed.

Arvin led it out of the gear room, into the mafic tunnel, and downward toward its opening over the lava chasm. It followed, gathering speed, and as Arvin got to the ledge it dropped from the ceiling and went into a leaping sprint.

*It figured me out.*

Arvin had nowhere to go, but to fall. Holding out both horns like downward daggers, he slipped off the ledge and dropped.

It was on him, horns forward and claws out, swiping for his face. But gravity was faster than its attack and Arvin fell away. The Chromium sailed clear over him into the yellow, sulfuric beyond.

Both of Arvin's horns caught the mafic and his locked grip held him steady, dangling from the lip of the opening. Behind him, below, he heard the rolling clang of the Chromium as it tumbled down the chasm. Peering under his armpit, he watched it barrel through the molten bank, and onto the roiling lava where it thrashed and blackened. The muddy nature of the lava sucked it in, its shape malforming from the heat. It thrashed, blackened, then fell still.

*I'm alive. I did it right.*

Arvin, relieved, thunked his forehead on the rocky lip only to be poked by the cruel mafic edges.

*Ow.*

He also realized he lacked the upper body strength to pull himself up. This made sense to him, because tightly sealed jars also gave him trouble.

*Didn't have much choice. Could just rest here, and hope they—*

Six hands reached over the ledge at once. Lovely, Mama, and Bastard all gripped Arvin by his sleeves and bandolier and even his hair. They yanked him up and as they did so, both horns slipped free from the rock and his cramped, sweaty hands couldn't hold them. They discordantly danced down the rocks of the chasm's descent and into the lava, following after the Chromium.

*Gods damnit. Those could have been really useful.*

Then came the cuddle pile. Mama's wounds had reopened, but that wasn't getting in the way of her nuzzling Arvin. Bastard flanked her as he licked Arvin's scrapes. And Lovely preened his hair with her teeth.

"Mama, I gotta restitch . . . in a minute." The collection of smothering love chased away his hunger and exhaustion, at least for the moment. He reached out and patted them back, drawing them in close. "Thank you," he whispered.

CHAPTER
# THIRTY-FOUR

Visteria

Dawn approached, and Visteria wasn't even tired. Fearfully checking over her shoulder kept her adrenaline flowing through the night. Riding atop the wagon, she constantly checked to see if she was being tracked, either by people or ovrens.

But that wasn't the most concerning thing.

Perhaps it was a mirage of the moonlight, but several times to the south, perhaps leagues away, Visteria saw silvery shimmering. She tried to dismiss it as reflections on the sand in the still air, but the harder she squinted at it, the more it moved around.

The mule didn't react at all. It was old and likely deaf and near-blind, so perhaps it just didn't notice the oddity. But Visteria wondered if it would even recognize whatever smell the polished killers gave off. Such an alien horror couldn't be easily processed by her own mind to say nothing of an idiot pack animal.

When the sun rose, she found no reprieve from her worries. She could no longer see the mirages in the distance to her left, but that hardly meant they were gone. Those things were still out in the world. Families slaughtered. Entire camps toppled onto reddened sand.

And it was Arvin's fault. He did this. Trapped Evrick below, leaving her to the mercy of the Children of Ramlagha. Her only hope was that Tunny could get below and free Evrick, but the truth of such impossibilities gnawed on her mind. She shoved the reality of despair back down. If she let it surface for too long, she'd stop moving, lay down, and die under the sun.

Redirecting herself, she took stock of her current situation. As the sun climbed free of the terrain behind her, she realized she had decisions to make.

First off, where to go. Visteria considered driving to Korris to catch a ship across the water. Once beyond the Yellow Sea, she would be out of the Children's reach. But Korris was notorious for collecting bounties on wanderers, and the Children would absolutely have a presence there.

The other option was to obey Booker's unsubtle westward directive and curve northward to Daynce, a wealthy mercantile city. Oppah had fled there after Skullhew chased him out of Vastard, and if he found the Lady Skullhew, he would take his revenge. But the benefit of being there was twofold: the large population would give her more autonomy and Oppah was an idiot. His shrewdness required crafty wording and signed charters, but the man was a dullard overall. It wasn't like he ran the city, but was instead a barely tolerated visitor in exile.

The choice wasn't a difficult one for her to make. Visteria would rather face Oppah and the enemies she made as Lady Skullhew far sooner than a single fellow Child. And if Booker had wanted her dead she would already be so. He may not be the enemy she feared him to be.

To Daynce, then.

Next, there was the decision of what to do with the stolen wagon containing the stiff, elderly body inside. But that one was also easy.

Tugging on the reins, she pulled the mule to a restful stop. She then gave it water and food and stroked its mane with a wary eye southward. Feeling almost normal, she completed the typical chores of a traveler. Collecting what she needed from inside the wagon, she filled the mule's side pouches with provisions and whatever valuables she could sell for traveling fare or lodging.

She wished she hadn't left behind her crossbow in Tent City. Anything in her hands would give her a sense of security right now that she felt desperate for.

Channeling her frustrations, she tore apart the inside of the assassin's wagon. She slashed the pillows and dumped their feathers, poured the cooking oil over the dead woman, and sliced up the sheets. Using one of the tiny stool legs, she bundled together a torch and balanced it on the highest shelf.

Striking flint, it lit easily. It might take a bit, but with the desert heat, any unmonitored fire was guaranteed to catch. And this way, Visteria would be far enough away to avoid any investigation of the smoke signal.

The dark satisfaction of a plan coming together calmed her. She left the wagon, locked it up with a padlock, and mounted the mule for the west. It might be a week or two, but soon she would be behind high walls, away from her assassins. And there she would keep an ear for Tunny Gontz's expedition and Evrick's reemergence. Assuming Evrick was alive.

When it bobbed up to the surface, she shoved her despair back down again. Tunny would find him. Skullhew would persevere and Visteria would return and stand next to her love. They would be safe from assassins while they raised the old world for *themselves*.

Visteria paused a moment. It startled her to realize she had gone almost all night without seeing Evrick's face in her mind. She wasn't sure if she had been away from him this long since she'd met him. His face couldn't materialize in her memory and her breathing became quick and shallow.

"Think of something. Think of something," she murmured in

desperation, closing her eyes. Forgetting his face was unforgivable. Forcing it just made his voice and face more obscure.

So she zeroed in on his smell, the smell of the sauna as they inhaled each other's sweat, the stress dripping off them as they made love slowly. It was her favorite way, slowly grinding back and forth on top of him.

His face came into view. He would look up at her, marveling. Sometimes she teased him by dangling her hair into his face, making him laugh.

It was the laugh. That did it. Visteria saw and heard him clearly, laughing under her. She kept his laugh ringing in her heart as she rode clear of the wagon, around a thatch of cacti, and toward the rockier parts of the desert.

A lizard crested a rock and tilted its head, examining her. She felt reassured by the tiny speck of life.

Westward until Daynce. Three days' ride.

CHAPTER
# THIRTY-FIVE

Arvin

Arvin couldn't remember walking to where he currently sat. The lake before him was the one they had escaped through, and the cavern's intricately etched ceiling dizzied him in the blue, fungal light.

*No time. Time not real. Construct of people.*

After the second Chromium had arrived, he felt it best to move them. Just because he couldn't figure out how, didn't mean they couldn't detect each other. And one with its guts out might be attracting more. But still, he didn't recall getting up and leading his three friends anywhere.

*Hunger. Or thirst. Or just growing madness. Is this what teleportation would feel like?*

With his hourglass lost and no day to night cycle, time had become meaningless. There was only hunger and the Chromium, and he was beyond caring which would kill him first.

But he continued his watch, his explosive bundles at the ready next to him, for when the last of the three metal hunters appeared.

He held the sling he made in his hand, an 'X' constructed of the Chromium's aluminum alloy ribs, with the bands dangling down. He occasionally tugged on them to keep himself awake.

*Haven't eaten in some time. What is my body digesting for energy?*

At least there had been plenty of fresh water. Every time his stomach clenched from hungry collapse, he'd fill it with water. Arvin had never peed more in his life, and he was confident his scent was all over the cavern. The Chromium had no olfactory system he could detect, so he knew he could pee wherever.

*Not much fat. Body digesting my brain.*

Through the dim fog of starvation, he found interest in the tragic experiment he was in. Water was precious in Vastard and the Yellow Sea beyond, and dehydration was a typical cause of death far sooner than starvation. If he had the presence of mind, he could be recording the journey of well-hydrated starvation. It could be the last pages in his journal.

*My stick-figure drawings would finally be an accurate representation of me.*

Sometimes he would close his eyes, just to rest for a bit. The lake was serene, its lapping song pure and devoid of echo pollution thanks to the cavern's etchings above. Every time he opened his eyes, he had forgotten the world was blue down here.

*Glowing fungus inedible. Unless we want to die vomiting blood.*

At this point, he wished he could swim back upstream to the cannibal's camp and help themselves. Mama, Lovely, and Bastard all deserved better than this, and they wouldn't carry the guilt of eating a dead human. Arvin could bring them a bundle of legs.

*Guard thigh muscle. Good eating. Boil the bones over the lava for a stew.*

The smell of the poor laborer cooking on the spit reminded him of a roast pig. Perhaps humans and pigs were more closely related since they smelled so alike while cooking.

Closing and opening his eyes again, several men stood before him. Their musculature was defined by the angled tattoos all over their bodies, and he couldn't tell where their minimal clothing ended and their decorated flesh began. Even their faces were covered, and the aesthetic was the same as the interior halls of the upper ruins; 45 and 90 degree angles in thick lines.

*Hallucination. Body finally digesting the last of my fat: my brain.*

The men gathered in closer, craning forward to examine Arvin as if he were a bizarre sculpture in the column he leaned against. They wore silken crotch pieces with polished greaves and heavy boots and gloves. Each had a short blade sheathed at their hip along with coils of thin cord and food satchels.

*Spelunking gear. Saw it all over the ruins.*

One reached out and set his thumb on Arvin's eyebrow. Pulling up, he examined his eyes closely.

*He's checking me out.*

Another pulled a bladder from his satchel, unscrewed the cap off, and placed the exposed tube into Arvin's mouth.

*I'm going to get spelunked. Thanks, brain. Way to go out.*

Infantile instinct kicked in and Arvin sucked on the tube. A berry paste, filled with crushed seeds but otherwise smooth, came out. It was instantly refreshing, and after four swallows, Arvin felt his limbs find a shred of strength.

*This is real. Real!*

Arvin snatched the bladder like the starving animal he was. He continued to swig, but then remembered that his friends were also starving just a short distance away. It took discipline, but he removed his mouth from the pouch, rolled free of the cave column, and wobbled back toward the gear room tunnel.

The men spoke in a language Arvin couldn't understand, either because he lacked the knowledge or starvation had melted his ability to understand. But he pressed on, his shoulder against the rocky wall. He only had to get there, to get there and put the tube in their mouths. It was his only purpose in life.

By now he had memorized the position of each gear, and he navigated them easily. Stepping around the dissected Chromium, he reached the secluded corner where the three huddled up. They, like him, were half-alive.

Arvin's desire was to put the tube in Bastard's mouth first. Bastard was his friend, and Arvin loved him. But Bastard loved Lovely and Mama, and would probably insist they be priority.

He put the tube into Mama's mouth and squeezed out some of the berry paste. She was first because of her wounds. Retracting it, he squished her checks a bit to make it move and wake up her tongue.

Next was Lovely, and he did the same, but there wasn't as much. In desperation, Arvin wrung at the bladder to get a drop out for Bastard.

*I did it wrong. My friend. Not my last friend.*

Wailing in self-hatred, Arvin stood to run back to the men for more, but they were already behind him. Each one stood, transfixed in shock, at the split Chromium on the floor. Its mercury blood had mostly trickled away into the gears' recesses, and Arvin had peeled away its hide and untangled its muscle fibers in curiosity.

"More!" he tried to shout, but it came as only a whisper. His lungs didn't have the strength to rapidly fill again, so he fumbled into one of the stupefied men and pulled his bladder free of his satchel. The victim of theft didn't even react, entranced by the Chromium corpse.

Arvin returned to Bastard. His knees gave out, and he collapsed into the three. Mama grunted, but swallowed her mouthful. Lovely had already done so, and was eagerly eying Arvin's new pouch.

He squished a third of it into Bastard's mouth, then shared the remainder equally with Lovely and Mama. Mama placed her free hand on Arvin's chest as she suckled.

Then Arvin went back for a third bladder. And by the fourth one, the men just handed it to him. They were now in heated debate, pointing at the dissected metal before them while gesturing with each other. Soon they reached some kind of nodding consensus. When Arvin went to them for a fifth pouch, they snatched him up, bound him with some of their cord, and sat him against a gear.

Pulling more cord free, they surrounded the other three. Slowly the tattooed ones approached, hands ready, expecting resistance. But the three of them were too weak to protest, much less fight. Even Bastard, when he tried to bite at their fingers, could barely open his mouth.

"Why?" Arvin squeaked, rolling his head on his shoulders to face them.

A look of recognition crossed their faces. One of them stepped over to Arvin and knelt nose-to-nose with him. He spoke, the word sounding awkward and untested in his mouth.

"Trespasser."

CHAPTER
# THIRTY-SIX

Visteria

The desert gradually evolved from just sandy mounds and rocky ridgelines to something more akin to life. Cacti farms emerged in the north with the farmers' homes under the shade of shrinking mountains. Bird calls became more frequent, lizards scampered about in front of her mule more, and the occasional traveling family fell in alongside.

More and more people appeared, most on foot but a few with carts hauled by camels or ponies, and each of their faces told Visteria the same tale: the metal menace had visited their lands. These people had been marching since their trauma and it showed on their dry, cracked faces. Children had tear lines where they periodically cried, mothers held what children they still possessed, and fathers receded into themselves as they tried to understand why their efforts weren't enough.

This horror, a horror visited upon the poor and destitute of Andos, was of Ramlagha's engineering and Arvin's unleashing.

Again, she found herself wishing he had died in the onslaught, but then if *Arvin* had died, so likely did . . .

She buried it yet again. Deep.

Digging her heels in, she spurred the mule forward in an effort to outpace the crowd. Everyone else reserved the strength of their animals, but Visteria intended to sell this mule just as soon as she dismounted.

Guard posts first appeared on the horizon. They often served as toll booths during such busy times, but now the guards simply stood agape and watched everyone funneling by. Each wore a wealth of armor and carried professional bearings. These were hardly the thuggish mercenaries that Evrick had had to work with.

"The coin has landed!" one yelled, his arms high like a proselytizing apostle. "The coin has finally landed, and we are the down side!"

Men, once committed to despair, were monsters. She would have to be mindful of that.

The trail continued several more leagues. The air shifted, gaining moisture either from the gathering mass of people or the nearby farms. Visteria was unsure. At every visible distance patrolled another guard of Daynce. They stood tall with a tin bullhorn and shouted the laws and expectations regarding the arriving refugees.

"You will gain entry via a fee. This fee will be determined at the gate based upon your cargo and situation. Labor and special skills will be taken into account. No sickly or dying are permitted."

By the third time it was shouted at her, she had it memorized. Hopefully, the mule would get her entry, and if not, she had a few baubles from the Children's assassin in her saddlebags to bargain with. And, as always, there was the oldest profession in the world she could fall back on.

She dismissed the thought. After Evrick, she could never defile herself. The Children of Ramlagha were right about men, at least. Not all men, but certainly enough of them.

After another league, she could finally see Daynce's spires in the distance, their black and gold flags flapping high. The golden coin was prominent in the center of a black background. Evrick once said even their flags were valuable, made of fine cloth woven with spun gold.

Her path led into another, larger stream of refugees. It stretched so far south she couldn't see the end of it, the trudging mass of humanity obscured by the haze beyond. Guards stood at the junction, guiding the two streams together and toward Daynce.

Here, the pace nearly halted. Horses stamped impatiently. Camels knelt stubbornly and children either flopped asleep or chased each other around. Visteria pulled her hood up to shield herself from the midafternoon sun. She took a sip of water and took in her surroundings.

From her vantage point on the back of the mule, she could see the carved palisades of Daynce far up ahead. At the base of the plateau that held the city, a massive gate stood open. Guards kept people from falling out of line to set up camp, and a few families turned back because of it. But nearly everyone stayed.

Someone set cooking stones into the sandy dirt and began roasting a bird they had shot down. A woman went from wagon to wagon, offering to wash clothing in trade for water. Two men argued heatedly about which of them should go first through the gate, despite it being half a league and hours of waiting.

Visteria wondered if this was what the line outside of Tent City was like. The desperate and despondent, carrying all they owned. It would have been so wonderful, though, if Evrick's vision had come to fruition. She would have powered up the ruins, Skullhew would have claimed the New Ramlagha mantle, and Visteria could have protected him from the Children's further attempts at intrigue. The world would have been theirs.

A Fourteenth Kingdom to grow and expand to every sea. Unshared except between Evrick and her.

Slouching in the saddle, the long journey piled on its weariness. She tried to daydream about an apartment in Daynce, a place to shelter and listen for Tunny's success, for Evrick's rescue. But her exhaustion was so strong that it took hold.

She drifted, chin resting on the clasp of her cloak.

It was brief, but nice.

And then the mule shifted under her. Her sense of equilibrium jolted her awake and she sat up. The beast shifted again, bothered by the commotion of everyone around them.

The entire crowd vibrated. Camels grumbled, dogs barked, a horse reared dangerously, and a woman screamed incoherent warnings somewhere behind.

Visteria spun in the saddle and looked to the south. The stream of refugees beyond, a league or more away, faded into a shimmering roil.

The metal horrors. They were here, and they were slaughtering the refugees in the south and working their way up the line.

The guards off to the sides didn't need orders to haul off toward the city gates. Refugees broke out in all directions, fleeing to the sides to get away from the mass of people. Her mule wriggled, expectant for direction, but Visteria was amazed that it didn't act out more.

"Go!" she yelled, snapping the reins. The mule ran with a power she hadn't expected and she nearly rolled off its back. She did her best to steer clear of the people, but the beast had a mind of its own and was intent on going over or through anything in its way.

The screams and shouts behind her turned into a consistent roar of terror. Dust kicked up as thousands of feet and hooves stamped about. People plowed into each other as complete bedlam took over.

As she got closer to the gate, someone crunched under her hooves. She was grateful not to have seen their face.

Horns blasted from the spires all over Daynce and the gates began rumbling closed. What few guards remained dropped their polearms and helms to enter a full sprint. Melees broke out and a wagon ahead tipped over onto its side. Visteria's mule tried to jump over the hitch, but a hoof caught and they lost balance.

The beast of burden rolled to its side. Visteria let go of everything and let the momentum throw her clear. She landed in a crowd of people, their arms and legs flailing about. Rolling to her knees, she looked back to see the mule had run off.

Beyond that, rolling metal death. She could see them clearly now. The things gripped each other, perhaps a dozen of them, into wheels that rolled across the sand. They crushed over people, slashing them open. Occasionally, one would spring free and hunt down those fleeing.

There were hundreds of the things, a metal tide rolling over the column of crying people.

All Visteria could do was run. She spun on her heel and ran toward the palisade. All other hopes and goals fell away leaving only survival.

"They're coming!"

"Gods, hear our call!"

"Why is the gate closing?"

"Stand! Stand and fight them back!"

She pushed through it all, eyeing the palisade for any sign of salvation: rocks she could climb, a recess she could hide in, or a drainage pipe without bars. Getting closer, she saw the top of the city wall. It had statues lining it, three times the height of men. Each held hammers, and one of them *moved*.

She kept running. Someone died close behind her in a gurgling rasp. A futile arrow from the wall zipped past her ear.

"Ropes!" a woman's voice cried from the top of the wall. "Climb the ropes!"

The statues tossed coils of rope from atop the wall, and people clamored to them. Some were too weak to ascend, and they either fell or were pulled down for others to try.

She aimed for the one that was furthest from the gate. The crush of people was less intense there.

A man running next to her yelped and was pulled back from her view.

With a dip to the side, Visteria rolled over a toppled wagon.

Something after her crashed into it, splintering the wood, as she found her feet and continued running.

Visteria could finally see that each statue was a giant. She had never seen one before, and they appeared as rocky and unfinished stone. They wore leather jerkins with troll skulls on their shoulders and iron helms adorned with tusks and drake teeth.

The rope was finally there. Right there. She ran at it with her arms out clutching for it. A woman was already on it, several heights up, and one of the metal monsters plowed into her, smashing her against the wall. They both fell in a streak of red.

Reaching the rope, Visteria gripped it and climbed with her arms, hand over hand, as fast as she could. She let her legs dangle since they couldn't keep up with her scaling grip. The rope was slick and warm with blood, but she got halfway up the palisade before her muscles started to lock up.

It was too high. She wasn't going to make it. Looking to her left, she saw the things leaping from below. They plucked their victims off the ropes and rocky crags with agile aplomb.

Visteria closed her eyes. She finally let the dark possibility of Evrick being dead reach the surface.

"I'll be with you soon, husband."

The rope jerked upward and it was all she could do to hold on. One of the giants was hauling her up. A human woman, dark-skinned with a mohawk, craned her head over the wall. "Hang on!" she called down.

Visteria came over the wall and the giant caught her with a free hand. He set her down with surprising gentleness, returned his attention to his hammer, and stood ready.

The mohawked woman threw her head back and called out to the giants. "Remember! Downward swing! Use the wall as an anvil!"

The giants grunted an acknowledgement in unison. They were a fighting force, and this human woman was their leader. Hoisting their hammers, they struck menacing poses.

A horror popped into view. They were scaling the palisade with ease. It was met with the iron head of a giant's hammer, squashed flat in a silvery splatter. Then another and another. They were coming in full force through the embrasures.

Each giant huffed and puffed as they pounded away. Several things leaped onto one giant, tearing at its leather jerkin and stoney skin. Fire broke out all over its body, but it just kept swinging and stomping them into the stone flooring of the wall walk.

"Keep going!" the woman shouted. It was only then that Visteria saw that she didn't have hands. Instead, both her arms ended in spiked morning star heads. "Pound them *down*."

"They easing!" one giant called as she paused between swings. "They are chasing off in other directions instead."

The woman looked grim. "Easier pickings. But keep an eye out in case these things come back. Fuckers can *think*." She then turned to Visteria. "Welcome to Daynce. The name is Gisela, and these Vulg are my tribe."

It was so much to process, but Visteria stood and walked to the wall to peek through the mercury slathered embrasure.

Below, beyond her as far as she could see, was absolute proof that the gods hated humanity.

# CHAPTER
# THIRTY-SEVEN

Arvin

**B**ound together in a tethered line, the tattooed cavemen led the four friends through the warren of tunnels and deeper still. Stopping to catch their breath, Lovely and Mama leaned against each other as Bastard fell asleep instantly. Here, they all received another pouch of berry paste.

The nutrients did wonders for the brain, and Arvin found his mind returning to its usual sharpened state. He sat as far as their bondage would allow as he curiously took in the scene.

They rested at the foot of a waterfall that had worn a hole into the cavern floor. Below was only perfect darkness and further down their intended track hung braziers.

*Eight men. No obvious hierarchy. Sideways glances mean they are curious.*

Arvin found most people difficult to read. The nuances of social gestures not only confused him, but held little interest. Yet their tattooed captors projected their feelings with childlike apparency. When they looked at Bastard and Arvin, they merely cocked their heads in interest. But with Mama and Lovely, they seemed almost in reverent awe.

*Are there not women among them?*

Everything they did with Lovely and Mama was gentle and measured whereas they used far more gruff gestures and shoves with Arvin and Bastard. Arvin himself had little experience with other sexes than his own, so he figured this was normal instinctive behavior among all men. The deference that Lady Skullhew received from Evrick's men reinforced this theory.

Having his brain fog lifted, Arvin evaluated the puzzle and how it had changed.

*Eight human captors. Armed. They are carrying all of my things. Don't know my sock balls are explosives. Similar markings to ruins' inner walls. Means they have been there or have adopted the pattern through cultural exposure.*

The men were shorter than most. Their skin tone was unhealthily pallid and their nails and hair seemed brittle. Arvin surmised that these men were not only denied the sun but also regular protein.

*Hopefully not cannibals.*

One approached Mama, humbly took a knee before her, and asked her a question in a language Arvin had never heard. Mama only gazed at him vacantly, so the man asked it again. After a moment of silence, he accepted she would give no answer, so he stood and stepped back.

"Trespasser," Arvin said to get his attention. At least this word, they knew.

All eyes fell onto Arvin. One pulled his short blade from its sheath and pointed it at his head. "Trespasser," he snarled.

"You recognized my language. At least some of it. What other words do you know?" Arvin shifted into curiosity mode to wrangle his fear.

"Trespasser."

"I got that. Thank you."

Another one slapped the back of Arvin's head.

Mama growled, and Lovely hissed. The men immediately backed off and all blades were sheathed. They each took a humble knee and bowed their heads at the two women, then uttered some brief mantra before standing.

*Women have a special place in this tribe. Must meet an indigenous one to learn more.*

Returning to the puzzle, he evaluated the cave. Stone markers were carved into the nearby walls in increments, and while the blue moss was no longer present to give light, sconces were visible further down the path as it narrowed.

This waterfall appeared to be the end of the river that streamed out of the lake. Several buckets sat tethered to long poles for refreshing water bladders. The ground, worn smooth from foot traffic, indicated centuries of usage. A new hypothesis took shape.

*Descendants. Of Ramlagha. When the ruins fell centuries ago, survivors fled down here!*

Pure fascination took over for Arvin. He couldn't believe it.

"You're ancient folk from above! Wow, you really did it wrong, didn't you?"

One went to slap him on the back of the head again, but Lovely shot him a withering glare.

"The Chromium. Either your doing *directly*, or you discovered them by mistake. Wait. Wait! Try this." Arvin wet his lips in preparation for the word. "Ramlagha."

They all froze.

*They sure know that word.*

"Good!" Arvin shouted in delight.

The word "good" caused Bastard to stir awake.

"Hey, do you know this?" Arvin tried to draw a rune on the smooth stone floor that he sat on, but there was no dirt or dust to do it in. He scrunched his nose in thought, then jutted his chin toward the tattooed man carrying his things. Among them was Visteria's lexicon with the rune.

His bonds were at the wrist and allowed Arvin to mimic a book opening with his hands. "Read. Read."

Their eyes all landed on the dangling tome. The man warily cracked it open as if something could spring out at him. His eyes explored the inside for a few moments, then he screamed out in alarm and flung the book into the waterfall. It vanished below.

Arvin tried to formulate a response to the man's bizarre behavior, but before he could arrange any words into a sentence, the man took his blade out and dragged it across both his open eyes. They gushed forth as he cried out a litany of pleas to whatever force he thought was listening.

Everyone stood in shock, but the tattooed men recovered far faster than Arvin, Bastard, Lovely, and Mama. They all pulled their blades and shook them about as they stamped their feet and gnashed their teeth. The only word Arvin could make out in their ranting was "trespasser."

"Don't be upset with them!" Arvin pleaded. Pressing his bound hands against his chest, he tried to keep their attention away from his friends. "My book. I told him to look. All my fault." He then touched Bastard's leg. "Good. He is good. Not trespasser. Good." Next, he walked on his knees to Lovely. "She is good. Good." And then, as he crawled toward Mama, something caught his eye.

All the men were facing him, blades out. Behind them knelt the blinded man, his hands clutching the air as he sputtered his prayer. But beyond that, something fell down the waterfall and disappeared below. It was brief, and difficult to discern of shape, but the reflection from it was distinctly chrome-like.

*It followed us.*

Arvin pointed at the waterfall behind them. "Look out! It's here!"

Mama had seen it, as well, and stood so fast that her bindings, connected to Lovely and Bastard, pulled them to their feet with her.

"Chromium!" Arvin cried.

Two men grabbed him, both blades at his throat as he gesticulated wildly at the hole the waterfall disappeared into. One kneed Arvin in the stomach and he doubled over.

Mama roared.

Things were escalating quickly.

Suddenly, the ranting prayer stopped. Arvin looked, as did several other men, but the self-blinded man was gone. Only the pile of Arvin's belongings remained.

Arvin took the moment of distraction to run the cords binding his wrists over one of the drawn blades. It sliced off easily and before the men could run him through, the Chromium leaped from below the hole's ledge. Claws wide and tail swinging, it dove into the nearest man. His blade skittered across the ground as the Chromium savaged him.

The others turned on the metal thing, harmlessly prodding it with their blades as its victim screeched in painful agony, his insides becoming outsides.

Arvin ran around them. Something wet and hot splashed on him as the thing's tail swung at the surrounding crowd. He reached his items, found his sling, and tested the rubber strap. Next, he took up one of his explosive balls, set it in the strap, but he couldn't take aim with all the men surrounding it.

"Move!" he cried. "Scoot! Scatter!" He tried every word he could think of, hoping at least one of them would be understood. "Skadoodle!"

Mama, Bastard, and Lovely gathered up the tether between them. They tossed it around the Chromium's head and pulled it backward. It clawed into its twitching target, dragging his gurgling body along underneath, as they hauled it clear of the crowd.

By now, the men realized their blades did nothing. One struck flint to fire up a torch, but the thing's tail swung about and took his fingers.

Mama placed her one boot square in the Chromium's back and pressed it into the stone. She was an imposing sight, her wounds now opened once again as her teeth gnashed and shoulders bulged.

When the tail came for her, Bastard gripped it with both hands and wrangled it like a viper. Lovely ran to its head, holding both of the horns, to keep it down.

But the joints in all four shoulders weren't like a regular animal's. They twisted around and the spine receded. Instead of laying on its front, it now lay on its back. It reversed itself without even flipping over.

With all four clawed hands, it slashed out. Lovely, Bastard, and Mama all stumbled away, their legs bleeding and slashed as it curled into a ball and sprung back onto its hands.

The opening was brief, and risky, but Arvin took it. Everyone was clear of the thing. Pulling the band back, he visualized where the explosive was supposed to land.

*Moist sock. Heavier projectile. Aim higher.*

He let go.

The band snapped forward, doing its work.

The Chromium swung its tail to bat the incoming explosive out of the way. It burst, deafening the world and knocking everyone over from the shockwave. Arvin fell backward, his head dangling off the ledge of the waterfall's abyss. After a moment of ringing, he sat up with a groan.

*Concussive blast. Overcompensated the mix. Too much sulfur? Powder?*

Mama and Lovely dragged Bastard further from the stunned Chromium. His legs were bleeding badly. The surrounding men cowered and held their ears from the ringing blast as Arvin readied the second explosive.

*Must hit torso. Won't rupture skin, but internal damage might do it.*

Arvin loosed the second one.

The Chromium snatched the explosive out of the air. It held the sock bomb for a moment, then lifted it up to its vibrating horns for observance.

Without taking time to think it through, Arvin reached for the nearest pouch of his discarded bandolier. He loaded whatever vial he could fetch into the sling, and loosed.

This one hit right between the horns. A sizzling hiss came, as the acid in the vial interacted with the moisture in the air to create a small, caustic cloud. It swung its head back and forth, disoriented as the perfect, glossy hide of its head and shoulders began to pit.

Arvin saw his concave reflection in the thing's face warp.

*Acid. Hydrochloric acid. Weakens chromium. Vulnerable.*

But it was still up, reeling, fingers out and tail high in an effort to judge its rapidly declining situation. There was no time to risk it going for anyone else.

Arvin charged, his metal bone sling forward, toward the Chromium's bubbling head. With all his middling weight, he hoped to drive one of the ribs through its skull.

It caught him, almost casually, with its other forward hand. The claws dug into his ribs, and he gasped for air. It held him high above the cavern floor and returned to its evaluation of the explosive in its hand.

Yet Arvin's arms were free. He plucked back the sling's empty band, aimed for the explosive in its chrome claws, and snapped away. The impact sent the claws into its own face, through its compromised metal skin, and crushing into its skull. There, in its own head, the explosive went off.

Arvin didn't even hear the explosion. Everything just turned bright and stayed bright. Then it faded dark. The stabbing pain in his chest pulled away. He hit the rocky cave floor. And hands, several of them, patted his limbs. A loving one stroked his hair.

*Mama.*

They were safe.

*I did it right.*

# THIRTY-EIGHT

Ovallin

Dead laborers and guards painted the walls, soaked the stone, and congealed in the stagnant and putrid air within. The orange glow of each chamber—the vaults, the listening dais, the pod chamber below—provided a hellish light.

The Ramlagha halls echoed with the skittering of the metal legion. Any heartbeat was their target. First the large ones in the chests of humans, but now only the rats remained and even they were hunted. If it had a heartbeat, it was found and pulled apart until silenced.

The Chromium, without the stimulation of targets to hunt, clawed their way to the surface of the desert and out into the open sky where their blindsight only discerned the wind-crossed dunes and flapping of torn tents.

To seek motion and end it.

To fulfill the renewed bargain.

But within the core of the ruins, at its brightest center, hovered the spherical portal. It led to another plane, one of only metal and unlife. Chromium birthed out of it en masse, scampering into the realm of Andos, each exact and focused on their singular purpose.

She floated around it, the bolt still embedded in her forehead and thin linens dangling from her like wisps from a ghost. Ovallin weaved her fingers at the portal as if conducting a symphony beyond the human ear. Its surface rippled. She watched her reflection twist and bend with each wave of her hand with unblinking, cruel eyes.

The Chromium pouring out changed, longer and bipedal. Human-like with womanly hips and more elegant lines, each molded in Ovallin's physique. They flopped into the round chamber, found their wobbly legs like newborn calves, and stretched their elongated claws up toward her.

It was an ancient bargain, one begun by a divine prisoner centuries ago. The Chromium were its salvation, in its own image. And now Ovallin had taken up the dark bargain, her mind only half present, as the living shadow of herself wove a new legion of her own making.

To serve.

To eradicate.

To cleanse.

To remove all that is lesser than she.

# Acknowledgments

Thank you, Kelly, for remembering me and, Kevin, thank you for not saying no. And a very special thank you to Jen and Shannon for suffering my mess and pulling the good stuff free.

# ABOUT THE AUTHOR

William LJ Galaini has failed at more things than most folks even attempt. Given his refined process of failure, he has streamlined his wordcraft and now produces books, short stories, and game narratives that are about what he knows best; idealistic losers that save the day. To learn more about William, check out his website at https://williamljgalaini.com/

X x.com/WGalaini

instagram.com/wgalaini

facebook.com/WilliamLjGalaini

# JOIN THE CURSED DRAGON SHIP NEWSLETTER

Love what you just read? Want more just like it? Sign up for our newsletter so you don't miss out on the adventure. You'll get:

- A free book for signing up
- Advanced notice of new releases
- First word of books on sale
- Opportunities for free books
- Most up-to-date information on author appearances.

We're busy and know you are too. We won't send more than one newsletter a month.

Register below.

# CHECK OUT THE SERIES THAT STARTED IT ALL

*Stealing the cash box of your mercenary unit as you run away probably isn't wise, but it sure is funny.*